Further praise for *So Far from God*

"*So Far from God* could be the offspring of a union between *One Hundred Years of Solitude* and *General Hospital*: a sassy, magical, melodramatic love child who won't sit down–and the reader can only hope–will never shut up. . . . As readable as a teen-aged sister's secret diary–and as impossible to resist."

–Barbara Kingsolver, *New York Times Book Review*

"Goddamn! Ana Castillo has gone and done what I always wanted to do–written a Chicana *telenovela*–a novel roaring down Interstate 25 at one hundred and fifteen miles an hour with an almanac of Chicanoismo–saints, martyrs, T.V. mystics, home remedies, little miracles, *dichos*, myths, gossip, recipes–fluttering from the fender like a flag. Wacky, wild, *y bien* funny. *Dale gas*, girl!"

–Sandra Cisneros, author of *The House on Mango Street* and *Women Hollering Creek*

"Ana Castillo is *una* storyteller *de primera*. . . . Her voice is distinctive–zany, knowing, rhythmic, with its very own mix of Latino-U.S. of A. cadences . . . able to hold our attention from the first to last page of this packed, picaresque novel. *So Far from God* is the novel that wasn't there before but which I'd been missing. Bravo, Ana!"

–Julia Alvarez, author of *How the García Girls Lost Their Accents*

"Haunting . . . surreal . . . lyrical, crazy, and wise . . . steeped in pungent folklore, with a flavor like Hieronymous Bosch meets Frida Kahlo and Diego Rivera. . . . It speaks in a totally original voice."

–John Nichols, author of *The Milagro Beanfield War*

"Castillo brings a warm, sometimes biting feminist consciousness to the wondrous, tragic, and engaging lives of a New Mexico mother and her four fated daughters. . . . Storytelling skills and humor allow Castillo to integrate and deliver folklore and political material with unabashed directness and disarming charm."

–*Kirkus Reviews*

"While reading, you may get an eerie feeling that you are 12 years old and back in your grandmother's kitchen smelling all those wonderful smells and hearing all her curious stories . . . wrenching . . . you will always pick up this book again because it calls to you until you finish it." —*Hispanic News*

"Raucous, realistic, yet mystical . . . memorable characters, radical politics, and storytelling skill that shimmers on the page."
—*MS*

"Ana Castillo is immensely insightful in every sense of the word. . . . A writer with enormous integrity, with common sense and lyric sense, yet one who passes back and forth between more than one psychic world . . . and is able to bring back what she has seen and sensed into the land of her intense and beautifully crafted writing." —Clarissa Pinkola Estés, Ph.D., author of *Women Who Run with the Wolves*

"Exciting and wonderful! I gave it to my mother, my sister, my daughter, my whole family. Anybody who's ever been the daughter of a mother will appreciate this book. There's just no way to get around it!" —Ntozake Shange, author of *For Colored Girls Who Have Considered Suicide When the Rainbow Is Enuf*

"A riotous and rascally novel . . . earthy and irresistible . . . sure to generate excitement . . . Castillo is simply dazzling, tossing off miracles, scathing social commentary, and smart-ass humor as easily and naturally as shaking water from a mane of wet hair."
—*Booklist*

So Far from God

Also by
Ana Castillo

I Ask the Impossible
Peel My Love Like an Onion
Goddess of the Americas
Massacre of the Dreamers
Sapogonia
My Father Was a Toltec
The Mixquiahuala Letters
Watercolor Women and the Opaque Man
Psst . . . I Have Something to Tell You, Mi Amor

So Far from God

A Novel

Ana Castillo

W. W. Norton & Company

New York London

Printed in the United States of America
First published as a Norton paperback 2005

Manufacturing by LSC Harrisonburg
Book design by Margaret M. Wagner

Library of Congress Cataloging-in-Publication Data

Castillo, Ana.
So far from God : a novel / by Ana Castillo.
p. cm.
I. Title.
PS 3553.A8135S65 1993
813'.54–dc20
92-34362
ISBN 0-393-03490-9 (cl)

ISBN 0-393-32693-4 pbk.

W. W. Norton & Company, Inc.
500 Fifth Avenue, New York, N.Y. 10110
www.wwnorton.com

W. W. Norton & Company Ltd.
15 Carlisle Street, London W1D 3BS

15 14 13

To all the trees that gave their life to the telling of these stories

y

A m'jito, Marcel, y a las siguientes siete generaciones

Contents

Acknowledgments

I am indebted to the members of the Southwest Organizing Project who assisted in my research; above all, for the inspiration I received from their consciousness, ongoing commitment, and hope.

Muchos thank yous to my apreciado editor, Gerald Howard, and, as always, thanks Susan B.!

"So far from God—So near the United States"

Porfirio Díaz,
Dictator of Mexico during the Mexican Civil War

So Far from God

1

An Account of the First Astonishing Occurrence in the Lives of a Woman Named Sofia and Her Four Fated Daughters; and the Equally Astonishing Return of Her Wayward Husband

La Loca was only three years old when she died. Her mother Sofi woke at twelve midnight to the howling and neighing of the five dogs, six cats, and four horses, whose custom it was to go freely in and out of the house. Sofi got up and tiptoed out of her room. The animals were kicking and crying and running back and forth with their ears back and fur standing on end, but Sofi couldn't make out what their agitation was about.

She checked the bedroom with the three older girls: Esperanza, the eldest, had her arms wrapped around the two smaller ones, Fe and Caridad. They were sleeping strangely undisturbed by the excitement of the animals.

Sofi went back into her own room where her baby, the three-year-old, had slept ever since Sofi's husband disappeared. Sofi put the baseball bat that she had taken with her when checking the house back under the bed—"just in case" she encountered some tonto who had gotten ideas about the woman who lived alone with her four little girls by the ditch at the end of the road.

It was then that she noticed the baby, although apparently asleep, jerking. Jerking, jerking, the little body possessed by something unknown that caused her to thrash about violently until finally she fell off the bed. Sofi ran around to pick her up, but she was so frightened by her little daughter's seizure she stopped short.

The baby continued to thrash about, banging her little arms and legs against the hard stone floor, white foam mixed with a little blood spilling from the corners of her mouth; and worst of all, her eyes were now opened, rolled all the way to the top of her head.

Sofi screamed and called out "Ave Maria Purisimas," and finally her three other precious children came running in. "Mom, Mom, what happened?" And then, everyone was screaming and moaning because the baby had stopped moving, lay perfectly still, and they knew she was dead.

It was the saddest velorio in Tome in years because it was so sad to bury a child. Fortunately none had died since—well, if memory served right, doña Dolores's last son. Poor woman. Eleven children and one after the other passed on her until she was left with no one, except for her drunken foul-mouthed husband. It seems all the babies were victims of a rare bone disease they inherited through the father's bloodline. What terrible misfortune for doña Dolores, suffering the pangs of labor through eleven births, all fated to die during infancy. Twelve years of marriage, eleven babies that did not survive, and to top it off, the husband drank up everything they owned.

A sad, sad story.

The day after the wake the neighbors all came out to

accompany Sofi and the girls to the church at Tome, where Sofi wanted the little baby's Mass to be held before they lay her into the cold ground. Everyone Sofi knew was there: the baby's godparents, all of Sofi's comadres and compadres, her sister from Phoenix, everyone except, of course, the baby's father, since no one had seen hide nor hair of him since he'd left Sofi and the girls.

That marriage had a black ribbon on its door from the beginning. Sofi's grandfather had refused to give the young lovers his blessing, the father had forbidden Sofi's querido to step foot in their house during their three-year courtship, and the local parish priest joined the opposition when he refused to marry the couple in church.

Nobody believed that Domingo was good enough for little Sofi, not her sister, not her mother, not even her favorite teacher in high school, la Miss Hill, who had nothing but praise for Sofi's common sense and intelligence. Nobody thought el Domingo would make a good husband because of the fact that he liked to gamble.

Gambling was in the man's blood. And gambling is what Sofi did when she ran off with him, sheltered by the dark night of a new moon, and came back a señora. And then, nobody could say nothing about it but wait for the inevitable failure of Sofi's marriage.

A month after he left, Sofi heard from her husband, a letter from El Paso with five ten-dollar bills and a promise to send more whenever he could. No return address. And no more news from Domingo ever again after that. After a year, Sofia was so mad, she forbade anyone to even mention his name in her presence.

It was 118 degrees the day of Sofi's baby daughter's funeral and the two pallbearers, upon the instruction of Father Jerome, placed the small casket on the ground just in front of the church. No one was quite certain what Father Jerome had planned when he paused there in the hot sun.

Maybe some last-minute prayers or instructions for the mourners before entering the House of God. He wiped his brow with his handkerchief.

In fact, he was a little concerned about the grieving mother, who at that point was showing signs of losing it, trembling and nearly collapsing between two others. Father Jerome thought it perhaps a good idea to advise them all on funeral decorum. "As devoted followers of Christ," he began, "we must not show our lack of faith in Him at these times and in His, our Father's fair judgment, Who alone knows why we are here on this earth and why He chooses to call us back home when He does."

Why? Why? That's exactly what Sofi wanted to know at that moment—when all she had ever done was accept God's will. As if it hadn't been punishment enough to be abandoned by her husband, then—for no apparent reason and without warning, save the horrible commotion of the animals that night—her baby was taken away! Oh, why? Why? That's all she wanted to know. "Ayyyyy!"

At that moment, while Sofi threw herself on the ground, pounding it with her rough fists, her compadres crying alongside her, saying, "Please, please, comadre, get up, the Lord alone knows what He does! Listen to the padre," Esperanza let out a shriek, long and so high pitched it started some dogs barking in the distance. Sofi had stopped crying to see what was causing the girl's hysteria when suddenly the whole crowd began to scream and faint and move away from the priest, who finally stood alone next to the baby's coffin.

The lid had pushed all the way open and the little girl inside sat up, just as sweetly as if she had woken from a nap, rubbing her eyes and yawning. "¿Mami?" she called, looking around and squinting her eyes against the harsh light. Father Jerome got hold of himself and sprinkled holy water in the direction of the child, but for the moment was too stunned to utter so much as a word of prayer. Then, as if all this was not amazing enough, as Father Jerome moved toward the child she lifted herself up into the air and landed on the church roof. "Don't touch me, don't touch me!" she warned.

This was only the beginning of the child's long life's phobia of people. She wasn't one of those afflicted with an exaggerated fear of germs and contagion. For the rest of her life, however, she was to be repulsed by the smell of humans. She claimed that all humans bore an odor akin to that which she had smelled in the places she had passed through when she was dead. Where she had gone she revealed from the rooftop that day within the limited ability of a three-year-old's vocabulary, in Spanish and English. Meanwhile everyone below was either genuflecting or paralyzed, and crossing themselves over and over as she spoke.

"¡Hija, hija!" Father Jerome called up to her, hands clenched in the air. "Is this an act of God or of Satan that brings you back to us, that has flown you up to the roof like a bird? Are you the devil's messenger or a winged angel?"

At that point Sofi, despite her shock, rose from the ground, unable to tolerate the mere suggestion by Father Jerome that her daughter, her blessed, sweet baby, could by any means be the devil's own. "Don't you dare!" she screamed at Father Jerome, charging at him and beating him with her fists. "Don't you dare start this about *my* baby! If our Lord in His heaven has sent my child back to me, don't you dare start this backward thinking against her; the devil doesn't produce miracles! And *this* is a miracle, an answer to the prayers of a brokenhearted mother, ¡hombre necio, pendejo . . . !"

"Ay, watch what you say, comadre!" one of Sofi's friends whispered, pulling Sofi from the priest, who had staved off her attack with his arms over his head. "Oh, my God!" others uttered, crossing themselves at hearing Sofi call the priest a pendejo, which was a blasphemy, crossing themselves all the more because although the verdict was still open as to whether they were witnessing a true miracle or a mirage of the devil, Sofi's behavior was giving way to the latter—after all, calling the holy priest a pendejo and hitting him!

The crowd settled down, some still on their knees, palms together, all looking up at the little girl like the glittering angel placed at the top of a Christmas tree. She seemed serene and, though a little flushed, quite like she always did when she was alive. Well, the fact was that she *was* alive, but no one at the moment seemed sure.

"Listen," she announced calmly to the crowd, "on my long trip I went to three places: hell . . ." Someone let out a loud scream at this. "To *pulgatorio* and to heaven. God sent me back to help you all, to pray for you all, o si no, o si no . . ."

"O si no, ¿qué, hija?" Father Jerome begged.

"O si no, you, and others who doubt just like you, will never see our Father in heaven!"

The audience gasped in unison. Someone whispered, "That's the devil," but refrained from continuing when Sofi turned to see who it was.

"Come down, come down," the priest called to the child. "We'll all go in and pray for you. Yes, yes, maybe all this is really true. Maybe you did die, maybe you did see our Lord in His heaven, maybe He did send you back to give us guidance. Let's just go in together, we'll all pray for you."

With the delicate and effortless motion of a monarch butterfly the child brought herself back to the ground, landing gently on her bare feet, her ruffled chiffon nightdress, bought for the occasion of her burial, fluttering softly in the air. "No, Padre," she corrected him. "Remember, it is *I* who am here to pray for *you*." With that stated, she went into the church and those with faith followed.

Once the baby was able to receive medical attention (although Sofi took her child this time to a hospital in Albuquerque rather than to rely on the young doctor at the Valencia County clinic who had so rashly declared her child dead), it was diagnosed that she was in all probability an epileptic.

Epilepsy notwithstanding, there was much left unexplained and for this reason Sofi's baby grew up at home, away from strangers who might be witnesses to her astonishing behavior, and she eventually earned the name around the Rio Abajo region and beyond, of La Loca Santa.

For a brief period after her resurrection, people came from all over the state in hopes of receiving her blessing or of her performing of some miracle for them. But because she was so averse to being close to anyone, the best that strangers could expect was to get a glimpse of her from outside the gate. So "Santa" was dropped from her name and she was soon forgotten by strangers.

She became known simply as La Loca. The funny thing was (but perhaps not so funny since it is the way of la gente to call a spade a spade, and she was called "La Loca" straight out), even La Loca's mother and sisters called her that because her behavior was *so* peculiar. Moreover, La Loca herself responded to that name and by the time she was twenty-one no one remembered her Christian name.

Her sisters, all born exactly three years apart from each other, had each gone out into the world and had all eventually returned to their mother's home. Esperanza had been the only one to get through college. She had gotten her B.A. in Chicano Studies. During that time, she had lived with her boyfriend, Rubén (who, during the height of his Chicano cosmic consciousness, renamed himself Cuauhtemoc). This, despite her mother's opposition, who said of her eldest daughter's nonsanctified union: "Why should a man buy the cow when he can have the milk for free?" "I am not a cow," Esperanza responded, but despite this, right after graduation Cuauhtemoc dumped her for a middle-class gabacha with a Corvette; they bought a house in the Northeast Heights in Albuquerque right after their wedding.

Esperanza always had a lot of "spunk," as they say, but she did have a bad year after Cuauhtemoc, who was Rubén again before she recovered and decided to go back to the university for an M.A. in communications. Upon receiving her degree, she landed a job at the local T.V. station as a news broadcaster. These were transitional years where she felt like a woman with brains was as good as dead for all the happiness it brought her in the love department.

Caridad tried a year of college, but school was not for her and never had been, for that matter. She was the sister of the porcelain complexion, not meaning white, but as smooth as glazed clay. She had perfect teeth and round, apple-shaped breasts. Unlike the rest of the women in her family who, despite her grandmother's insistence that they were *Spanish*, descendants of pure Spanish blood, all shared the flat butt of the Pueblo blood undeniably circulating through their veins, Caridad had a somewhat pronounced ass that men were inclined to show their unappreciated appreciation for everywhere she went.

She fell in love with Memo, her high school sweetheart, got pregnant, and they married the day after graduation. But two weeks had not passed before Caridad got wind that Memo was still seeing his ex-girlfriend, Domitila, who lived in Belen; and Caridad went back home.

All in all, Caridad had three abortions. La Loca had performed each one. Their mother had only known about the first. They didn't tell anyone else about it but said to Memo and his family that Caridad had miscarried from being so upset about Memo's cheating on her. It was agreed by all that the marriage be annulled. It would have been a terrible thing to let anyone find out that La Loca had "cured" her sister of her pregnancy, a cause for excommunication for both, not to mention that someone would have surely had La Loca arrested. A crime against man if not a sin against God.

The occasions when La Loca let people get close to her, when she permitted human contact at all, were few. Only her mother and the animals were ever unconditionally allowed to touch her. But without exception, healing her sisters from the traumas and injustices they were dealt by society—a society she herself never experienced firsthand—was never questioned.

Caridad kept up with Memo for several years until he finally made his choice. It was not Domitila of Belen and it wasn't Caridad of Tome. It was the Marines. And off he went to be all that he never knew he was. For while it was said that the Army made men, the Marines' motto, he was told, was that they only took men.

Three abortions later and with her weakness for shots of Royal Crown with beer chasers after work at the hospital where she was an orderly, Caridad no longer discriminated between giving her love to Memo and only to Memo whenever he wanted it and loving anyone she met at the bars who vaguely resembled Memo. At about the time that her sister, who was definitely not prettier than her but for sure had more brains, was on the ten o'clock nightly news, you could bet that Caridad was making it in a pickup off a dark road with some guy whose name the next day would be as meaningless to her as yesterday's headlines were to Esperanza la newscaster.

Fe, the third of Sofi's daughters, was fine. That is, twenty-four, with a steady job at the bank, and a hard-working boyfriend whom she had known forever; she had just announced their engagement. With the same job since high school graduation, she was a reliable friend to the "girls" at work. Fe was beyond reproach. She maintained her image above all—from the organized desk at work to weekly manicured fingernails and a neat coiffure.

She and Thomas, "Tom," Torres were the ideal couple in their social circle, if one could call a social circle a group of three or four couples who got together on weekends to watch football on wide-screen television at Sadie's, or to go to a Lobos game at the university, or rent videos or once in a while got all dressed up and went to Garduño's for dinner.

Tom ran one of those mini-mart filling stations, sometimes working double shifts. He did not drink or even smoke cigarettes. They were putting their money away for their wedding, a small wedding, just for family and a few close friends, because they were going to use their savings for their first house.

As it was, while Fe had a little something to talk to Esperanza about, she kept away from her other sisters, her mother, and the animals, because she just didn't understand how they could all be so self-defeating, so unambitious. Although, by anyone's standards it was unfair to call her mother unambitious, since Sofi single-handedly ran the Carne Buena Carnecería she inherited from her parents. She raised most of the livestock that she herself (with the help of La Loca) butchered for the store, managed all its finances, and ran the house on her own to boot.

But as for Fe's antisocial sister, sometimes, when she came home from her job at the bank and saw La Loca outside the stalls with the horses, always in the same dirty pair of jeans and never wearing shoes, even in winter, she was filled with deep compassion for what she saw as a soulless creature.

She had only been six years old when La Loca had had her first epileptic seizure and her mother and community (out of ignorance, she was sure) had pronounced the child dead. She did not remember "El Milagro," as her mother referred to La Loca's resurrection that day in front of the church, and highly suspected that such a thing as her little sister flying up to the church rooftop had never happened.

Usually, Fe did not feel compassion for La Loca, however, but simply disappointment and disgust for her sister's obvious "mental illness," the fact that her mother had encouraged it with her own superstitions, and finally, fear that it was, like her own Indian flat butt, hereditary, despite everyone's protest to the contrary.

Fe couldn't wait until she got out—of her mother's home as well as Tome—but she would get out properly, with a little more style and class than the women in her family had. Except for Esperanza these days, whose being on television every night was lending some prestige to Fe at the bank. Although when Esperanza was in college, being a radical and living with that crazy Chicano who was always speeding on peyote or something, Fe hadn't known what to make of her older sister and certainly had no desire to copy Esperanza's La Raza politics.

Fe had just come back from Bernadette's Bridal Gowns, where she had had herself fitted for her dress, and the three gabachas (my term, not Fe's) she had chosen from the bank as her bridesmaids, instead of her sisters, had met that Saturday to have their pink-and-orchid chiffon gowns fitted too, when La Loca, sweeping the living room, pointed with her chin to the mail as soon as Fe came in.

"What? A letter for me?" Fe said cheerfully, recognizing Tom's neat, small printing on the square envelope. She smiled and took it to the bathroom to get a little privacy. La Loca had that look like she was going to stick close to her. Sometimes she did that. She had this sixth sense when she suspected something was amiss in the house and wouldn't let up until she uncovered it.

Dear Honey, it began, a short note on yellow paper from a legal pad. This was a little unusual, since Tom always sent cards, cards with lovers kissing, with irises and roses, with beautiful little sayings that rhymed to which he simply signed, "Your Tom." *Dear Honey.* Fe stopped. She heard a faint rap on the door. "Go away, Loca," she said. She heard her sister move away from the door. Fe read on: *I have been thinking about this for a long time, but I didn't have the nerve to tell you in person. It's not that I don't love you. I do. I always will. But I just don't think I'm ready to get married. Like I said, I thought about this a long time. Please don't call to try to change my mind. I hope you find happiness with someone who deserves you and can make you happy. Tom.*

When La Loca and Sofi—along with the help of Fred and Wilma, the two Irish setters that immediately joined in the commotion of the women's breaking down the bathroom door, and Fe's screaming and tearing the tiny bathroom apart—finally got to Fe, she was wrapped up in the shower curtain in the tub. "You're gonna suffocate, 'jita, get outa there!" Sofi called and with La Loca's help unwrapped the plastic from around Fe, who in her ravings had inadvertently made herself into a human tamale—all the while letting out one loud continuous scream that could have woken the dead.

Sofi shook her daughter hard, but when that didn't silence Fe, she gave her a good slap as she had seen people do on T.V. lots of times whenever anyone got like that. But Fe didn't quiet down. In fact, Fe did not stop screaming even when Sofi announced ten days later that she was going to get Tom. She decided to go personally to Tom's house when he did not return her calls.

"I got a daughter who won't stop screaming," she told Tom's mother, Mrs. Torres.

"I got a son who's got *susto*," Mrs. Torres replied.

"*¿Susto? ¿Susto?*" Sofi shouted. "*You* think that cowardly son of yours without pelos on his maracas has *susto*? I'll show you *susto!* My daughter has been screaming at the top of her lungs for ten days and nights. She spent hundreds, maybe even a thousand dollars already on their wedding plans. She has people at work that she can't even face no more. And let me tell you something, Mrs. Torres, don't think that I don't know that your son had her on the pill for a long time."

"Wait, just a minute, señora," Mrs. Torres cut in, holding up her hand. The two mothers, believe it or not, had never met before. Fe had been too ashamed of her family to bring Mrs. Torres over to her house. "My son . . . my son is a good boy. He hasn't eaten for days, he's just so upset about this breakup. But he said he had to do the honorable thing. He hasn't cost your daughter nothing he himself hasn't lost as well. What's money when in the long run he spared her from an unhappy marriage? I don't know why he changed his mind about marrying her. I keep out of my son's business. Just be glad he left your daughter when he did. You know how men are . . ."

"Ay!" Sofi moaned, because she knew full well that *that* last remark was meant to hit below the belt regarding her own marriage, and thanks to Fe, she knew next to nothing about Mrs. Torres to come back with a good rejoinder. But finally Tom came out of his room and she convinced him to come over so that he might make Fe stop screaming.

"What's that?" he asked, obviously spooked by Fe's shrill cries that were heard from outside the house. "Is that La Loca?" He had heard of her, but had never met Fe's so-called retarded sister. "Are you crazy?" Sofi said, unlocking the door. "That's *your* girlfriend! Why do you think I brought you here? If I know Fe, she'll snap out of it—maybe by you talking to her. We'll see."

But Tom stopped at the threshold. "I can't go in," he said. He looked nauseated. "I'm sorry, I just can't." And before Sofi could think of something to say to stop him, Tom was back in his car, smoking down the road. Damn, Sofi thought, seeing him speed away, maybe he *does* have susto.

Unfortunately, nothing and no one could quiet Fe down.

She wanted her Tom back. And even when Caridad managed to get some tranquilizers from her hospital friends, Fe would only shut up for an hour or two at a time when she slept. She even screamed while she was being fed (because now it was Sofi and her daughters who took turns feeding, cleaning, and dressing poor Fe, who was truly a mess and who—if she were in any way capable of realizing it—would have been horrified at that thought).

Meanwhile, La Loca did what she could. She sewed a padded headband for Fe so that when she banged her head against the wall, as she increasingly did while she screamed, she wouldn't hurt herself as bad. She also prayed for her, since that was La Loca's principal reason for being alive, as both her mother and she well knew.

Above all, however, she prayed for Tom, because like so many hispanos, nuevo mexicanos, whatever he wanted to call himself, something about giving himself over to a woman was worse than having lunch with the devil. Yes, he had susto. But no tea and no incantations by the curandera his mother brought over to relieve him of it would ever cure him. The mere mention of Fe was enough to set him off into a cold sweat. So La Loca prayed for him because in a few years he would probably look for a new novia to marry while no one, not even Mrs. Torres, not even he himself, would know that he was still suffering from the inability to open his heart.

Fe and her bloodcurdling wail became part of the household's routine so that the animals didn't even jump or howl no more whenever Fe, after a brief intermission when she dozed off, woke up abruptly and put her good lungs to full use. But it was Caridad who, being selfless would never have thought of becoming the center of attention, ultimately caused the entire household, including animals, to forget Fe when she came home one night as mangled as a stray cat, having been left for dead by the side of the road.

There was too much blood to see at the time, but after Caridad had been taken by ambulance to the hospital, treated and saved (just barely), Sofi was told that her daughter's nipples had been bitten off. She had also been scourged with something, branded like cattle. Worst of all, a tracheotomy was performed because she had also been stabbed in the throat.

For those with charity in their hearts, the mutiliation of the lovely young woman was akin to martyrdom. Masses were said for her recovery. A novena was devoted to her at the local parish. And although Sofi didn't know who they all were, a dozen old women in black came each night to Caridad's hospital room to say the rosary, to wail, to pray.

But there are still those for whom there is no kindness in their hearts for a young woman who has enjoyed life, so to speak. Among them were the sheriff's deputies and the local police department; therefore Caridad's attacker or attackers were never found. No one was even ever detained as a suspect. And as the months went by, little by little, the scandal and shock of Caridad's assault were forgotten, by the news media, the police, neighbors, and the church people. She was left in the hands of her family, a nightmare incarnated.

When Esperanza finally managed to get her mother to come home to try to rest a bit, they found Fe dozing off in her room and La Loca nowhere around. They didn't find her in the roperos, under the beds, not out in the stalls with the horses. The dogs would not reveal where she was, staring blankly at Sofi when she asked them about La Loca's whereabouts. Esperanza suggested calling the police. La Loca never left the house except to go out in the stalls, or walk down to the ditch, and though she rode, she never went out at night. Surely, the two women thought, after their having been gone for more than twelve hours, the two women thought, La Loca must have wandered off, not knowing what else to do.

But just as Esperanza was dialing the emergency number she heard a distinct clunk sound from inside the wood-burning stove in the living room. Sofi and the dogs heard it too and they all rushed at once to pull La Loca out. "Mom, is Caridad dead?" La Loca asked, soot-covered, arms around her mother's shoulders. She was crying. "No, 'jita, your sister is not dead. Gracias a Dios."

Just then Fe woke up and the walls began to vibrate with her screaming and since everyone including the dogs and cats had been concentrating on La Loca for a moment, they gave a start, in unison. La Loca began to cry harder and Sofi, who couldn't take no more the reality of a permanently traumatized daughter, another who was more ghost than of this world, and a third who was the most beautiful child she had given birth to and who had been cruelly mutilated, let herself sink into the couch and began to sob.

"Mom. Mom. Please, don't give up," Esperanza called out, but she did not come to put her arms around her mother's hunched shoulders. "Aw!" Esperanza said, clearly trying not to give in to it all herself. Although this was far from the right moment to spring her news on her family, she found herself announcing, "I've just been offered a job in Houston. I don't know for sure if I should take it . . ."

No one heard her anyway. Being the eldest, she was used to her mother's preoccupation with her younger sisters. Caridad, because she was too beautiful; Fe, because her compulsions wound her up too tight; and the baby, La Loca, because she was kind of . . . well, *loca*. Esperanza threw her hands up in the air and went to bed.

The next day, Esperanza went straight to her boss and gave her notice. The staff was pretty excited for her since the job in Houston was definitely a step up and things were looking good for Esperanza in the way of career opportunities.

As it turned out, she got a message before the end of that week from a certain Rubén out of her past. *Lunch tomorrow?* the message read. Sure, why not? Esperanza thought. Enough time had passed so that she could almost say she bore no hard feelings against her college sweetheart. She was doing all right for herself and she was certain he had seen her on the nightly news, so he knew it, too. Soon she would be getting out of New Mexico, broadening her horizons, freeing herself from the provincialism of her upbringing, and Rubén with his blond wife and their three-bedroom house, coyote kid, dog, and minivan could just live happily ever after as far as she was concerned.

But as it turned out there was no more house in the Northeast Heights and no more minivan. Rubén was driving an old clunker, and Donna had split with their kid to *Houston.* (Apparently she too was intent on starting a new life, broadening her horizons, freeing herself from her provincial upbringing, and so on.)

"I have thought of calling you for a long time, Esperanza," Rubén told her. "I have gone back to the Native-American Church and everytime I go pray at a meeting at one of the pueblos or go to the sweat lodge, I think of us, and how it coulda been." He had put on a few pounds, well, more than a few, but to Esperanza, he still had that kind of animal magnetism she always felt toward him.

"You remember, vieja, when we used to go to the peyote meetings together, when we sweat together at the lodge back in the days when we were in college?" he asked, giving her a nudge with his elbow. He was holding a mug of beer in his hand, and she saw as he waved his arms with great animation that he didn't spill any of it, but instead chugged it right down and grinned at her. No, he wasn't drunk, just feeling good. It was good to see him again, to be back together, and she ordered herself another beer too.

Esperanza didn't go back to work that day, but they ended up picking up where they left off, and to make a long story short, she didn't get to Houston that year, either. Every two weeks she was right there with Rubén, at the teepee meetings of the Native-American Church, Rubén singing and drumming, keeping the fire, watching the "door," teaching her the dos and don'ts of his interpretation of lodge "etiquette" and the role of women and the role of men and how they were not to be questioned. And she concluded as she had during their early days, why not?

After all, there was Rubén with his Native and Chicano male friends always joking among themselves, always siding with each other, and always agreeing about the order and reason of the universe, and since Esperanza had no Native women friends to verify any of what was being told to her by Rubén about the woman's role in what they were doing, she did not venture to contradict him.

At this time a virtual miracle occurred in Esperanza's house and which eventually caused her to decide about her relationship with Rubén. Well, actually she had been thinking about it for a while. Every time they went to a meeting, which was maybe once every two or three weeks, everything was good between them. They went to the meeting. Sometimes they also did a sweat. Afterward, they went home and made love all day. The problem was that then she would not hear from Rubén again until the next time there was a meeting. She was beginning to feel like part of a ritual in which she herself participated as an unsuspecting symbol, like a staff or a rattle or medicine.

As the months went on, their separation between meetings and sweats had become unsettling. It completely closed her off from her other life, the life which Rubén referred to derogatorily as "careerist." She felt just plain sad and lonely about it. She wanted to share with him that part of her life. She needed to bring it all together, to consolidate the spiritual with the practical side of things. But whenever she suggested to Rubén that they have lunch again like they did that first time or to go out on a regular date in between meetings, he simply declined with no apologies, regrets, or explanations.

What was left of Caridad had been brought home after three months in the hospital. In addition to caring for Fe la Gritona (as her mother had begun to refer to her, although never to her face), it was Sofi's main job to care for Caridad, or as stated more accurately above, what was left of her.

It was La Loca who took care of the horses and the other animals as well as helped her mother with preparing meals for her sisters. One evening, right after one of La Loca's infrequent seizures, the miracle that Esperanza witnessed occurred. Sofi was tending to La Loca, who was on the living room floor, the tray with Fe's carne adovada and green chili all over her, Esperanza standing nearby, and of course, all the animals that had given their perfunctory warnings just beforehand stood nervously around as well. Then movement in the adjacent dining room caught their eyes at once. Dogs, cats, and women, twenty-eight eyes in all, saw *Caridad* walking soundlessly, without seeming to be aware of them, across that room. Before anyone could react she was out of sight. Furthermore, it wasn't the Caridad that had been brought back from the hospital, but a whole and once again beautiful Caridad, in what furthermore appeared to be Fe's wedding gown.

"Mom?" Esperanza said, hesitating, but eyes still fixed on the empty space where Caridad had passed.

"Dios mío," Sofi gasped. "Caridad."

"Mom," La Loca whispered, still on the floor, "I prayed for Caridad."

"I know you did, 'jita, I know," Sofi said, trembling,

afraid to pull herself up, to go to the room where she suspected Caridad's corpse was now waiting be taken care of.

"I prayed real hard," La Loca added and started to cry.

The dogs and cats whimpered.

The three women huddled together went to the bedroom where Caridad was. Sofi stepped back when she saw, not what had been left of her daughter, half repaired by modern medical technology, tubes through her throat, bandages over skin that was gone, surgery piecing together flesh that was once her daughter's breasts, but Caridad as she was before.

Furthermore, a calm Fe was holding her sister, rocking her, stroking her forehead, humming softly to her. Caridad was whole. There was nothing, nothing that anyone could see wrong with her, except for the fact that she was feverish. Her eyes were closed while she moved her head back and forth, not violently but softly, as was Caridad's nature, mumbling unintelligibly all the while.

"Fe?" said Esperanza—who was equally taken aback by Fe's transformation. She had stopped screaming.

Sofi, sobbing, rushed over to embrace her two daughters.

"I prayed for you," La Loca told Fe. "Thank you, Loca," Fe said, almost smiling.

"Loca." Esperanza reached over to place her hand on La Loca's shoulder. "Don't touch me!" La Loca said, moving away from her sister as she always did from anyone when she was not the one to initiate the contact.

Esperanza took a deep breath and let it out slowly. She had spent her whole life trying to figure out why she was the way she was. In high school, although a rebel, she was Catholic heart and soul. In college, she had a romance with Marxism, but was still Catholic. In graduate school, she was atheist and, in general, a cynic. Lately, she prayed to Grandmother Earth and Grandfather Sky. For good measure, however, she had been reading a flurry of self-help books. She read everything she could find on dysfunctional families, certain now that some of her personal sense of displacement in society had to do with her upbringing.

But nowhere did she find anything near to the description of her family. And now, Caridad's and Fe's spontaneous recoveries were beyond all rhyme and reason for anyone, even for an ace reporter like Esperanza. It was time to get away, Esperanza decided, far away.

"I'm going to call Rubén," Esperanza announced, but at that moment her mother was too overwhelmed by her two daughters' return to the living that she didn't hear Esperanza either.

"Rubén?" Esperanza said, when Rubén answered his phone.

"Yeah? Hey, how's it goin', kid?" he asked with his usual condescending manner, adding a little chuckle. Esperanza paused. He talked to her on the phone like she was a casual friend. A casual friend whom he prayed with and whom he made love with, but whom he could not call to ask on a given day how she was doing. When it was her moon-time the estrangement between them widened since she was not permitted to go to the meeting or to sweat, nor did he like to make love to her. A casual friend who accepted her gifts of groceries, the rides in *her* car with *her* gas, all up and down the Southwest to attend meetings, who called her collect the month he left on a "pilgrimage" to visit the Mayan ruins throughout southern Mexico, where she had not been invited to join him, who always let her pick up the tab whenever they stopped someplace for a few beers and burritos just before she left him—after the meetings, sweats, lovemaking, to go home so she could get herself ready for that job which he suspected her so much of selling out to white society for but which paid for all the food, gas, telephone calls, and even, let's admit it, the tens and twenties she discreetly left on his bedroom dresser whenever she went over, knowing he could use it and would take it, although he would never have asked her directly for it.

"It's my sisters," she started to say, but already something else was on her mind more pertinent than the recent recuperation of Fe and Caridad.

"Yeah, your sisters," Rubén said. "You got your hands full, huh, woman?"

"No," Esperanza responded with sudden aloofness. "As a matter of fact, they're taking good care of themselves. I just wanted to tell you that I'm accepting an offer in Washington. And that I think it's better if we just don't see each other anymore, Rubén."

"Well, uh . . ." Rubén was groping for a response that would reinstate the pride just demolished by Esperanza's abrupt rejection, when he was cut short by a *click*. Esperanza didn't mean to simply hang up on him but she had just caught sight of a man peering in through the kitchen window. What made it really eerie was that instead of barking the dogs were waving their tails. Just then the man opened the door and stepped in. She recognized him right away since she was already going on twelve when he had left. "Dad?"

Yes. It was their father, Sofi's husband, who had returned "after all those years" as they would say around Tome for a long time to come. Some say, *that* was the true miracle of that night. All kinds of stories circulated as to what had happened to him "all those years." Most of the rumors he would start himself, and when he would get tired of hearing them played back always with some new variation or detail of exaggeration added to them which did not quite suit his taste, he pretended to get angry about them, stopped them, and started a new story all over again.

For example, the favorite chisme that went around about him was that he had been living down in Silver City, running a gambling operation and living the high life. After the story circulated awhile, the gambling operation became part of a house of ill-repute. Domingo found this addition to the story amusing, even something to boast about with his friends down at Toby's Package Liquors, or after Mass in the church courtyard. But when people started to say that Domingo had married the woman who owned and ran the brothel, Domingo got angry. He was many things, but a bigamist, nunca.

With regards to his own adventures, he quickly realized he had considerable competition with La Loca's life, which she herself didn't relate but which he invariably heard about from everyone else. When he tried to get her to fly to the roof or stick herself in the wood-burning stove, she simply stared at him as if such suggestions were absurd. However, the one thing she did confirm was her repulsion for human contact when ever he came close to her, unless she was the one who initiated it, which, believe it or not, once in a while she did.

She would approach him when he was eating or watching television and sniff him. Since he didn't want to scare her off, he'd remain still and pretend he didn't notice what she was doing.

" 'Jita," Sofi asked her daughter one day when they were alone, "what is it that you smell when you smell your father?"

"Mom," La Loca said, "I smell my dad. And he was in hell, too."

"Hell?" Sofi said, thinking her daughter, who didn't have any sense of humor at all, was trying to make a joke.

But instead Loca replied quite soberly, "Mom, I been to hell. You never forget that smell. And my dad . . . he was there, too."

"So you think I should forgive your dad for leaving me, for leaving us all those years?" Sofi asked.

"Here we don't forgive, Mom," La Loca told her. And

there was no question at that point in Sofi's mind that La Loca had no sense of humor. La Loca's voice empathized. "Only in hell do we learn to forgive and you got to die first," La Loca said. "That's when we get to pluck out all the devils from our hearts that were put there when we were *here*. That's where we get rid of all the lies told to us. That's where we go and cry like rain. Mom, hell is where you go to see yourself. This dad, out there, sitting watching T.V., he was in hell a long time. He's like an onion, we will never know all of him—but he ain't afraid no more."

2

On Caridad's Holy Restoration and Her Subsequent Clairvoyance: Both Phenomena Questioned by the Doubting Tomases of Tome

After Caridad's "Holy Restoration"—as her mother referred to her phenomenal recovery—she moved out with her Corazón. It was all very sudden and no one could really explain it, not even Caridad, but she was beginning to say and do a lot of things that could not be explained since her Holy Restoration, so Sofia did not protest the move too much.

Caridad insisted on finding her own place without asking no one, so it was no surprise to anyone neither that she took the first place she found without considering that there was no stall to keep her mare. Her new home was in a trailer complex which lay in the heart of the South Valley in Albuquerque. Some neighbors had horses and other assorted farm animals, so Caridad's Corazón in and of itself did not stand out. Except when it got loose it pretty much wandered about on its own. There was no corral for her and at night, she simply came close to Caridad's kitchen window and stuck her head in through an open window.

Caridad's landlady, doña Felicia, looked like she was at least ninety years old. Sofia suspected that the old woman was much older than that—as hard as that was to believe, she was so agile and self-sufficient—but her vivid memories of fighting in the Mexican Civil War with her first husband, Juan, meant that she *must* be over a hundred! Sofia finally decided that doña Felicia must have picked up the memories of her own mother and incorporated them into her storytelling.

How could she possibly be a hundred years old and still put on her red "*lipistick*" to go to Mass every morning and walk a mile to the market for her own groceries? When you stopped in at her own little traila, she was busy embroidering with perfect eyesight a beautiful mantel for a bride-to-be, keeping up with her favorite telenovelas on Spanish cable T.V. in between "patients," and ready with a pot of coffee and plate of beans to make you feel right at home.

Sofia entrusted her daughter, whom she referred to as una inocente—despite her lively history in every cowboy bar in el Rio Abajo—to the centennial old woman, and doña Felicia graciously assured the preoccupied mother that she would keep an eye on Caridad, adding that she did not see nothing too unusual about Caridad insisting on keeping her young mare with her, with or without a stall.

Corazón had become Caridad's only companion. "Los animales entienden más que la gente a veces," doña Felicia said to Sofia. Sofia was more concerned for Caridad's Corazón, who had never been away from their home in Tome, than for her daughter, who had shown an uncanny ability to survive anything. Caridad's Corazón, however, was easily frightened by strangers, the revving up of car engines and other loud sudden noises, even the playful shrieks of small children.

"Just make sure she remembers to keep her Corazón tied up, so it don't take off," Sofia asked doña Felicia, who nodded and gestured with liver-spotted hands that Sofia could count on her.

After Caridad's physical recuperation, she had run a fever for many weeks. Loca and Sofia spoon-fed her and took care of all her needs until Caridad was strong enough to get up and do things on her own. During her convalescence Caridad rarely spoke, but they knew that she understood all that was said to her because she responded with little nods and shakes of the head.

However, they also knew that she had changed in an even bigger way when, on four distinct occasions before she left home, she drifted off into a trancelike state and took on an otherworldly expression. Each time, both Sofia and Loca were witnesses.

The first time, Sofia was feeding Caridad her usual breakfast of blue corn atole and one huevo tibio and suddenly, her mouth still open, Caridad seemed to go paralyzed. Loca was sitting nearby, combing Bringraj hair oil through Caridad's chestnut brown locks, which had gone brittle from a year of being bedridden. She couldn't see Caridad's hypnotized expression, but suspected immediately that something was wrong. "Mom?" Loca said when Caridad abruptly "went away" (as Loca called it later), and Sofia started to gently shake Caridad by the shoulder, but she did not respond.

"Domingo! Domingo!" Sofia called her husband, who was in the living room watching a football game on television. He came medio asustao because he knew by his Sofia's tone that something had her frightened.

None of their attempts to revive Caridad worked. Instead,

slowly on her own she broke out of the trance. And when she looked around, as if wondering what these people with frowns on their faces were concerned about, she announced, "Esperanza is here . . ."

Esperanza had blown the job offer in Houston back when she first got together with Rubén. Maybe that had been for the better since as it had turned out that was where his ex-wife and child had gone to start their new lives; and Esperanza was the kind of woman who felt that no town was big enough for the two exes of one man. But come to think of it, Esperanza was the kind of woman that no town was big enough for no matter what category one might put her in.

That's why, when another big-time opportunity came along not long after for Esperanza, local star reporter, that time she did take it. By then, aside from it being a great career break, it was pretty clear to her that there was no need of her on the homefront. Her sisters had recovered. And with the reappearance of her father a likely resurrection of her parents' marriage seemed forthcoming, which was one more reason why Esperanza thought that her mother might not need her around no more. Finally, after playing out the renewed romance with her ex-love, Rubén, she concluded that fatality for them as a couple was only inevitable. They had one last sweat up at Taos Pueblo and parted at dawn as amigos. With little left to keep her locally, Esperanza had left for Washington, D.C., a month before to take a post as an anchorwoman with a major television station and had not been back since.

"Esperanza is going far away . . . and she's afraid . . .," Caridad continued. "We should keep her home, Mama . . .," Caridad finished, her voice drifting off as she fell into a sound sleep.

Don Domingo scratched his head of thick salt-and-pepper hair, relieved that his daughter was back to normal, and without comment went back to his Lazy Boy chair in the living room. But Sofia and Loca stared at each other and waited.

Momentarily they heard don Domingo call from the living room, "Jesus Christ!" The screen door opened and closed with a little squeak. Esperanza's mother and sister went to the door to greet her and with artificial levity she told them that she had just decided to see them all because she was homesick. "I just got to thinking how much I missed everybody, so I got on a plane and here I am!"

"Who got you at the airport, 'jita, Rubén?" Sofia asked.

"No, I didn't tell him I was coming either. But I am going to call him . . ." Esperanza's voice trailed off. She hadn't seen Rubén since they broke up, but she wasn't surprised at Sofi's question because mother and daughter had always been that way, anticipating each other's words. The truth was that she hadn't come home just because she missed everyone and all during the flight to Albuquerque she had thought of calling Rubén because no kind of white woman's self-help book and no matter how many rosaries she prayed, would result in giving her spirit the courage she got from the sweat lodge and which she surely needed now more than ever.

"Where are they sending you?" Sofia asked. Don Domingo stopped watching television and stared at his wife, who he realized had taken Caridad's mutterings seriously.

"Saudi Arabia . . . ," Esperanza answered. She smiled nervously as if she wanted it to sound like Paris or London or even Los Angeles but there was no way that this faraway and frightening place could be made to sound inviting. She looked at her mother, then at her father, then at La Loca, and she saw in their eyes that despite their naïveté about the things that happened in the world, they were well aware of what that assignment meant. So many men and women throughout the state had been shipped off in the last months because of the imminent global crisis.

Don Domingo, who had barely got past high school

himself, was proud of his college-educated, career-oriented daughter, but what had the world come to when a daughter also went off to the frontlines of a war as part of her "career"? What business did she have there and what right did her bosses have to send someone so obviously unprepared to defend herself?

While Domingo was still away from his family, imagining his four daughters growing up without him, he was actually glad he hadn't had no sons. When he was drafted for Korea, he had claimed mental instability and was made exempt. In his youth he belonged to a theater company and it was easy to improvise a performance for the draft board that sent him home rather than to war although he had to undergo a week's testing in the hospital first. Call him a pacifist or a chicken, Domingo did not believe in war, which he felt only benefited los ricos.

It had not occurred to him that a daughter could be as enticed by the idea of serving the military as a son. In any event, when he went back home, he was happy to find them all there, pretty much minding their own private lives. So what kind of trick of fate was this now to send his only college-educated civilian daughter off to war?

"Well, they don't send reporters out to where there's fighting or real danger or nothing, do they, honey?" don Domingo asked.

"Sometimes they do, Dad. That's the whole point of being a journalist," Esperanza said quietly.

"Well, how come they're sending you? You just got started. How come they don't send someone with more experience, like la Diana Sawyer . . . !"

"Papi, it's part of my job . . . I'm leaving Tuesday."

And that was that.

Sofi prepared Esperanza's favorite foods that weekend, like posole and sopa and lots of chili, because feeding is the beginning and end of what a mother knows to do for her offspring, even when she doesn't know what to say. Esperanza did go and spend the night with Rubén, but no one asked how it went between them nor did she say, and Monday morning she went back to Washington.

Caridad's second prediction had to do with don Domingo; well, it didn't have nothing directly to do with Caridad's father, but after the success of her first prediction, don Domingo made it his business to pay special attention to Caridad's don, this faculty of prophecy that even don Domingo could not have imagined having in his wildest dreams. After Caridad's second trance, Caridad told of a spectacular dream she had. She saw her horse Corazón leading a herd of one hundred and thirteen horses along a creek. There was some snow on the ground and the horses were all at a gallop, happy and free. "It was magnificent," she said, stroking Corazón's dark mane. "I felt like I was one with them."

Don Domingo, who was never one to miss a cue where he might have an opportunity to make a profit, called his brother in Chicago to play the state lottery for him. "Put a buck on 113 today, will you?" That night, don Domingo's brother called him to tell him that he had won eighty dollars on the daily number.

Needless to say, for the next few days it was don Domingo who insisted on feeding his daughter and keeping her company, hoping that again she might reveal a winning number through trance or dream. But no more numbers came to her head and within a week, he returned the task of caring for Caridad to his wife and youngest daughter.

The third occasion for a prediction caused Caridad to come out of her trance with a smile. "Wilma's coming home," she said. "And we're all going to have our hands full with her . . ." La Loca was gleeful to hear this news because they had given up their Irish setter for dead months before.

The next morning, they found Wilma in the stall, having

just given birth to a litter of six mixed-breed puppies. "I don't know how Fred's going to take to these puppies . . ." Sofi laughed. "He's got quite a wife here, taking off on him and coming back with a familia!" But as it turned out Fred, noble and gentle creature that he was, accepted Wilma and her brood playfully and showed no indication of resentment for having been abandoned.

Finally came the last instance of Caridad's domestic prophecies, which although significant to her family, could not have been very interesting to the world at large. Sofi thought this to herself in deciding to not mention any of it to the neighbors or to her confessor. Especially since this last one foretold Caridad's own departure from home and therefore it is quite a matter of individual opinion whether one wants to consider it a prediction or simply an announcement. In any case, Caridad, like the other times, fell into a trance beforehand. "Corazón and I are leaving," she said to Sofi and Loca when she came to. "But we won't be together for very long . . ." And then, whatever it was that she "saw" but could not tell in words caused her to cry unconsolably.

Remembering this prophecy Sofi requested of doña Felicia to make certain that Corazón was tied up because her trance-susceptible daughter was not reliable regarding such responsibilities, having only recently resumed the basic one of caring for herself.

As soon as Caridad was up and around she returned to her job at the hospital, because after all, she did need to support herself since neither Domingo nor Sofia had ever been able to do more than give her a roof over her head and food to eat. This was all the work she had ever done since high school—change starched linen, clean out bedpans, help make patients comfortable, fluff up their pillows, and get hold of doctors to prescribe heavier doses of medication when they couldn't sleep because of so much pain and misery. As before, she worked the second shift and, if asked, sometimes she also stayed on for the third shift, and then she didn't get home until seven in the morning.

During this time she tended to be distant, although she was able to function well enough and did her job as well as before, and even more conscientiously, as her supervisor observed. It was hard for her co-workers to pinpoint the change. It wasn't like she was unfriendly or had undergone a major personality overhaul. Caridad was still the sweet disarming woman she had always been. The only marked difference that everyone agreed upon, and of course found perfectly understandable, was that she had quit drinking and "dating."

They were quite relieved about that, since it had been pretty obvious that that road was leading to some form of self-destruction or other, and surely what had happened to her was warning enough, if one could call what she experienced a warning and not in fact a second chance at life.

Otherwise, Caridad seemed content enough, with her job and with her new trailer home, which she had begun to decorate herself, buying pieces of furniture at the flea market and the segundas on Fourth Street, making her own curtains and chair covers. And although Corazón had never been ridden and did not seem ready for the idea, Caridad spent a lot of time with her horse, who stuck its head into whatever window she left open, trying to follow her from room to room while she went on telling Corazón whatever it was that she didn't tell no one else. Which was quite a bit, because Corazón had become her best friend.

Caridad trusted her mother implicitly, and even Loca, but she had a few reservations about her father, whom she had not grown up with and who was always anxious to cash in on something she was apt to utter without thinking—but after she left home she hardly didn't see her family no more. Loca didn't come to visit because who knows what atrocious-smelling individual she might be forced to be in contact with, so neither Caridad nor Sofi insisted. Don Domingo came by only when Caridad needed a hand bringing home a piece of furniture too big or heavy for her to handle alone.

One morning when Caridad came home, doña Felicia's soft rap followed almost immediately. "Ay, m'jita!" she said, and spoke to her in Spanish as she almost always did. "What a night I had taking care of that animal of yours!"

Caridad didn't say nothing. Instead, she moved aside, letting the little old woman enter and continue with her story, which by her expression had caused her a great deal of anxiety. "Do you want some tea, doña Felicia?" interrupted Caridad, who had recently become very interested in herbs and knew just what she would give the poor old woman for this anxiousness of hers. Caridad was not worried because Corazón was busy feeding outside, and so she knew that whatever could have happened, it had not ended badly.

"About one o'clock in the morning," doña Felicia said as Caridad went to put the kettle on, "I noticed that your horse was gone! Ay Dios Mío, I was so worried, I called the sheríf's office. You know where they found her? Halfway down the road to your mother's house! Fortunately she was taking the back roads and did not get on the freeway!"

"Well, she's home safe now," Caridad smiled, while she mixed a little sage into the te de demiana she was preparing for doña Felicia. "What a beautiful day it's going to be, don't you think?" Caridad asked, stroking Corazón's muzzle. Corazón's head was inside the kitchen window. Doña Felicia drank her tea and went back to her trailita shaking her little head, around which was wrapped her long thin silver plait.

She considered Caridad a decent tenant and liked her mother well enough, but it was apparent that Caridad was not being realistic about her horse. The horse needed better attention, she thought. She could not pass another night worried about it if it decided to take off again. She herself could not get close to it because the mare was not used to no one except for Caridad and got very agitated when doña Felicia or anyone else was nearby. She called Sofi to tell her all this, and while Sofi was in agreement, she hesitated to take the horse back home because it seemed to be the only source of comfort and friendship for her daughter.

The two women decided that yes, maybe it would do Caridad more harm than good to take her Corazón away and so they let the matter go. "If it takes off again, doña Felicia," Sofi assured her, "call me. I'll have my husband take care of finding it. You shouldn't have to worry about it." And that was that.

But only eight days later Corazón was dead. And nothing that doña Felicia nor Sofi could say to each other could make them think they had not made the wrong decision about leaving the young mare in Caridad's care. It wasn't really Caridad's fault either, however, since she had done nothing but feed it the best oats, brush its sable brown coat, and give it all her love.

It seems that after doña Felicia fell asleep watching an early Catinflas movie that fatal night Corazón pulled herself away from the post where she was tied. It probably wasn't a good thing that Caridad took on those double shifts. To a waiting horse perhaps that time passed with torturous languor. There was a party going on down the road, with the loud voices of drunken men and cars screeching away, and finally Corazón took off for home to Tome.

The sheriff's deputy was waiting for Caridad when she came home the next morning. He said that he and his partner had found the horse lying by the road having broken its hoof jumping over the cattle guard. They did what they thought they had to do and shot it. One bullet just above its left nostril.

"My Corazón is dead?" Caridad asked in a whisper of

disbelief. Just then doña Felicia came out to see what was going on. She had just woken up from her easy chair from which she had not moved since the night before, having had a rare full night's sleep. As usual when she first got up, she peeked out her windows to see how things were with the world, and to her alarm the horse was gone again. But no sooner did she make that observation when she saw the deputy's vehicle parked right in front of Caridad's door.

The deputy left promising to take the horse's carcass out to Caridad's mother's property. Caridad was sitting on a banco. "They killed my Corazón . . . ," she said looking up at doña Felicia. It was obvious she had taken quite a blow from the news and couldn't get herself to stand up. Doña Felicia let out a little gasp, her hand going over her mouth, "Ay, cheri," is all she said in consolation. But she was not surprised. Something like that was bound to happen.

This poor girl did not have the sense even to take care of herself, from what her mother had recounted to her about her terrible mutilation. How could anyone expect her to take care of something so delicate and demanding as a horse? Her mother should not have let either of them go, and doña Felicia decided she would tell Sofi as much when she went back in and called her with the news.

For the moment however, she helped Caridad to her feet and led her into her trailer. "Ma cheri," doña Felicia spoke, and taking care to be as tactful as possible with what she had to say to Caridad, "your mother tells me you have developed the don to see into the future . . . how is it that you didn't foresee this tragedy?"

"I did," Caridad said. Doña Felicia went about the kitchen preparing tea for both. "But knowing and preventing are two very different things, aren't they, doña Felicia?"

"Yes," the old woman nodded, glad to hear that no matter how innocent, naive, or just plain "loca" Caridad was said to be she knew the difference between these two important aspects of the laws of the universe. This was an indication of the true healer, as she had suspected.

"Esos salvages del sheríf's department did not have to shoot your horse," she told Caridad. "I could have set its bones. If it's true where they say its hoof was broken, it could have been mended."

A revitalized expression took over Caridad's face. "You know how to set bones?" she asked. Doña Felicia laughed and placed a cup of raíz de valeriana in front of Caridad to drink. "Of course I do! That was what I did during the Revolución! I put more soladados back together and sent them back to work in their fields than I can remember! I set bones, I removed bullets, and more importantly, I gave them courage!

"Women endure the labor of childbirth and men send themselves to war! But I gave birth to eight children and never once did I cry like I saw some of those men out there before they even fired their first shot! I think it has something to do with the unnaturalness of killing compared to the naturalness of giving birth. What do you think, cheri? But then, you've never given birth yet! No importa. You endured a tremendous battle and just look at you! By God's grace you're like new! Which brings me to tell you something I've been thinking a lot about since you came to live here. How can I say this? I believe you are meant to help people a lot more than just wiping their behinds as they make you do in the hospital. Don't think I am degrading your work. It's honest work and necessary work, ma cheri, and I more than anybody know about hard work. But you are destined to help people as even those trained doctors and nurses down there can't do. Look what you did for yourself! All they did at the hospital was patch you up and send you home, more dead than alive. It was with the help of God, heaven knows how He watches over that house where you come from . . . but *you* healed yourself by pure will. And yes,

I will show you all I know. It will be my pleasure and it is el Señor's wish."

"How do you know?" Caridad asked.

"¡Mira! Look at how the pelitos on my arms are standing up!" doña Felicia responded, putting out her goosefleshed arms as proof of God's approval of her plan. "That's a sign that I always get when He wants me to do something!"

Caridad stared at the old woman who was to become her mentor. How she wished already that she knew how to listen to the Lord, had her own surefire signs that came directly from Him, and knew even some of the wondrous healing secrets that doña Felicia had at the tip of her fingers. Caridad had always been charitable. She had faith and hope. Soon, she would have wisdom from which she had sprung, and sooner still her own healing gifts would be revealed.

So it turned out that a tragic morning in Caridad's life turned out to transform itself very much the way it is when we wake up to an overcast day and suddenly the sun breaks through. That's how she took doña Felicia's offer to teach her to heal.

"But I will miss my Corazón . . . ," she told doña Felicia. "It was my only friend . . ."

"I, too, am your amie—tu amiga," doña Felicia assured Caridad, patting her hand with her shriveled one. Caridad smiled as best as she could because one look at doña Felicia and anyone could tell she wasn't exactly destined for too many more years in this life. On the other hand, how many had she already endured, and how many wars had she witnessed, and how many children had she borne herself as well as helped bring into this world? It was very possible that doña Felicia had no intentions of leaving the earth until she said she was good and ready.

"I'm tired, doña Felicia," Caridad said.

"Yes, I know, ma petit, go to bed, get some sleep . . ."

"No, I mean, I'm really tired, doña Felicia," Caridad went on.

"Yes, I know, cheri," doña Felicia said again. "Go to bed now. Descansa."

Caridad let doña Felicia take her to her room and put her under the covers. She did not even change out of her orderly's uniform nor remove her "*pantinghose*" (as doña Felicia called them), and her head had hardly touched the pillow when she went into a deep sleep.

In the meantime, doña Felicia called Sofi and told her to expect the sheriff's office to deliver the remains of Corazón, and this was done. La Loca wanted to go to her sister but could not bring herself to travel into the unknown terrain of the city, so she prayed, as she so often had done for the women in her family. Don Domingo simply said they should never have let Caridad take the mare. For that matter it was obvious that since Caridad's trauma, despite her unexplained physical recovery, she had no business on her own either. And by the way, did anyone get the number of the license plate of the deputy who had gone out to Caridad's trailer?

"How the hell can you think of such things when your daughter has just had such a tragedy!" Sofi scolded her husband.

"The death of an animal always foretells something," he replied, shrugging his shoulders. "That mare was a beautiful creature. I don't see what's wrong with thinking somehow its death could bring us good fortune. And anyway, I would do it for Caridad to get back some of her losses . . ."

Sofi lost her temper. "You can't recuperate that kind of loss with money!"

"M92183," La Loca announced, between Hail Marys, passing through the living room at that moment with a rosary wrapped around her fingers. Sofi and Domingo both stopped arguing to watch Loca go out the back door. Immediately don Domingo went to the phone to call his brother to play the Illinois State "Big Lotto" for him. This time he was going to go for the big one and skip the daily number.

Of course by this point you can guess that Domingo won with that number because it was his destiny now, having not just one, but two daughters with unusual dons. Eventually it would be revealed that none of the women in that family was without some unusual trait—and even though a fortune was not in Domingo's cards, he was not going to suffer the same economic hardships he had experienced all his life especially during those years that he didn't like to talk about when he had left his wife and 'jitas.

As La Loca had told her mother, her father had indeed been to hell and back, which is what may be said of the life of the compulsive gambler. Only God knew what depths he had sunk to during those many years that no one had heard of him; and though he seemed at first to have made a recovery from his addiction no less incredible than that of his two daughters who had undergone their near-death experiences, he understandably had relapses, such as wanting to play the numbers related to Corazón's death.

While it is the gambler's nature to fall prey to superstitions, in a household such as Sofi's it was becoming increasingly difficult for her husband to determine what was a definite "sign" to play a hunch on and what was just part of its daily activities. And in order to ensure his luck even more, in the bargaining style of gamblers, he made an unselfish promise to himself that if he won—and indeed he did—one day when Caridad woke up (since after doña Felicia had put her to bed Caridad slept without stirring for nearly fourteen days) he would grant her anything she wanted with the winnings that had come from the death of her heart.

3

On the Subject of Doña Felicia's Remedios, Which in and of Themselves Are Worthless without Unwavering Faith; and a Brief Sampling of Common Ailments Along with Cures Which Have Earned Our Curandera Respect and Devotion throughout War and Peace

First and foremost, doña Felicia will tell you that nothing you attempt to do with regards to healing will work without first placing your faith completely in God. Yes, the last apprentice of her life nodded when asked if she believed. Thus, her apprenticeship began.

When doña Felicia was a child of about eight years of age in Méjico Viejo, near Veracruz, just before she lost her mother to malnourishment and disease gone untreated, she accompanied her mother to a woman's "home" (really just a room in their vecindad) where her mother went to have her cards read. The woman, a mother herself of who knew how many little children all running in and out, eyed the little girl suspiciously from the moment they entered the room.

Finally she said, "Señora, I must ask you to have your little girl wait outside. She is obstructing my ability to see anything in your spread. Her presence is too powerful—I think she is a non-believer and I can't concentrate!" Doña Felicia's mother did not understand what the fortune-teller meant by "non-believer," but she did not want to offend the woman so she sent her only child out to play.

That woman, whom doña Felicia never forgot because on their way home her mother told her that the woman had predicted that she was going to die soon and then she did, was right about her. Felicia was a non-believer of sorts and remained that way, suspicious of the religion that did not help the destitute all around her despite their devotion. Then her first husband, Juan, died in Zapata's army and she was left to find her way home with their two infants, and finally, she did develop faith, based not on an institution but on the bits and pieces of the souls and knowledge of the wise teachers that she met along the way.

But as the decades wore on, doña Felicia came full circle, reaching a compromise with the religion of her people when she became caretaker of the House of God in Tome. And finally, she came to see her God not only as Lord but as a guiding light, with His retinue of saints, His army, and her as a lowly foot soldier. And she was content to do His work and bidding.

She had been a young mother, illiterate, the orphaned daughter of mestizos who had both died without leaving her, to put it in a few vulgar words, so much as a pot to piss in. Many years would pass, and eventually doña Felicia not only learned to read and write in her native Spanish, but also in French during the Second World War and English as well. She usually mixed two or even three of the languages, still making herself somehow quite understood by all.

She would have two more children by a second husband who tied railroad tracks in the United States just before the Depression, and they enjoyed a brief life of fine clothes and a brand new Studebaker. Then they lost everything when they were deported back to Mexico in cattlecars along with the rest of the Mexicans who had been brought in as laborers during the days of prosperity. That husband also died, he was not shot in the head as Juan was before her eyes, but rather died of tuberculosis, the only thing that the United States had allowed him to bring back to his country.

As a bracera during World War II, doña Felicia ended up joining the U.S. Army rather than letting herself get deported again and trained as a nurse. She took her two youngest children (the two eldest were grown by then and on their own) with her to Europe when she was sent to mend soldiers in the frontlines.

She married a French soldier and had two more children. But when the war was over she discovered that her husband was already married to a woman in Lyon and he went back to his first family and doña Felicia (by then she could be considered a "doña") returned to America alone, and made her home in the United States.

And while she did not marry officially again, she had one more true though brief love and bore her last two children during the era when families throughout the United States were rushing out to buy television sets. If those two youngest children had lived, the rest of doña Felicia's long life might not have been absorbed by her role as devoted community servant. But at the age of ten, her boy was kidnapped and found dead months later facedown in a riverbank and later her daughter at nineteen was found raped and murdered—and from that point on, doña Felicia lived alone.

The six older children had gone their own ways, away from the land she finally decided to settle in; sometimes they wrote and less frequently visited her with their own families and even their families' families and doña Felicia, who as a child was said to have no faith, had nothing but faith left and devoted herself to healing with the consent and power of God, Tatita Dios en Sus cielos, the only lasting caretaker of her life.

Caridad observed and assisted doña Felicia for several months before she was even asked to diagnose a "patient." At first it was all too confusing and scary to Caridad, who tended to drift off into her own thoughts and did not know if she could truly decipher the symptoms and complaints of other people, nor could she determine which were based on physical ailments, which were spiritual factors, and which were "psychological"—and therefore to be treated solely with generous doses of compassion.

Could Caridad even be said to know how to listen at all, much less listen properly so as to not misdiagnose an illness? A curandera not only had the health of her patient in her own hands but the spirit as well. What if Caridad gave out the wrong remedio and caused the sick one to get worse, or to go mad, or even to die?

So for a while, Caridad just paid very close attention, observing her teacher at work. "Everything we need for healing is found in our natural surroundings," doña Felicia told her and put up her two hands in front of Caridad, palms facing her. With those hands she had repaired more bones and muscles and rubbed out more intestinal obstructions than you could shake a stick at. Yes, those two wrinkly instruments of ancient medical technology were in the final analysis all doña Felicia could count on.

Among the most common ailments Caridad learned were empacho and bilis; mal de ojo, caída de mollera, and susto (not to be mistaken with espanto or corage) had to do as much with the body as with the spirit; and aigre, which could be translated to a number of things, the most common being just plain gas. Yes, there were many others and a wide range of variations even among these. These illnesses could be a result of physical causes or, as said before, the result of someone's bad intentions. "Watch that you never give people reason to envy you!" doña Felicia warned her. Oh, envy was a formidable force, doña Felicia told Caridad, which could cause a victim to suffer the worst pain imaginable, even death!

Quite often these symptoms were not only treated with herbs, decoctions, and massages but also with "limpias"—cleansings. Depending on the ailment the cleansing treatment might range from employing tobacco smoke, an egg, or a live black hen, herbal baths, or sweeping the body with certain branches and incense.

No, the work of the curandera was anything but simple. But one thing was sure, as Caridad saw for herself, as long as the faith of the curandera was unwavering, successful results were almost certainly guaranteed—the only thing that could prevent them was the will of God.

When they were not treating patients, life became a rhythm of scented baths, tea remedies, rubdowns, and general good feeling for Caridad. Her body, already externally repaired from the mutilation it had undergone, now was slowly restored internally by the psychic attentiveness she received from her teacher and which she learned to give to herself.

Ritual, in addition to its potent symbolic meanings, was a calming force. Tuesdays and Fridays she prepared a baño for herself. Sundays she cleaned her altar, dusting the statues and pictures of saints she prayed to and the framed photographs of her loved ones—with special care to the one of Esperanza who by then, it was known, was a famous prisoner of war. Every night on the ten o'clock news, instead of Esperanza giving the news live in person like she did in the old days, her picture was flashed and an update was given on her status. It was still assumed by the press that Esperanza was alive but being held captive.

Sofia and Domingo wrote letters and made telephone calls to congressmen and senators and were even invited by one big shot to Washington, but nobody had yet found out anything about what happened to Esperanza and her crew.

Loca prayed.

Doña Felicia tried to divine some news through the Tarot, sticks, and a raw egg dropped in a glass, but only had vague images of Esperanza.

On three occasions Caridad woke from a deep sleep in a sweat and felt her sister's presence. All Caridad could say of it was that Esperanza wanted to come home.

On Sundays Caridad always lit at least one white candle so as to start the week with her head clear, changed the manta on the altar, and cleaned out the incense brazier.

Her "moon" became regular by taking rue at least three days before she estimated that it was due. Te de anis she drank for anxiety and she also prescribed it on a regular basis for her sister Fe. Romero, the woman's herb, she also took a cup of each day.

She kept to a diet of mostly fruits and vegetables; once a week she and doña Felicia shared a small piece of medium-rare hormone-free steak for added protein. They liked yogurt fruit liquados as a snack with a piece of rennetless cheese. They worked long days, going to bed around midnight, the last of their clients (or patients, if you will) being seen no later than 10 P.M. Since many people worked and had to go home first to make supper for familias and put their hijitos to bed, they often could not get away any earlier to see doña Felicia and Caridad.

The two women were usually up just after sunrise, except during those occasions when Caridad fell into trance, which usually were followed by bouts of sleeping for days and nights on end. On most days doña Felicia went to seven o'clock Mass but she was no longer as fixed about such habits as when she was the keyholder and dressed the saints of the church at Tome. Caridad never went to Mass; instead, a new student of yoga, she rose with a salute to the sun.

A Brief Sampling of Doña Felicia's Remedies

Empacho (gastrointestinal obstruction): "Now, there are many kinds of causes of empacho—eating too much of one item, too many oranges, let's say, or food that's too 'cold' for your system, food that's gone rancid and so on—or perhaps you have been given something to eat by someone who wants to do harm to you and it gets 'stuck' somewhere in your intestines . . .

"First you must determine that it is empacho and not bilis, which is related to the bladder and kidneys and not the intestines. You can do this in various ways. A gentle massage of the person's belly is usually the fastest way. You feel around carefully, like this, using the index finger of each hand and when the patient feels a little pain, you usually will also feel something like a bolita inside and there you will know is the obstruction.

"If you can't determine it by feeling, you can try using an egg to tell you. The egg, as you know, is used to divine many things, as well as used for cleansing people of mal espiritus. Bien. So, you lay your patient down, arms spread in a cross-like fashion. You reveal the stomach area, not forgetting to commend yourself to Dios and to repeat the Creed at least three times while you are concentrating, you move the egg on the patient's belly in the sign of the cross, then you break it. Yes, the person may put her hands up so that it doesn't spill off, but where the yolk breaks on her stomach is where the obstruction is. To be truthful, I don't trust this method as much as my own feeling and my fingers, but I have a lot of practice, so maybe it comes easier to me to just know these things than it will for you right now.

"Now, the part about treating empacho which is not very pleasant is that sometimes you may have to go in through the rectum to loosen the obstruction, but if it is necessary then it must be done. If it is too far up for your finger, use a candle. For these difficult cases, I later recommend a good enema—but believe me, except in the cases of small children I leave that to the person to do for herself when she goes home!

"Tomatillo is very good as a decoction for treating empacho. You take a little crushed root mixed with lard and rub the abdomen until you loosen the obstruction. You can tell because the bola starts to break down. You can also give some of the root to be drunk for three days—before breakfast.

"Other teas that are very good for treating empacho are raíz de valeriana and estafiate. You may chew a sprig of sage, that is very soothing too. Te de canela, te de manzanilla—I usually recommend to children for empacho, they are very mild teas and very good for curing their little tummyaches!"

Aigre (internal draft): "Anyone at anytime can be susceptible to air, which is another way of saying 'catching a draft,' only it's on the inside. Aigre can even be caught by the dead! But in their case it is a matter of a bad spirit entering their bodies and not just the wind that sometimes causes headaches, an earache, stomach pain, and so on. In the case of the dead catching aigre, we used to have the custom of putting pieces of cotton soaked in alcohol in all their orifices to ensure their protection from such invasions, back in the days when one laid a body out at home. Now they take your people off to a funeral parlor and who knows what they do to them there.

Anyway, you see now how easy it might be to mistake aigre for something much more complicated like empacho when the person comes to you simply complaining of a pain in the stomach.

"Usually the point is to 'warm' the person up, with teas if they are children, a nice massage with alcohol, and if they are gente grande, you can even give them un tragüito!" Doña Felicia herself was not averse to a little drink now and then, at which time she liked to "toast" with the following verse:

Un doble y un sencillo quitan cualesquier resfrío.	A double and a single get rid of any chill.
Si es grande la pena, copa llena; si no se quita que se repita.	If the grief is big, fill the glass; if it remains fill it again.
Contra todo mal, mezcal. Contra todo bien, también.	Against all bad, mezcal. Against all good, as well.

"Ventosas are a tremendous treatment for getting rid of aigre from various places in the body. Sometimes it gets into the shoulders and back, not only in the stomach! I do ventosas to treat my patients who have rheumatism, too. Candles, as we know, are very special for helping us with our prayers and the ventosa requires the use of a candle. In the old days, I used candles that were brought from the church, but now I use store-bought candles. If I remember I take them to be blessed by the priest and if I can't do that, I dip them in holy water, and when I can't get to the church to have the priest do it, I just say an Our Father over a jar of water. A small candle is placed on a penny on the troublesome spot on the patient's body. Steadily, you light the candle. Then you place a clear glass directly over the lit candle. You will see how it sucks out the mal. You can repeat this as many times as you like until the patient feels some relief."

Mal de ojo (evil eye): "This is something that is usually given to children, mostly infants and sometimes even to one that is still in its mother's womb. People don't usually give mal de ojo on purpose. It comes from admiring the child too much and the way to prevent making the child sick, as we all know, is to simply touch it, a little stroke of the manita or a pat on the head y ya. The parent understands and you will be free of worry that you have made the baby sick because you admired it too much. When I have seen a pregnant woman who has mal de ojo I recommend for her to eat the meat of a black hen. Usually the black hen is not a good thing for people to eat, it is more for the use of cleansing and to be thrown away, but because of the daño caused to her child within, it is not too potent for her. In the case of children, I lay the little child down, arms spread in the form of a cross, to diagnose whether it is mal de ojo or not. While I rub an egg over his little body I pray the Apostle's Creed, and always I say at least one Our Father. It doesn't hurt to commend oneself to the Virgen Maria either, by the way. Afterward, I break the egg into a clear jar of water and leave the jar with the egg underneath the child's bed for the night, right under where his little head rests. In the morning, if it is mal de ojo, you will see the "eye" there—in the form of a clotted substance that clings to the yolk. If the white has risen high up, the mal de ojo was given to the child by a man. If the white stuff stays around the rim, it was a woman. Then you take the jar and throw the contents in the toilet—or if you are out where you can dispose of them in a river or ditch, do that. Just get rid of it for good."

Limpias (spiritual cleansings): "Over the years I have come across many different ways in which people cleanse—cleanse persons, houses, stalls, trucks, things that have come in contact with los malos espiritus. But I don't want to say that it is as simple as that—as if there are all these unhappy souls floating around us just looking for a vulnerable person to ruin. No, it's not like that at all. Although I will not say that there aren't unhappy souls that sometimes do that to people! Many times that terrible state of being comes from within the person himself, a sorrow too great to contain any longer, anxiety over not having work to support one's family, or misery caused by an unfaithful lover. The purpose then of a cleansing is to restore peace of mind to the individual, to give him a clear head so that he will know what practical things he must do to improve his lot.

"Throughout my years of practice and my travels I have learned many different ways to cleanse but I will tell you right now only of two as examples, very simple and very quick, for cleaning a house and cleaning an individual. Sometimes someone who has bad feelings about us comes to our home, that's why it's always a good idea to keep a jar of fresh water somewhere near the door. It absorbs the bad vibrations that people bring with them so always remember to change the water when visitors leave. You will know right away when bad vibrations linger because you will not feel at ease in your house soon afterward. It's not always something noticeable like a foul odor left in the air, it's just a feeling. Sometimes you keep getting gooseflesh when passing the place where the person sat. Sometimes you feel all right when you are at work but when you come home you cry all the time or can't sleep. These are indications that it is the house and not you. Of course, we also know that sometimes when a person has died or grieved terribly in our home that that person's sorrowful energy may also linger there, and we must get it out if we are to feel peace at home again. Salt, in my opinion, is maravilloso as a cleanser. We may form salt into the shape of a cross beneath our beds, under where we rest our head. You may go as far as spreading salt all along the baseboards of your rooms . . . turpentine is also good for this, applying it the same way. Incense, like sage, is also a good fumigation. Let us not underestimate garlic and even onion as similar cleansers. It is good to have a string of garlic near the door—it will avert people with bad intentions from coming in! Sprinkling holy water around the rooms is helpful, and you don't need a priest for this. Don't forget to give your house a good cleaning with plenty of ammonia! There are many cleaning agents for ridding a house of bad vibrations, but always one must remember to commend herself to God, praying the Apostle's Creed and always at least one Our Father.

"Giving a person a limpia is extremely delicate work since you are dealing with the person's spirit. I will tell you of one of the early ways I learned to do limpias. It was called 'a sweeping' by my first teacher, doña Jovita, I'll never forget her, from Nuevo Leon de Méjico Viejo! I've never known a woman más buena, may she rest in peace. She made a small broom with branches from the rue bush, rosemary, and hierba de cruz and brushed it over the person, up and then down in sweeping motions. The person usually stood in the center of the room, with arms spread in the form of a cross. On the floor, she burned incense in a brazier, close to the feet of the person getting the sweeping so that the fumes reached up to him. When she knew that the person was afflicted because of intentional harm done by someone else, she might cleanse the person by rubbing the egg of a black hen over his body, or sometimes use the chicken itself as a sweeping instrument, that would consume all the mal out of the person, and then she'd take it out, kill it, and bury it.

"As you have already seen, mi'ja, there are many ways to cleanse but what we must remember above all is that it is He who performs the work and we are only His servants made of vulgar flesh here on this earth. So when people come to me, resentful and bitter because catastrophe has struck their homes, their houses have burned down or their cow was hit by lightning . . . I always tell them to humble themselves before the magnificence and the power of Our Father in heaven and before anything we offer a prayer in which we begin: Thank you, Señor, Tatita Dios. Más merecemos. ¡Ay! We deserve even more, lowly beings that we are!"

4

Of the Further Telling of Our Clairvoyant Caridad Who After Being Afflicted with the Pangs of Love Disappears and Upon Discovery Is Henceforth Known as La Armitaña

At daybreak on Wednesday of Lenten Week doña Felicia readied herself for her yearly pilgrimage to Chimayo. She prepared a lonche to last three days, put on a cap with "Raiders" written across it to protect her head from the sun, and gave another one to Caridad, signaling to her that she was going along and that was that.

El Santuario was not far from the little adobe that don Domingo was having built for his daughter, and Caridad, who had chosen that spot because of its holy reputation, had only passed through the village. This was Caridad's first pilgrimage. Sofi never took her girls to Chimayo during Holy Week. As a matter of fact, during their growing-up years it had been difficult to take them all together anywhere because of La Loca's inability to be around people because of their all-too-human smell. But of course Caridad, through her dreams and from people's accounts, knew all about Chimayo, which was why she had chosen to have her house built there with her father's lottery winnings.

In that valley in the Sangre de Cristo foothills nearly two centuries before, a Penitente Brother performing his penances during Holy Week ran toward a bright light coming out of the ground not far from the river. He dug at the spot where the light emitted and found a statue of Our Lord of Esquipúlas.

Now, of course there are a lot of amazing aspects to this legend because Nuestro Señor de Esquipúlas was the black Christ of the far-off land of the converted Indians of Esquipúlas, Guatemala, and how He got to the land of the Tewa is anybody's guess! But he most certainly had a mission, which was to let people know of the healing powers of the sacred earth of Tsimayo—just like he had done in Esquipúlas—so shortly after his appearance, the Catholic Church endorsed as sacred what the Native peoples had known all along since the beginning of time.

With this in mind, Caridad was more than willing to go but not all that thrilled, frankly, at the prospect of *walking* all the way there, which was the only way doña Felicia said that they would get there, refusing to jump in Caridad's pickup when Caridad opened the door for her.

"If *I* can make it on these rheumatic legs filled with varicose veins—certainly a young girl like you can make it there skipping all the way!" doña Felicia told Caridad who, without responding, reluctantly followed the old woman as she started down the road.

Doña Felicia nimbly led the way in the direction of the penitente procession she told Caridad that they were going to join, only stopping occasionally to take a swig of water from the jar that she had handed over to Caridad to carry along with the rest of their provisions.

"Doña Felicia—how hot do you think it is today?" Caridad called out to her guide after they had traveled a long while. At that point it really didn't matter how hot it was, because hot can only be so hot before it's just *hot*. The sun was pounding on Caridad's head right through the Raiders cap, sweat dripped down the sides of her face and down her neck. She was drenched under her breasts and armpits and her T-shirt was soaked. Caridad had only asked so as to make conversation, since she was lonely walking in single file all that long way.

"Don't talk," doña Felicia responded over her shoulder.

"¿Por qué no?"

"Because it's hotter if you talk . . ."

They walked, rested, slept in a huddle at night, rose at dawn, and walked some more until Good Friday, when they caught up with the penitente procession. While it's not every day that you see a crowd following a Christ-like figure carrying a cross along the highway (unless your people are from Chimayo or Tome or similar places throughout the territory controlled by the Spanish queen and friars for centuries with such ferocity that neither Mexican nor U.S. appropriation diluted the religious practices of the descendants of the Spaniards who settled there, including this procession that has been performed annually for two hundred years and will probably go on for two hundred more, such is their fervent devotion), Caridad, who had not been in love with anyone since Memo, fell in love that Holy Friday, and this took her by such surprise that every other marvel around her paled in comparison.

So, the telling of the penitente procession, the description of Francisco, doña Felicia's godson, who carried the huge wooden cross over his bare shoulders for miles under the piercing sun, and all the rest of that impressive spectacle will be forsaken because it was surpassed by the one of Caridad falling in love.

When they reached el Santuario it was swarming with tourists and others also making their Lenten Week pilgrimage. Caridad stayed close to doña Felicia. "You're getting more like your sister Loca everyday," doña Felicia scolded her, pulling her faded tapalo away from Caridad's grasp.

Caridad tried to hide her tension about the crowd and let herself move away from doña Felicia just enough so that she no longer was able to cling even to the reassuring smell of ground comino and chili that came off doña Felicia's pores. Yeah, she was getting more like Loca more and more each day, she agreed to herself. Now, like Loca or like a blind person or even a dog, she was sensitive—although not averse—to individual body odors. Well, ni modo, she concluded, because after all, Caridad did not go in for psychoanalyzing that which just was and it was enough for her to know something without having to question it.

It was about then, however, that she stopped short at the sight of the most beautiful woman she had ever seen sitting on the adobe wall that surrounds the sanctuary. At that moment the woman also turned toward Caridad, but since she was wearing sunglasses, Caridad wasn't sure whether her gaze was being returned.

"Come on, come on," doña Felicia summoned Caridad the way one does with children, with a little sweeping gesture of the hand. Caridad, completely overwhelmed by the sight of the woman, blushed and followed doña Felicia into the church without a word. They lined up to go through the small rooms adjacent to the chapel where there is a pozito opened to the holy earth with which, since the early part of the nineteenth century, Catholics (really, it wasn't their fault that they came so late to this knowledge, being such newcomers to these lands) have healed both their bodies and spirits.

Both doña Felicia and Caridad bent down and rubbed

some of the earth along their brows and temples and on their forearms and put a little on their tongues. Doña Felicia also scooped some up and put it in a small coffee can she brought for that purpose, and then they slowly made their way out.

All the while, Caridad could do nothing but think of the woman on the wall. Maybe she had sunstroke and had just imagined her. She was exhausted and nearly dehydrated and surely she could not have experienced what she felt throughout her entire body just from the sight of a woman! But as soon as they were outside, coming around from the back of the church, she saw the woman in question, more real than before, still on the wall. Moreover, the woman on the wall was looking over her shoulders in Caridad's direction!

Doña Felicia and an uneasy Caridad went to the front of the church and found a little shady spot under a cottonwood to have their lunch. Each one ate four oranges but couldn't touch any of the tacos de papitas doña Felicia had prepared, their stomachs were so unsettled from heat and fatigue. They peeled one orange after the next, sharing without a word, just sucking hard to end their thirst.

All the while, Caridad kept sneaking glances over at the woman on the wall who, as far as she could tell, was unabashedly staring at her as well.

"Maybe she thinks you are a long-lost cousin . . . ," doña Felicia said out of nowhere.

Caridad blushed because the feelings she was having were not the ones one has for a long-lost cousin and yet, she couldn't explain them. Memo had been her only love. After Memo, all was a blur for her. She could not tell you the name or identify the face of one man among all those who had followed her out of the bars at night where she had spent entire years of her life.

It was a funny thing because you might figure that after what happened to her, not only with Memo, but especially because of that nightmarish night in Caridad's life, she might have become an embittered woman, who hated men for having served little purpose in her life but to bring her misery and shame. But she didn't. Caridad was incapable of hating anyone or anything, which is why doña Felicia had elected her heiress to her healing legacy. Hating came quite easy in this life of injustices, doña Felicia figured, but having an abundant heart took the kind of resiliency that a curandera required.

Caridad had never talked about that night to anyone, but there were two people besides herself who knew what had happened because she had let them know through dreams and that was La Loca and doña Felicia. And they three knew that it wasn't a man with a face and a name who had attacked and left Caridad mangled like a run-down rabbit. Nor two or three men. That was why she had never been able to give no information to the police.

It was not a stray and desperate coyote either, but a thing, both tangible and amorphous. A thing that might be described as made of sharp metal and splintered wood, of limestone, gold, and brittle parchment. It held the weight of a continent and was indelible as ink, centuries old and yet as strong as a young wolf. It had no shape and was darker than the dark night, and mostly, as Caridad would never ever forget, it was pure force.

The night doña Felicia dreamt of the *malogra*, she jumped up and ran about the house with her escopeta—the one she had used in the Revolución, a little rusty, but still operable—in a half-sleep until she realized it had been a dream and that the thing was not there in her rooms. When La Loca dreamt it she went out to the stall and slept between two of the horses. "Oh my God! Oh my God!" Sofi said, crossing herself when her daughter described her dream the next morning, coming in and carrying her blanket covered with hay that Sofi snatched from her and threw out the window. (Loca's hypersensitivity to human smells had shortchanged her response to the odors of the animals.)

In Loca's dream it had taken the shape of sheep's wool, large, voluminous, not in animal form but something just evil. "That was the *malogra*, 'jita! It was looking for you! Oh my God! And you went outside . . . that's where people see it, out in the dark, at night! Thank God it didn't find you out there!"

Caridad dreamt of it often, and while it still frightened her, on each occasion she built courage against it. One day, or rather night (for it seems the *malogra* only comes out at night), she would wrestle it to the ground, that wicked wool spirit, at the crossroad where she knew it still waited with nothing better to do.

"Doña Felicia, I'm too shy . . . ," Caridad ventured to say to her friend. "Will you go up to that woman for me and ask her where she thinks she knows me from . . . if that's why she keeps looking at me?"

"She's gone, mi'jita," doña Felicia answered casually, unaware of the importance it had to Caridad. Caridad looked up and sure enough the woman on the wall was gone. Caridad quickly scanned the area but didn't see a trace of her. She bit her lip. Suddenly she jumped up and declared, "I'm going to look for her . . ."

"And what are you going to say?" doña Felicia asked without budging from her spot. "And what is the purpose, anyway?"

Caridad sat back down. Her whole body was affected by a stranger and she couldn't explain why. And now the woman on the wall was lost to her in the thick of the crowd. In total despair, sitting on the ground with her legs tucked beneath her, she threw her body forward, arms stretched out, and let out a deep sigh of despair like a prayer.

"Oye, niña, this is not Mecca!" doña Felicia teased Caridad. Doña Felicia let out a little "hee-hee" laugh afterward because she still didn't know what Caridad was going through with Woman-on-the-wall. Caridad shook her head but did not get up. How could she tell doña Felicia that for the first time in years, since way before the attack, her heart was renewed, moved by another human being? Admit it, Woman-on-the-wall was the most beautiful woman she had ever seen—but she had scarcely had more than a glimpse of her. And what had made her so exceptional to Caridad in any case?

In and of herself there was nothing about her that was unusually striking. She was dark. Indian or Mexican. Black, black hair. Big sturdy thighs. She could tell that because the woman was wearing cutoffs. There was just something about her, and suddenly Caridad got up and without a word to doña Felicia began to wander about in search of her because she knew that she could not bear the thought of living without that woman.

For twenty minutes, Caridad searched without success and then she spotted Woman-on-the-wall, who by then was sitting on a small hill, legs spread out in front of her the way a child sits on the ground. She was pulling food items out of her backpack and talking with another woman; and for the first time Caridad realized that Woman-on-the-wall-now-on-a-hill had been with this other woman all along, but like a close-up lens, Caridad had focused only on the dark woman. Even now that she had become aware that Woman-on-the-wall-now-on-a-hill was not alone, she perceived the other woman as a blur rather than an actual person.

Then Woman-on-the-wall-now-on-a-hill looked over in Caridad's direction, and Caridad was certain that she was being looked at this time, because without realizing fully that she was doing it, she was climbing the hill toward the two women.

"Hi," they all said to each other when Caridad had reached them. A rather anticlimactic opening for the most dramatic moment in Caridad's life thus far. Well, then again, perhaps "dramatic" is not the best word here, considering who we are talking about, but to Caridad such events as her Holy Restoration, her clairvoyance, the Screaming Sister (as some unkind people back in Tome still referred to Fe), and such were just part of life. Falling in love . . . now *that* was something else altogether! In any event, that brief meeting overwhelmed Caridad, who, having nothing else to say, turned right around and went back down the hill.

When she returned to doña Felicia, they gathered up their things and began their strenuous walk back to Albuquerque with the only consolation that at least the sun had begun to set and would not leave them like a couple of dried peach pits by the side of the road before they had a chance to curl up somewhere to sleep.

Caridad returned at dawn on Easter Sunday to her little trailer with her inner being blooming bright red like the flowers on a prickly pear cactus. She swept, mopped, changed the linen, cleaned the kitchen appliances, scrubbed her bathtub and toilet bowl, and sang Aretha Franklin tunes. About 5 A.M., just as the sun was splitting the sky, doña Felicia knocked on Caridad's door. "What's going on?" she asked, looking at Caridad with a cleaning rag in her hand just about to start wiping off the venetian blinds.

"I can't sleep," Caridad said cheerfully.

"Well, nobody can say that cleaning is a waste of time, ma cheri, but why don't you try praying? Whatever you're trying to figure out will come to you, believe me. And you can give that little body of yours a rest," doña Felicia told Caridad and went back to her own trailita with its smell of chili sauce, herbs brewing, and its fresh Yerba de la Vibora hanging from the window panels to dry.

So this is what Caridad set out to do as soon as doña Felicia left. Sometimes, however, she had a tendency to follow doña Felicia's advice to a fault, which may explain why it wasn't until the following Tuesday, when doña Felicia had to revive Caridad who had passed out at some point before her altar that she *stopped* praying for light to be shed on her regarding Woman-on-the-wall-later-woman-on-a-hill-with-someone-else.

"Ay! doña Felicia," Caridad said. "I'm a lousy student for you! I see mirages and am filled with bad dreams! Right now I was dreaming of being pursued by a creature with huge wings like a giant eagle, but he had these small horns—or maybe it was a she—and he or she was wearing armor and I was flying as fast as I could to escape it until I hit a telephone wire and crash-landed. Good thing you woke me up and saved me!"

"Why don't you go up to Ojo Caliente?" doña Felicia suggested. "And take yourself a nice mineral bath, cheri!" She slipped Caridad a ten-dollar bill knowing that since Caridad left her job at the hospital her finances were tight. Since the assassination of Caridad's Corazón, doña Felicia no longer charged her rent. So Caridad packed her vinyl overnight bag with hair blower, toiletries, and a change of clothes (badly needed since she was still wearing the T-shirt and jeans she had on during her long trek to Chimayo and back, and she had cleaned house in the same apparel), got in her pickup truck, and left.

This was the last that anyone saw of her for a year. To begin with, Caridad had no sense of direction and could not read a map, so consequently she did not carry one; also, she had never been to Ojo Caliente. That by itself might explain her getting lost. But then I shouldn't have said that no one saw her because she did make a stop at the NuMex gas station just off I-25, where Francisco el Penitente happened to be working at the time as a mechanic, and *he* told his godmother later that Caridad had stopped and put ten dollars even in her tank. This was when doña Felicia knew something was up because she knew that Caridad only had ten dollars and would not have gone up to the hot springs for a mineral bath without money to pay for it. Still, doña Felicia decided not to call Sofi and don Domingo, since that would only serve to worry them, until a few nights had passed and doña Felicia herself could not divine what had become of Caridad.

First, the old curandera lit a special candle for St. Anthony who helps people find lost things. Well, of course Caridad was not a thing, but la inocente was lost like a broken compass just the same. But St. Anthony kept silent and did not give doña Felicia so much as a clue, not even when she turned his small statue upside down to persuade him to cooperate. Instead, he kept more tight-lipped than ever. The truth is St. Anthony probably just didn't know where Caridad went, since like I said, he is for finding things, not people.

Now, El Santo Niño de Atocha is another matter—and he more than likely had probably guided Caridad to a refuge. But many years before doña Felicia and El Santo Niño had had a falling out, so she no longer entrusted her prayers to the child Jesus who once saved Christians from Muslims in conquered Spain and in North America saved conquering Catholics from pagan Indians. (This was part of doña Felicia's problem with the little saint in Spanish regal dress, trying to accept that he saved souls or abandoned them depending on their nationalistic faith.)

Doña Felicia used divining sticks and then she took out her dog-eared deck of Tarot cards given to her by a woman in Veracruz back in '27, but neither of these gave her any specific information. All she knew was that Caridad was alive and that she had left on her own accord. She told Caridad's family as much on the third day after her disappearance.

"Ay! How could you let esa inocente out of your sight,

doña Felicia!" Sofi wailed, hands up in the air. She came over directly to Caridad's trailer as soon as she got the news from doña Felicia, as if she had to see with her own eyes that Caridad was really gone. Sofi feared the worst for her daughter.

"Now, now, Sofi," said one of doña Felicia's vecinas, "reprochas ain't gonna do nobody no good . . ."

"I say we call the police. That's what they're there for! St. Anthony might help you find a ring that has fallen behind a trastero, but he can't bring a grown woman back against her will!" another comadre contributed.

"And what makes you think that Caridad doesn't want to come back?" Sofi asked, somewhat put off by the neighbor's presumptions about her daughter, whom she hardly knew.

"And what makes you think that the police would find her?" Sofi's husband added. From what he understood the local police had done next to nothing to find his daughter's attacker or attackers when she was left for dead by the road. If they knew who it was that had disappeared they probably would do little more than a routine hospital and jail search for Caridad, such had been her reputation. Domingo had heard many insulting stories about his daughter and had defended her honor more than once in Valencia County bars when it was suggested that she had for all intents and purposes "asked for it" when she was attacked.

"No, we'll get some people together and we'll go out to look for her ourselves," he said. And that's what happened. For weeks, Caridad's father and those concerned about Caridad spread themselves out throughout the state posse-style in hopes of finding her. Somehow they were certain that she had not left her homeland. But where could she be? Not in Albuquerque, Santa Fe, Taos, or any of the villages where they put out the word. They asked the peoples from the pueblos all the way from Taos to the Zuñi to see if she had turned up on any of the reservations. But there was no sign of her no place.

Meanwhile, Esperanza was still missing in the Persian Gulf. The last traces of her and the other three members of the news crew were their abandoned jeep, six thousand dollars in cash, camera equipment, and footsteps in the sand leading toward enemy lines.

Domingo's and Sofi's invitation to Washington by the only senator who seemed interested in discussing their missing daughter brought them little reassurance. It was an election year and Domingo decided afterward that the senator's only concern was getting some good publicity out of their meeting, which had been on national television news. The couple returned home feeling worse about Esperanza than ever.

"God gave me four daughters," Sofi told Father Jerome her confessor, who was still saying Mass at the church at Tome, "and you would have thought that by now I would be a content grandmother, sitting back and letting my daughters care for me, bringing me nothing but their babies on Sundays to rock on my lap! But no, not my hijitas! I had to produce the kind of species that flies!"

"Your daughters fly?" Father Jerome interrupted and cleared his throat a little. He had never gotten over the sight of the infant who had risen from her little casket and ascended to the church roof, but he did not know of any other incidents since then.

"Well, Padre," Sofi explained, "you remember when La Loca went to the church rooftop the day of her funeral when she was three years old? Then, just before Caridad's disappearance, doña Felicia told me that Caridad had a dream where she was flying and being pursued by Lucifer or some other horrible winged monster like that, and if I know Caridad more than likely she is flying around somewhere in the mountains, keeping out of the way of telephone wires! And then my Esperanza flew—not with her own wings, of course, Esperanza is much too practical for that—but in a jet to another continent and she too, is gone! The only one who stays earthbound is la Fe . . ." At this point, Sofi began to cry.

"Well, be thankful for that much," Father Jerome sighed and put a hand on her shoulder to comfort her. He had once talked to the bishop about the case of the resurrected child, but had not brought himself to mention the details about her flying or her announcement regarding her otherworldly travels. The bishop had dismissed it as an example of the ignorance of that community and added that such "resurrections" were commonly reported where proper medical attention was not given.

"And what do *you* think happened to your sister?" Sofi had asked Fe's opinion one evening out of desperation. She knew Fe did not have clairvoyant faculties, but her calmness about the matter puzzled her mother so that she wanted to hear Fe's speculations.

"Which ____?" Fe asked. Sofi could not hear the second word to her question because of the fact that Fe had severely damaged her vocal cords during the days when she had so violently and ceaselessly screamed; as a result, when she spoke now her voice was scratchy-sounding, similar to a faulty World War II radio transmitter, over which half of what she was saying did not get through, something like talking to Amelia Earhart just before contact was broken off altogether and she went down.

Sofi understood her daughter, while exercising to the fullest the patience granted to her to endure the particular life she had been given. Nevertheless, being only human, she answered with exasperation. "Of course I mean Caridad! I'm too scared to even think of la Esperanza . . . bombs falling, prisoners of war paraded on the television every night. ¡Dios mío! God only knows what has happened to m'jita . . . !"

"Did you __ think ______ Cari____ eloped?" Fe suggested. Poor Fe, she never did get over Tom. All she seemed to think about were bridal gowns, floral arrangements, and the June wedding she never had.

"Caridad get married? To whom?" Sofi asked.

To whom indeed.

A year passed before Caridad was found one day living in a cave in the Sangre de Cristo Mountains. It was Francisco el Penitente and two of the hermanos from his morada who found her quite by accident. No one knows *why* they were up there just before Holy Week, all on horseback that afternoon, when they spotted the traces of a fire someone had made and followed their noses to the cave that turned out to be Caridad's home.

The young woman was hardly recognizable. You can imagine what she looked like after not having changed her clothes or been in contact with a single human being for four seasons!

More than likely she had bathed in the stream that ran a few miles down below, but Francisco would not have ventured to gamble on it. At least we know what her water supply was and from the other things the men found that day, jackrabbit pelts and the bones of other similar small animals, it was also apparent as to how she kept herself alive. Now, how she kept herself warm during that bitter winter that had just passed, besides with animal skins and maintaining a fire, no one will ever know.

"You're coming with us!" one of the brothers said sternly to Caridad once they all were able to agree that she was indeed the woman that everybody had been looking for for so long.

Caridad shook her head. The man dismounted from his Arabian steed and went over to her to pull her firmly toward his horse. She resisted and let herself drop on the ground. He bent down to take her up in his arms, figuring she would be even easier to get on the horse without any resistance but he couldn't lift her. "What the . . . !" he said, dumbfounded at how heavy she was although she was only half his size.

The other man joined him and finally Francisco el Penitente and yet the young woman could not be budged. The first brother, irate that his strength seemed no match for such a slight person, motioned to yank her along by the hair. "Stop!" Francisco el Penitente called, dropping to his knees. "It is not for us to bring this handmaiden of Christ back to her family. Can't you all see that? It is not our Lord's will."

He said a quiet prayer on Caridad's behalf and the men left, resigned that it was for them to simply relieve her mother of her worry by reporting that they had found her.

The word spread quickly, however, that a woman hermit was living in a cave up there and that she had resisted with passive yet herculean strength three men who tried to carry her back home. Many people remembered the stories regarding La Loquita Santa and were not surprised that her sister also showed out-of-the-ordinary abilities.

So it was that during that Holy Week, instead of going to Mass at their local parishes, hundreds of people made their way up the mountain to la Caridad's cave in hopes of obtaining her blessing and just as many with hopes of being cured of some ailment or another. Not only the nuevo mejicano–style Spanish Catholics went to see her but also Natives from the pueblos, some who were Christian and some who were not, since for more than a year Caridad's disappearance had been a mystery throughout the state and her spartan mountain survival alone seemed incredible.

The three men whom Caridad resisted by making herself into lead weight turned into a score of men as the story spread. Francisco's humble gesture of delivering a prayer for her well-being became the act of many men brought to their knees before the holy hermit, all begging forgiveness for their audacious attempt at manhandling her. It was said that she lifted the very horse in the air that the hermano had tried to force her to mount—with him on it—but out of benevolence brought it back down safely without so much as spooking the horse with her defiant magic.

The word had even gotten as far as Sonora to Yaqui land. The stories grew until some began to say that she was the ghost of Lozen, Warm Springs Apache mystic woman warrior, sister of the great chief Victorio who had vowed "to make war against the white man forever." And Lozen, among the last thirty-eight warriors, was the only woman. It was Lozen who alerted the others when the enemy approached, being warned herself first by the tingling of her palms and her hands turning purple.

When left by herself, Lozen turned toward the four directions and sang to her god Ussen to guide her through the wilderness.

Yes, perhaps this mountain woman was not the one the Penitente brothers thought her to be, but a spirit-memory, and that was why she was not overcome by them.

Don Domingo, who could spin a good tale himself, was amused by these accounts and although he knew his daughter was not of the common strain, he strongly suspected that she was not lifting horses nor bringing droves of men to their knees.

Sofi refused to join the Easter Week throngs, convinced that if that was la Caridad up there she would make herself invisible rather than let herself become a spectacle. She decided she would wait it out. Now that she knew her daughter was safe, living in a cave but safe nonetheless, her heart was calm.

Doña Felicia took her yearly pilgrimage to Chimayo and decided that she would go and get Caridad afterwards. It had been decades since she had done any mountain climbing. She did not drive and didn't trust no one to take her up there neither. But she would tell her godson to point her in the general direction and she was certain she would find her apprentice and convince her to come back home with none of the resistance that Caridad had shown to the men.

Fe, who had not once worried over her sister's disappearance but had continued with a business-as-usual attitude (she still worked at the bank and drove everybody up the wall with her perfectionist's manias), continued to maintain that her sister's departure from society must have something to do with being in love. In all fairness to la Fe, it must be admitted that her theory did coincide with the fact that Caridad disappeared right after she was bowled over by la Woman-on-the-wall-later-woman-on-a-hill.

Caridad herself could not explain, even if she were inclined to try, what led her up those mountains that day. She could not say why, after having slept for four days and nights before her trip, she was so overcome by sleep that after getting lost she pulled up in that secluded area, thinking it was as good a place as any to rest, and abandoning her pickup, curled up that first night at the mouth of a cave and slept undisturbed by the cold mountain winds.

The following dawn, when she woke to a delicate scar in the horizon that gradually bled into day and saw the sun then raise itself like a king from its throne over the distant peaks, Caridad only knew that she wanted to stay there and be the lone witness to that miracle every dawn.

Until those three men rode up on their horses she did not think of time or of no one, not doña Felicia, not her mom or the other members of her family, not even herself, but not a sleeping or waking moment went by when her heart did not long for Woman-on-the-wall in Chimayo.

Once the three men had gone away that day the spell of solitude under which Caridad had lived peacefully was broken, but she remained in her cave home in a daze, trying to remember what her life was like before she got there.

There followed another disorienting event, worse than the abrupt appearance of the penitentes who tried to make her do something she didn't want to do. After so many, many months of tranquillity—through heat, winds, snow, and blooming cactus again, her entire mountain was invaded up to the threshold of her very cave home by hundreds of people!

What did they want? As the first dozens arrived, she thought they had come to get her by force—like those three men—and she went deep inside the cave to hide. But later, she heard them call to her: "Oh Holy One! We beg you, please take pity on us!" "Your blessing, Little Hermit!" "I beg you, santita armitaña, help my mi'jito!" or "Cure my dying padre!" or ". . . a mi abuela!" or "a mi pierna coja que ya no sirve pa' nada!"

Of course, all this was confusing to Caridad, who, having been away from society for so long, made no connections between those please and her recluse existence and she just went deeper into the cave until all the voices finally went away.

Unbeknownst to Caridad, however, down below some of the daily newspapers had reported the pilgrimage to her mountain with "eyewitnesses" who had supposedly seen her. Some claimed to have been touched and blessed by her and still some others insisted that she had cured them! One man said that when he laid eyes on her, he saw a beautiful halo radiate around her whole body, like the Virgen de Guadalupe, and that she had relieved him of his drinking problem. One woman showed the press a small scrap of cloth that she said she had torn from la Santita Armitaña's robe!

"Robe?" Sofi said, after she read the article. "What was my daughter wearing when she left here anyway?" she asked doña Felicia, who was at the stove making fideos in one pot and preparing a purification baño for a neighbor in another.

"Distracted" as she tended to be at that stage in her life, she accidently sprinkled a little camphor oil in the fideos that was meant for the baño in the other pot for a woman down the road with espanto. But decided that it couldn't hurt too much, even if it gave the food a suspicious taste.

"I can tell you she wasn't dressed for the occasion, cheri!" doña Felicia laughed. "But then, who's to say how a handmaiden of Christ should dress!"

"A handmaiden of Christ? Now *who* is calling her that?" Sofi asked.

"My godson Francisco. But I think he's in love with la Caridad . . . No matter. Tomorrow I'll start up there and she'll be back home soon enough!"

But as it turned out, by the time the old lady made her way up to the cave home of her apprentice who had absentmindedly let a year pass without letting her know where she was, not even in a dream, Caridad had found her truck, had some trouble starting it up, but had been able to take off, remembering only that she was on her way to Ojo Caliente to take a mineral bath.

She didn't have money and the price for a bath and wrap had gone up a buck anyway since the year before, but fortunately Caridad had brought with her some animal pelts and she traded a flawless deer skin for the bath. It was worth much more than one bath and the woman behind the counter gave her credit for a series of visits before she sent the bewildered-looking mountain woman in filthy rags off to the locker room.

Slowly Caridad took off her handmade deer-skin moccasins. She laid her Raiders cap beside her on the bench. And finally she pulled off her T-shirt. She scarcely noticed the attendant, who had placed a clean towel next to her, pick up her Raiders cap. "I'll be a sonofagun!" the attendant said, and still Caridad did not look at her, more shy than ever around people after not having been around no one for so long. The woman had a kind of singsong accent that Caridad took to be Native American. Slowly she glanced up, sensing the woman was waiting to meet her eyes.

"I remember you! You're the woman who was at Chimayo last year! You came up to me and my friend and then went off right away!" The woman spoke as if she had just run into an old high school chum and wasn't being recognized because she had gained too much weight or had had too many babies or didn't wear bangs no more. She looked straight into Caridad's eyes, expecting Caridad to respond to her own enthusiasm at any moment, but Caridad's stare was dull and blank.

This woman before Caridad had nice teeth. She had shiny black hair pulled back, half in a ponytail and half down. She was confident and kind and full of stories of good times and bad times—all this Caridad was sure of. But she could not possibly be la Woman-on-the-wall-later-woman-on-a-hill that had obsessed her to such an extreme that she had all but abandoned life itself . . . could she?

Not because it wouldn't have made perfect sense to run into her at the first stop she made after returning to the world, for Caridad believed that her life had to have a turn for the better at sooner or later and this would have been as good a time to start as any.

But this attendant—who now, disappointed or just confused that Caridad had only stared at her and said nothing, had concluded that Caridad was burnt out on drugs or something and went about her business picking up wet towels off the floor—was just a woman.

The woman led Caridad to her bath after Caridad had showered for no less than an hour, feeling hot water run down her back for the first time since we all know when, and after a while, she called Caridad out of the tub to wrap her up and let her sweat out her body's toxins.

Then the woman began to talk again, as she arranged

Caridad with a huge flannel sheet and a kind of wool Army blanket, leaving her neatly wrapped like a human burrito. All the while, she went on talking as if Caridad wasn't hearing her. "I just thought you were someone I had seen at Chimayo last year, but I guess I was wrong . . . Anyway, you looked so much like a cousin of mine that I ain't seen since we were girls. She's Pueblo, like me. Well, I'm half. My father was Mexican, so my grandma tells me. I didn't know my mother either. She died of a bad liver, you know how that goes. That's why I got to live with my grandma in Acoma.

"I ain't seen none of my cousins for a long time . . . I sure miss 'em. My friend, you know, the one I was with that day when I thought I first saw you? She's kinda like my roommate, you know? She didn't think you were my cousin. You're not Indian, are you? But I had this feeling like we knew each other . . ."

Caridad closed her eyes. Then she felt the woman's breath close to her face. "Are you *sure* you wasn't that woman in Chimayo last year?" the woman whispered.

"Yes," Caridad finally said. "That was me." A hot tear was escaping down her left eye, making its way to her ear when the Acoma-Mexican woman caught it with her finger and wiped it off. "Shhh," she told Caridad. "You rest now. Just rest."

5

An Interlude: On Francisco el Penitente's First Becoming a Santero and Thereby Sealing His Fate

Francisco el Penitente was not always Francisco el Penitente. As a boy at Our Lady of Sorrows School and to his pals in the playground, he was Frank. To his six older brothers and to his father he was el Franky. To his Mexican godmother, la doña Felicia, however, he was Panchito and, sometimes, Paquito and as he grew up, her Paco. But to his buddies in 'Nam he was Chico.

He didn't like Chico—which back home meant a roasted corn.

Or just a hard kernel.

He didn't like Chico no more than the Navajo who was also in his platoon went for the nickname "Chief," or the Puerto Rican from Rio Pierdas, just shy of finishing his Ph.D. when he was drafted, liked to be called "Little Chico." Francisco el Penitente (who was not a penitente then) was a lanky six feet in height compared to Little Chico's five feet eight inches, and to the white and black soldiers all "Spanish boys" were "Chico."

It was much later, at the age of thirty-three, that Franky joined his uncle's morada up north, over ten years after he undertook his uncle's vocation of santero for himself. Thus he sealed his fate to play a role in the religious belief system of his people and his land as both santero and penitente and from there on became Francisco el Penitente.

There were many signs throughout Francisco el Penitente's life that indicated such a destiny for him, but they were never so blatant that anyone like doña Felicia, his father, or his tío Pedro would have readily detected them.

Signs that pointed to a special fate came to him rather like his third-grade teacher Sister Prudence used to say, "Remember, children, God writes straight with crooked lines!" For example, Francisco was the seventh son but not of a man who was the seventh son of his family; instead, it was his uncle Pedro who was the seventh son. Francisco's own father, in fact, had been the first son, and as such, had only known a life of family obligation rather than spiritual aspiration.

His tío Pedro, a seventh son as was just said, inherited his father's gift for making santos at a very early age. Francisco was not sure if his grandfather had also been a seventh son because his grandfather did not live to see his youngest grandchildren and his own children were not as intent upon knowing such ancestral details as Francisco, who was in search of a divine sign to reveal to him his role on earth. Thus, the crooked line of God passed the seventh son's gift to a seventh son although not in direct lineage, and for the time being Francisco had to settle for that.

Being a santero means many things in many places, which Francisco discovered when having a conversation with Little Chico about his tío Pedro one night while they shared a joint and waited to be killed if they didn't kill first. "Hey, no kidding?" Little Chico laughed. "My uncle in Carolina, Puerto Rico, is a santero, too!" But no, as Francisco discovered when they got into it more, that Little Chico's santero tío practiced a very distinct variation of the Catholic influence on the New World—a Yorubic adaptation of the names of European and Hebrew saints to African gods.

The Caribbean santeros maintained a kind of secret membership, just as the penitente brothers of Francisco's land did. However, theirs included women as much as men and were not based on medieval Catholic rituals seeking absolution through penance and mortification, but on ancient African rites, with drums and frenzied dance and much more, in which the santero himself contained the power to answer prayers, perform miracles, and cast out demons from the possessed.

No, Francisco, explained, a santero in Nuevo Méjico was a simple man, often given to solitude, who worked alone. Sometimes a woman succumbed to the vocation, but this was rare. The santero, in and of himself, had no divine powers except during the time he was preparing a bulto, a wooden sculpture of a saint. His expert hand was not guided by the aesthetic objectives of artists, but by the saint himself in heaven, as permitted by God, because that wood-turned-bulto would become the saint's own representation on earth to aid those who were devoted to him.

The santero used the artistic talent granted to him humbly as a creative individual, and with the same deftness which he applied to his fields, to the care of his animals, and perhaps even to the love he had for his woman, he prepared the materials for his bulto. Not every man or just any man who decided to produce such holy icons for his church and community had the stamina to make it his life's vocation. And while a santero received a certain amount of respect for his work, it was nothing in comparison to that recognition that artists have aspired to since the Renaissance when all work—secular and sacred—began to be signed with the illustrious name of the individual who designed it.

El tío Pedro never expected no one in his own family to follow his path because although times changed slowly for him, he knew the world around him was transforming beyond comprehension. But when his nephew came back from the war in Vietnam and visited with him so many times and finally asked to try his hand at a bulto he considered that perhaps it was possible, after all, that the family tradition of over two centuries was not ready to die out yet.

Francisco or el Franky, as his tío Pedro still liked to call him, was the youngest born to his sister-in-law, and while an unquestionably sensitive child—something which don Pedro tended to attribute more to being "spoiled" by his mother as the youngest boy and later by his godmother—he showed no early indications of being special in any way.

Pedro's eldest brother insisted on yet another child after the birth of his seventh son because although it had been a good thing as a rancher to have so many boys, his heart yearned for a daughter. And so it was that the eighth and last of his brother's children was a beautiful little girl, Reinita, named after her mother, Reyna.

When Franky started school at the age of six, both his mother and baby sister, who were not vaccinated as had been all the boys in school, became very ill and died of smallpox, leaving Franky's father alone with the seven boys.

The youngest boys were sent to their respective padrinos and the oldest ones stayed to help their father with the ranch. When el Franky was ready for high school he left his godmother Felicia's home, where he had been treated like a little prince without so much as ever being expected to fix his bed in the mornings, and went back home to help his father with the laborious tasks of farming.

Doña Felicia, because of her advanced age, was more of a grandmother to Francisco than a substitute mother and as the years went on his mother ever ascending toward heaven became more remote as a former human being and more akin to a celestial entity. To Francisco, yes, his mother was no less than a saint. Many men say this of their mothers, of course, who sacrifice themselves to their children and husbands, but for Francisco, what else could his mother be at that moment when he found himself a small child with his large family gone from him, if not una santita en el cielo watching over all of them to make sure that they completed the tasks she had labored so hard to bring each into the world to do?

In doña Felicia's home, at that time she lived in Tome near the church and was, in fact, the keeper of the keys and the caretaker of the santos there, there was always something good and satisfying on the stove when he got home from softball practice, his denims were patched but clean, his shirts ironed; in short, he was well cared for by the old woman. And the little house was anything but gloomy, since it was always bustling with all kinds of gente from the community who came to get massaged, receive consultation for family dilemmas, be "cleansed," or to get herbal remedies from the old healer woman.

Many times Francisco assisted, glad to help his nina but not completely aware of what all the details of the remedios meant or whether they in fact helped, although of course they had to help, since people held her in the highest regard and they always came back, and moreover recommended others to her as well.

So Francisco learned a little about being a diagnostician of physical and spiritual ailments, and which symptoms were caused by something physical and which were caused by the bad intentions of ill-wishers. But Francisco did not like to talk about these things too much with people, not even with his brothers once he went back home, who, being practical men, tended to find his godmother more an eccentric than someone to turn to for medical attention.

His father, however, did often go to doña Felicia for

massages although he never followed the tea prescriptions she advised. He also managed to get Francisco to give him a massage at the end of a day in the field on occasion or a ventosa treatment when his rheumatism acted up.

Francisco watched his tío Pedro prepare to make a bulto many many times before he went to him one day after a philosophy class at the university to ask him to teach him the work of the santero. Francisco was attending college, but he was not pursuing anything in particular. He had learned to be a mechanic in the Army and he could always work at that to earn a living; in fact as it turned out, he ended up doing that to get by most of the time. But when he came back from Vietnam it was hard for him to concentrate on things, to take a steady job, so he spent nearly a year doing little more than wandering around the streets of Albuquerque, usually stoned on pot.

As it turned out, as it usually does with young romantic men, it was the love of a "pretty girl" that persuaded him to enroll at the university. She was to Francisco the epitome of loveliness, with sky-blue eyes and long blond hair, her loveliness was that much more enhanced by her lack of encumbrance by material things like money, that "just didn't matter" as so many youth felt in 1969—at least those who did not go to Vietnam, or who did not live in barrios and housing projects.

She took Francisco home to her parents' house and fed him gringo food—nothing like the blue corn tamales, posole, and green chili he was raised with, but a little closer to the Army food he was fed for two years, only better tasting, things like mashed potatoes, string beans, and steak. She made love to him under the stars. We may not say, in this case, "with" him because Francisco was in a kind of mummified state when he came back from the war; and during their sexual encounters, while he went about the motions, he never quite felt present.

So it was because of this young woman, whom he was as close to being in love with as he had ever been, that he acquiesced to the idea of enrolling in college, but no sooner was his angel on to other men as earthbound as himself than Francisco lost all interest in being a student.

He also lost interest in being a lover, not just a lover of privileged white college girls, but all women. It was not within Francisco's scope of imagination to be a lover of men, neither, by the way. Although it may be said that with the exception of la sublime Armitaña and his godmother, he only loved men, even if only in the platonic sense.

He loved the strength and tenacity of his father and each of his brothers who—except for his brother James who seemed to find it easier staying in jail than out—were all family men devoted to their homes and land. He loved his tío Pedro above all his tíos and tías for maintaining the religious tradition of their ancestors. Above all, he loved Christ, his heavenly Lord. He loved God, too, of course, but God was too great and too remote for Francisco to have a fixed picture of in his head or to presume any direct contact with Him. At least that is what he felt for a long time until the day he took his knife to a piece of wood and began to carve out his first santo.

He and his tío Pedro went out on his uncle's land one morning and felled a pine, one that was as straight and healthy and as perfect as their eyes and hearts could tell. They each cut a log for themselves approximately three feet in length. Next, they trimmed the front and back with a hand-adze and knife, then smoothed it with a stone just as one would use sandpaper for refining a surface.

Without too much pondering over his first subject, Francisco began to carve the image of the pious Saint Francis of Assisi, for whom of course, he was named. His tío Pedro approved and offered guidance but sparingly, knowing that at best all he could do was educate his nephew on how to handle his tools and the wood, but not tell him what his bulto should look like, that is, what would be correct or incorrect about the representation of his image. For that, St. Francis himself could only guide Francisco's hand since it wasn't St. Francis the holy man whom Francisco was imagining, the one who had cared for the poor, the infirm and the hungry, the orphaned children and all the innocent creatures on earth, but St. Francis in his rightful eternal place in heaven, from which privileged place he was able to work miracles for the all-too-human beings left on earth.

Francisco's first bulto was just three feet high, angular, much like himself, a thin, undernourished monk with hands stretched out before him. He was barefoot and although Francisco did not have the patience to carve out little details like individual toes or nostrils or pupils, he did take the time to shape each small round bead of the rosary hanging around the saint's neck, repeating all the while the Our Father or the Hail Mary, depending on which prayer pertained to the bead he was carving.

When the figure was done (although one leg ended up uneven with the other and tío Pedro advised against Francisco trying to do anything about it, lest he end up with a truly cojo bulto), jaspe or gesso was manufactured out of gypsum to prepare the wood for painting.

Their paints, too, were manufactured by their own hands—gathered from earths and plants and carbons from charcoal or soot; their brushes were made from yucca fronds and chicken feathers tied together and from horsehair. In other words, nothing was store bought because everything that went into making a bulto must be prepared with the utmost reverence; and although they did not have the actual relics of the saints to mix with their paints like the Russian monks who produced Byzantine icons, they labored with the natural elements, sun, air, and earth and prayed all the while as they worked together in silence—like their Spanish ancestors had done for nearly three hundred years on that strange land they felt was so far from God.

6

The Renewed Courtship of Loca's Mom and Dad and How in '49 Sofia Got Swept Off Her Feet by Domingo's Clark Gable Mustache, Despite Her Familia's Opinion of the Charlatan Actor

"Ay, comadre!" Sofi's neighbor said one day when she stopped by to borrow Sofi's portable Singer. "Can you believe it? My husband is finally taking me out to someplace besides a wedding in the familia!"

Sofi sighed wistfully because she herself had not been taken out for close to a quarter of a century. The years, they did pass quickly, she reflected without admitting nothing about her long sparse social life out loud. She handed her forty-year-old sewing machine to her vecina, explaining its quirks, and then put various hilos into a paper sack for her as well, since the woman hadn't quite decided on the color of her dress for the dance.

"Out of the blue, the man tells me, 'Saturday there's a baile in Belen at Our Lady of Belen Church'!" the neighbor continued, laughing and elbowing Sofi, who only listened, remembering her teen years when she was courted by the handsomest man she had ever laid her betraying eyes on. " 'What say we go, honey?' he says to me. And I just looked at him and tried to smell his breath, thinking maybe he had taken to the bottle again. Since it has been mucho tiempo since we went dancing, you know what I mean, comadre? Yes, he waltzed with me at our son's boda and at our grandson's baptism he got up and two-stepped with me and our daughter-in-law a *few* times, but it's not the same thing as saying, 'let's go and kick up some dust'! Is it, comadre? That just leaves me 'ora ora with four days to make myself a dress! So I'd better get going!"

Well, Sofi's vecina from down the road was like a novia all over again, eyes gleaming, rushing out with a little swish of the hips leaving Sofi to her memories of when she was like that a lifetime ago, always happy and over nothing. When she was a young girl there didn't seem to be nothing that could dismay her. She had one of those personalities that ingratiated people around her, sweet like Caridad's but without the melancholy absentmindedness that was particular to that daughter.

And then one day when she was still in high school, she met a young man who was miel in the flesh, and after that, only when she was with him was she able to smile. How it bugged the you-know-what out of her family, who said there was just no living with her no more after she got together with Domingo; "ese tirili," her grandfather called him with obvious disdain for her dandy lover.

Domingo was an actor, so he said. (Well, he did do a lot of acting, even if it wasn't on stage. And no matter how many times he did it, Sofi always felt a little rush whenever he'd lean over and whisper, "Frankly, my dear . . ."

He never finished that line because he did not curse in her presence. Instead he'd give her a sly smile from beneath his

Clark Gable mustache and Sofi would blush.) He also did magic tricks for her, making a coin appear from behind her ear, a bouquet of paper roses for her from out of his sleeve, a real dove from inside his jacket.

Ayy! And how that sinvergüenzo could dance!

When he left her with their four daughters all she could think of was that thank God her mother (que en paz descanse) had not lived to see that day, for she surely would not have let her live it down, with constant reminders of how everyone tried to tell her that he was no good. What honorable man would pretend to be crazy so as not to go do his duty in the Army? Not to mention the fact that he had little by little hocked all of Sofi's jewelry, the silver-and-green-turquoise necklace she had been given on her wedding day that had been passed down to her from her great-grandmother, and the sapphire ring that her father had bought her for her fifteenth birthday? Worst of all, Domingo had sold the ten acres parceled out to them by Sofi's grandfather as a wedding present without even consulting Sofi. At least, Sofi thought to herself over the years, he had had enough sense to leave her the house so that she could have a home for their children when he left.

It was at the feast day dance of Santa Flora de Cordova in Belen that she first met Domingo. She and her sister, her sister's comprometido, and their parents and grandparents had all gone. She was wearing one of her sister's fiesta dresses because her older sister, being engaged, had been going to social functions with her novio that year and Sofi, who was not quite fifteen and had not yet had her quinceañera, had no need for party dresses.

It wasn't until a girl had her coming-out ball at fifteen that she got to go out and be seen at such events, but because the rest of the familia was going to the dance, Sofi's father reluctantly gave his approval. So in a soft pink chiffon dress and pink pumps (she and her only sister wore the same size in everything—at least back then), Sofi made her unofficial debut.

He—who was to become the lifelong source for both her heart's misery and joy—was standing with some other young men looking as wily, as tirili, as he, right near the door of the church hall when Sofi and her family came in. Although he denied it thereafter, Sofi was never convinced that the purpose of their being at the entrance was not to get the first chance at the girls as they came in, since that is exactly what Domingo tried to do when he saw Sofi. Without even bothering to get permission from her father, that brazen young man with a charlatan's black mustache and spit-shined boots came right up to her and tried to take her out to dance.

"¡Orale, tu!" Sofi's father said, putting a hand firmly on Domingo's arm just as that tirili was about to pull Sofi away from her family without a word. Sofi, in the meantime, was transfixed by the handsome stranger's even white teeth, with just a slight gap that added to his charm in a sneaky kind of way and which he showed off with a wide grin, and above all, by those dark, sinful eyes. Even the Frank Sinatra records her future brother-in-law played for them when the chaperons were not in ear's reach did not conjure up a more seductive image of a crooner. Her parents would not let her go to the movie house in Albuquerque, not even with Chencha, her sister and her comprometido—so convinced were they that la little Sofi would see something inappropriate for the child, such as they still considered her to be—so she did not have the slightest idea what Frank Sinatra looked like.

Meanwhile, Domingo, who Sofi knew at a glance was no less a dreamboat devil than el "Franky," backed off at the father's insistence, all too familiar with the restrictions of such fathers who protected their daughters' virtue with unflinching vigilance, and with a subtle glance of regret at

Sofi that said "too bad for us" he went off. Then, to Sofi's further dismay, a minute later she saw him going round and round in a tight two-step embrace with another girl.

Her eyes stuck like chewing gum on that forbidden heartbreaker while the rest of her was made to sit between parents and grandparents the whole evening. She swore she saw him making goo-goo eyes at that mocosa as they waltzed, polkaed, and two-stepped one number after the next right in front of her. She never forgave Domingo for that demonstration neither, although he swore that he only danced with that girl because Sofi's father had not let him have his first choice!

Sofi could not even think about no one or nothing else those next six months before she saw Domingo again. Even the big mitote made over her quinceañera did not help her forget that enchanter, tirili or not—especially since her escort was chosen for her: a cousin once removed, suffering from severe acne and three inches shorter than Sofi, who in her white satin pumps was tall for a "Spanish girl" of her generation.

She wore a splendid lace full-skirt gown befitting a bride, and the fourteen girls in attendance had on the most beautiful chiffon formals in rainbow pastels that anybody had ever seen in Valencia County—the fabric imported by one of her many quinceañera madrinas from Durango. Well, just everything was perfectly matched and perfect: the church hall was decorated with real rainbow-dyed carnations, the queque was strawberry filled and looked as beautiful as a wedding cake, her rosary, the beads of which were made of pressed rose petals, was blessed by the bishop in Santa Fe, who, although he was unable to come and give the Mass himself, sent his blessings, the bouquet for la Virgen was of white and pink long-stemmed roses.

All of Sofi's quinceañera godparents competed with each other at sparing no expense with regard to their contributions, since her family, so respected throughout the county, would do no less for them when their turn came to host such an event for their own 'jitas. Yet Sofi was heartsick at not having for an escort the guy she had seen only once and whose name she did not even know and who, as far as she knew, had already eloped with that . . . puta (yes, that was the word Sofi actually used, although only to herself) from the dance in Belen.

There she was, the prettiest debutante in Tome's history, and sadder-looking than a week-old clavel. And then, after the traditional waltz that launched off the fiesta, where all the girls in the quinceañera were introduced with their escorts, and Sofi with her too-short and homely cousin in the middle where everyone could witness her humiliation (being the vain young girl that she was), her sister leaned over and whispered, "Mira, who had the ñervo to come—party crasher!" And it was him, walking in with a family of invited guests who was vaguely related to her own and who turned out to be his cousins.

That night she was allowed to dance with whoever asked, and when Domingo walked over to her she thought her heart was going to leap right out through her mouth like a scared rabbit. They danced and danced, and even though she knew her father was fuming while keeping an eye on their every move and would reprimand her the next day, she took advantage of an occasion when she was no less than a princess holding court, and avoiding eye contact with all of her familia—but especially her father—she had the most memorable time of her life. As it should be for a debutante at her coming-out ball.

And that was that after that. Domingo courted her for the next three years and a week after her eighteenth birthday they eloped, because despite their three-year courtship her familia, not even la Chencha who almost always sided with her on everything, could not even see Domingo pintado, as the Spanish saying goes, and who, they said and never stopped saying, was just plain not good enough for their sweet Sofi.

"What are you thinking of, silly Sofi?" Domingo asked, breaking Sofi's reflective mood, when he came in from a day of fruitless fishing.

"My mother, que en paz descanse, never did like you," she said.

"I know," he responded, still wondering where his wife's thoughts were at at that moment when he had come in and found her sitting on the banco by the window, just staring outside at nothing.

"Neither did la Chencha . . . she still doesn't."

"I know that, too."

"Neither did my dad."

Domingo stared at Sofi and waited. He had come home last fall and Sofi and he in an unspoken way had picked up as husband and wife again as if only a day of estrangement had passed between them and not nearly twenty years. They acted like a couple who had actually been together for the better part of their nearly thirty-five-year marriage and had become so used to each other that they didn't even notice one another no more, like an old chair in the corner of the room or a table passed on from one generation to the next that is just there for the purpose of eating off. They slept not only in separate beds but in separate rooms, and hardly shared a meal together.

Sometimes when Sofi wasn't looking Domingo indulged himself in watching her, like when she ran around in fishing boots feeding the horses, or when she was squatting at work in her vegetable garden, or when she came home from the Carne Buena butcher shop, bloody apron and all, and what his reminiscing eyes saw was the radiant señorita whom he had made fall in love with him the night of her quinceañera.

"And don't call me 'silly Sofi' no more neither."

"I always used to call you that and you liked it, don't you remember?" he said, trying to get on her good side because he had a funny feeling that some long-held-off reproaches from the past decades were imminent.

The night he had shown up at the back door, she had come out of the girls' room when Esperanza called to her, sizing him up and down, and she said dryly, "Did you forget something?" Then she went back to tend to the two daughters in crisis who had become women during his absence. He brought in his bag and made himself at home in the spare room in the back, and trying to be as innocuous as possible, spent the first days after his reappearance keeping out of everybody's way.

Little by little Sofi started to talk to him, but she confined their verbal exchanges to things that pertained to the household. Yes, she had let him return, he was after all her husband and the father of their children, but he was sad to accept the reality that his presence was little more than tolerated.

"Do I look like a silly woman to you, Domingo?" she said, cocking her left eyebrow. EEE, Domingo thought, remembering her temper, at least he was getting some kind of response from her. "Not at all," he said. "You look like a beautiful woman to me . . . especially right now, with the glow of the sunset against your face . . ." There was a time when Domingo had only to look at Sofi and she would go to him, dissolving in his embrace like liquid gold . . . a time when Domingo looked forward to every sunset with Sofia, his Sofi. But that was before the cockfights, the horses, the card games, the nickel-and-dime bets that turned into acres of land he bet away and knowing there was no end and no limit to his impulses, he went away for twenty years without looking back.

"I just ran into your comadre getting into her truck with your sewing machine . . . ," he started to say.

"She's making a dress for the feast day dance at Belen," Sofi told him, looking again out the window and wondering if Domingo still found the hazy hue of the falling sun as flattering to her profile as once upon a long time ago.

"So the compadre's taking her out finally, huh?" he said, meaning to make Sofi smile, but she was not in the mood and looked at him again sternly.

"Do you know how long it's been since *I* went to a fiesta, Domingo?" she asked. He shook his head and lowered his eyes like a boy who was about to be scolded, but he looked more pitiful because he was a man about to be scolded.

"Since our last daughter's baptism . . . a year and a half before you disappeared on us. And since that child out there died there hasn't been one evening when I have been away from this house! Even the night that Caridad was attacked by the malogra and I could barely tear myself away from her at the hospital, so worried was I that she wouldn't make it through the night, I forced myself back home—just as worried for the two daughters I had left here who were as helpless as two babies—and for good reason too! That poor thing out there"—she pointed toward the window where Loca at that moment was out by the ditch—"had somehow got herself hiding in the stove!

"Look at me, Domingo! While you were gone, doing who knows what—gambling your soul away, dancing with every loose . . . woman you ran across, and who knows what else—I have been hanging the rumps of pigs and lambs and getting arthritis from the freezer and praying to God to give me the strength to do the best by my girls alone and with the wits I had left after what I'd been through with them, starting from when Loca died!"

"Loca's not dead," Domingo protested, although just barely daring to speak up, since he knew this was not a good time to assert his own observations or opinion of things and it was best for him to just listen if he was ever going to win la

Sofi back at all. Strangely enough, with the hunch of the gambler, he was getting this tingling feeling all over that told him that his honey was just about to come around again.

"Well, she was! ¡Chingao!" Sofi stood up, her body trembling with the rage of twenty years of celibate living. Had she been able to have a lover, she would not have hesitated a year after that son of a gun had taken off without the decency of even letting her know that he was all right, but that was when Loca had died and "come back" and after that people really couldn't come to visit because of Loca's "condition." As Sofi had just told Domingo, she herself could not go out at night and leave her little girl, even though Esperanza after a while was old enough to babysit.

The fact that Loca never let no one near her but her mother made it impossible for Sofi to feel comfortable leaving her alone, except to go to work during the day, with the number of the butcher shop right by the phone at home and Sofi just a ten-minute drive away. So, needing to earn a living for her family, she took the risk of being away for eight hours a day, six days a week.

For a whole minute Domingo and Sofi stared at each other. It was the first time that they had looked directly at each other since his return. Then Domingo lowered his eyes again and suddenly with three quick steps he was at Sofi's feet, his head on her lap, "I'm so sorry, Sofia. Perdoname, honey, for all the grief I've caused you."

For a moment Sofi softened, but a man's remorse must translate into a little more than a few tears and an apology on weak knees, even one whose mustache and smoldering eyes were crowned with Omar Sharif eyebrows. (Since once Sofi got to see what the gangly Frank Sinatra looked like she decided her querido looked more like what the singer should look like than what he actually did; and later, once she got to go to the movies, Sofi decided he had more of a Rudy Valentino–Omar Sharif–Prince of the Desert look about him.) But still made the pelitos on her arms rise a bit, so she only made a half-earnest gesture of moving away from him, although not quite pushing him away.

He looked up at her, the sky streaked purple and red, the last of the day's sun wiping Domingo's tear-stained cheeks, and the twenty years of separation between the two lovers dissolved. "Take me to the baile," Sofi told him, with that same demanding haughtiness she had shown him the night of her quinceañera.

So it was that on the evening of August fourteenth, leaving Loca under the supervision of la Fe, Sofi, in the only party dress she had bought for herself ever in her life, since she made all her clothes, a kind of dark green to match her eyes, went out to two-step to the famous fiddle of Cleofes Ortíz at the Our Lady of Belen Fiesta with her one and only honey, who was still, in her estimation, as enrapturing as when her father kept him from taking her out to dance at the feast day baile of Santa Flora de Cordova in Belen when she was fourteen years old and known to the world as la niña.

7

Caridad Reluctantly Returns Home to Assume a Life as What Folks in "Fanta Se" Call a Channeler

While doña Felicia would have wanted to keep Caridad's traila just as she had left it the day of her disappearance—with the red Formica kitchen table and four red-and-white matching chairs (only one of the chairs needing reupholstering badly), the flea-market wooden-trunk coffee table that the mexicano merchant who sold it to Caridad swore he bought from some indios in Chihuahua, the foam futon single bed that doubled as a couch and all the little things, the silver and glass nicho with a papier-mâché skeleton on a cart inside and the three-dimensional picture of La Virgen de Guadalupe, San Martin Caballero, and El Santo Niño on the wall, which Caridad had brought to make her little trailer "home"—out of economic necessity she was forced to rent it.

Usually, doña Felicia had a nose for sniffing out unreliable tenants from the dependable ones, but this time she really missed the mark. She gave Caridad's furnished traila to a young couple with a baby on the way, feeling compassion for their troubles rather than listening to her own better judgment, since neither was employed at the time they moved in and whether or not they could afford it remained to be seen. They gave her the first month's rent and only half the deposit but their sad faces and promises to make good on it in a few weeks managed to soften doña Felicia, who in any case could not stand to see an expectant mother without a home for her future baby.

But baby to come or no, within a few weeks doña Felicia did not receive the other half of the required deposit as promised. Instead there arrived more family members who never left the young couple's trailer. First there was the young man's mother and two teenage siblings. Later came the wife's sister with her three small 'jitos. As if that were not enough, after that the sister apparently reconciled with the father of the children and then *he* moved in. This last moocher had un parna who supposedly helped him do odd jobs for a living, and although this one spent his nights, unless it got too cold, sleeping in the truck they used for their work, he did use the traila's bathroom facilities and joined the rest inside at mealtimes.

On top of that, the sister's husband also had a dog that for the life of him he would not give up despite the fact that the dog hated him. Worst of all, it hated everybody. Doña Felicia lived in dread that the dog might one day take a chunk out of one of the man's own little children, or even her, and so she took to carrying her escopeta, the very same firearm that her first husband Juan used in the revolution, all around the grounds with her, even when she just went out to check the mailbox down the road. It went against all of doña Felicia's principles, of course, but the idea of mixing a little rat poison into the dog's food did cross her mind more than once whenever she saw how those children trembled when that four-legged beast bared its teeth, eye-to-eye with their little faces.

Now doña Felicia was not only out of the income she had depended on—because although the excuses at the first of the month came in abundance the rent money being delivered continued to dwindle, until the sixth month of the family's occupancy when she ultimately received nothing, not even an excuse—but with six adults, five children, and a mean, ugly dog occupying Caridad's little home, there was no telling in what condition they were going to leave it.

And leave it they did, without notifying doña Felicia, of course. She had slept all too soundly, to their advantage, that night, for they had taken in tow all of Caridad's stuff. Crayon marks and the dog's teeth and claw marks on the doors and baseboards were one thing, not paying the rent was another, but outright theft was wrong indeed.

Doña Felicia felt compelled to tell Caridad's parents about the disgraceful loss, expressing all her regrets. But even though she offered to replace Caridad's possessions, there remained the fact that Caridad herself was still lost and don Domingo and Sofi thought that anything short of the replacement of their daughter was unnecessary.

"¡Hijola! Doña Felicia! Those good-for-nothings were just taking advantage of you all along! They saw a woman your age, all alone, and they thought, ¡Chingao! We can dance all over her property and nobody will tell us nothing!" don Domingo said to doña Felicia while Sofi nodded. Doña Felicia looked at each of them. They were right. She was able-minded and certainly got around admirably well despite her age, but she had let those sin vergüenzas take advantage of her in a way that she would not have done when she was younger, or perhaps if she had been less in need when she rented out the trailer to them.

She loaded up her escopeta and placed it by the door that very night, especially remembering the brother-in-law's helper who lived in his truck and that demon dog. Quite often such thieves, seeing that they had gotten away with something the first time, returned to see what else they could get away with until there was nothing left to be got. Well, she was an old lady, as don Domingo had pointed out, with perhaps too big a heart for some people to appreciate, but defenseless, never! So, for two weeks after the sneaky departure of her unsavory tenants, doña Felicia slept in the living room with one eye open and Juan's escopeta, which had not been fired since 1910, ready at the door.

It was during one of these nights of vigilance that Caridad returned. Doña Felicia's ears, long-lobed from the weighty gold earrings she had worn all her life, pricked up, not like a rabbit's but like a wolf's when she heard the soft steps outside. She was hardly able to scramble out of the easy chair where she had dozed off while on guard when already the light was on in Caridad's trailer.

But just as she swung her door wide open, aiming Juan's escopeta in the direction of Caridad's trailer, Caridad came out. A second later, doña Felicia noticed Caridad's Chevy pickup parked just a few yards away. Caridad, at seeing doña Felicia's escopeta pointed directly at her, froze in the doorway, and doña Felicia, startled to see a barely recognizable Caridad in deer-skin mocassins and raggedy clothes, took a few seconds to get her bearings before she put down her weapon.

"Ma Cheri! ¡Dios mío! You look like you just crossed the Jornada del Muerto!" doña Felicia finally said, referring to the treacherous desert road that traders used in times past to travel from Méjico Viejo to Méjico Nuevo. "¡Qué diablos te pasó qué we lost sight of you for so damned long, muchacha?"

Caridad walked slowly over to doña Felicia and with her usual candor and unadorned manner she said, "I don't know, doña Felicia."

But in a week's time, Caridad's family got over their excitement about having Caridad back safe and sound and were tired of badgering her about her whereabouts and why she had made such a big retreat, and the vecinos and strangers who had heard of La Armitaña finally gave up on her when she was not disposed to performing daily miracles no matter what the newspapers reported.

Nevertheless Caridad's psychic don was fully honed after her return. Her dreams were not hits and misses no more like in the beginning, but very clear messages which, with the help of her mentor, doña Felicia, she became adept at interpreting. For example, if a client came and asked Caridad about a particular situation Caridad set her mind to dreaming about it and in a few days, she almost unfailingly came up with a satisfactory answer for the client. Take the case of the comadre who had inquired as to the fidelity of her husband, she brought Caridad the clairvoyant her husband's underwear. Caridad put the man's underwear under her pillow and concentrated on the man for three days and nights. On the fourth night, she saw the good-for-nothing husband in her dream sneaking through the bedroom window of his neighbor at night.

Caridad was perplexed because she knew that the neighbor was a married woman with three small children. She investigated: "Doña Felicia, isn't la señora from down the road still married?"

"Yes, of course she is!" doña Felicia replied. "Where would she go with three little babies?"

Caridad scratched her head. "Where is her husband then?"

"Where is he?" Doña Felicia stopped her needlework which she liked to do between clients. "Hmm. Oh! Sí, sí! I remember now! He's been going up to Mora on the weekends . . . his father is ailing and can't get around no more. The old man probably won't last very long."

When Caridad's client returned for Caridad's answer and for her husband's tale-telling underwear, Caridad had the unfortunate task of telling the woman that her suspicions had not been wrong.

Sometimes Caridad did not even have to dream as a channeler, or as doña Felicia called her, a medium. She often fell into semiconscious trances and communicated with spirit guides as a way of communicating messages to clients. Eventually the word got around and Caridad earned herself a respectable reputation as a medium, if not as a miracle worker.

Her cynical sister Fe, however, stood by her original conviction about her sister's year-long disappearance and insisted: "It had to have some____ to do __ fall__ in love."

After all, Fe had no reason to think that Caridad (strange though she was by anybody's standards!) was exempt from suffering the inevitable consequences of falling in love with the wrong person. For example, some people might constantly scream and beat their heads on the wall for a year. Others, perhaps, went to live in a cave. Big deal. After her experience with Tom, to Fe it was simply a matter of women just being "more in touch" with their feelings than men, just like she had heard a panel of jilted ex-fiancées say on the "Oprah Winfrey" show.

And just as la Fe's fate was not to marry Tom, the convenience store manager, but her very own cousin—whom she first met that arid day of her little sister's funeral, a boy who kept pinching her little arms black and blue while she clung defenseless next to her grieving mother and who remained vivid in her memory—as far as Fe was concerned, Caridad's heart's fate was sealed, too. No matter how much la Caridad—strange and stoic and even holier-than-thou as she had become—refused to admit it.

8

What Appears to Be a Deviation of Our Story but Wherein, with Some Patience, the Reader Will Discover That There Is Always More Than the Eye Can See to Any Account

The sorrowful telling of Francisco's demise takes as its point of departure an adventure (or what was seen by some people as a *warning*) that started in a small town far away, not scattered with tumbleweed but skirted by seaweed, known as Santa Cruz.

Now, neither the woman nor her companion in this account was Caridad's Woman-on-the-wall in Chimayo, but with some patience (a virtue no one could ever have too much of) a few people actually made the connection in the end, like in one of those connect-the-dots games. It seems that these two Californian women would be thought of somehow as being responsible for Francisco's end since who had asked them to come here in the first place? But this all depends on who is telling the story, and as far as anybody has been able to put it all together, it begins something like this:

Helena and Maria, although both born in Los Angeles, had met each other at a grass-roots organizers' conference in Oakland. But their real friendship did not blossom until later, after each had done quite a bit of living and learning from that living. Finally, they came together and made their home, with their three cats, Artemis, Athena, and Xochitl, in a rented two-bedroom nestled in the redwoods just outside ese village called Santa Cruz. There they lived productive and peaceful lives, Maria as a tarot reader and social worker and Helena as an independent landscaper.

They had gone on that way being more or less happy until the summer when they decided to explore the land of Maria's ancestors. Helena and Maria were the adventurous types so their plan was to make it a road trip, camping along the way, until they reached the ruins of the Anasazi, the mysterious ancient ancestors of the Zuñi and Hopi peoples, that they had both read about.

Maria, who tended to have the distracted nature of the poet, upon arriving at the great abandoned ruins described them in her journal like this: "It was as if the Great Cosmic Mother had tossed her broken pottery to the ground." But then, more reflective than sad, she went on, "No, it was not the rage of the Goddess that caused this disastrous doom . . . but man's own shortcomings in dealing with his home, the Earth." Then she added in Spanish because she liked to mix a little Spanish into her writing, even though it made her nervous since she didn't speak it too well: "su Madre."

On the other hand, Helena, less philosophical, or perhaps just not as poetic as her parna, simply had let out a loud whistle at the impressive sight and uttered, "*Cool.*"

At the time of this excursion, the two women were no longer in love.

At least not as they had been once—like the summer they traveled down to southern Mexico and Guatemala to see the Mayan ruins and that unforgettable year when they worked and worked and saved and saved so that they could spend the summer in Athens with Helena's grandparents. No, not in love like when one got a thought and the other got it too at that same unspoken moment, both having merged in mind and dress so that sometimes neither friends nor family could tell one from the other no more. But what had really happened, unfortunately, as ideal as it started out to be, was not that they had succeeded in becoming one, but that they had become neither.

On the positive side, there remained between them sincere affection and general concern if not burning love, so they made the best of their intense and isolated journey together, just as a pair of astronauts must do, having been launched into outer space knowing that the person next to her, however much a stranger, is really the only other human being that exists.

So they forged ahead—sometimes talking up a storm and laughing like old times and sometimes in brooding silence, each wondering what was to become of her once she got back home—stopping in villages and cities, occasionally picking up a souvenir, like a heart-shaped stone polished by the shallow waters of the Rio Grande for a favorite nephew, or a pair of silver-and-lapis-lazuli earrings in the shape of the "Story Teller" for a comadre or a necklace of coral and shell or animal-shaped fetishes for herself.

Their destination point was the village where Maria's ancestors had been buried for the last nine generations—until her father had left New Mexico to try his luck in California, where indeed, he had done well with a string of taquerías in East L.A. Her father had been successful because he had the collateral, but it had been her Mexican mother's taco know-how that was the key to the business's popularity.

Taco know-how that Maria had grown up with and that had played no small part in winning over her Grecian goddess, oh—once upon what seemed so long ago as the trip wore on, as it became obvious that no kind of taco know-how was going to bring them back as they once were.

Anyway, it was early that morning when they started out toward Truchas—Maria's ancestral village just northeast of Santa Fe—where they had indulged themselves the night before at an overpriced bed and breakfast inn and taken a hot tub bath at an equally overpriced West Coast lifestyle spa.

Helena was at the wheel as usual, and Maria, who admittedly had little sense of direction, did her best at co-piloting with a state map. Somewhere along the road, they found a convenience store and stocked up on some not-all-that-healthy but at least survivable edibles, like buffalo jerky and Blue Sky sodas, thinking that farther along they would find a nice picnic spot where they would relax and enjoy the view of the magnificent Sangre de Cristo range. But as it turned out, the pair did not have a picnic that afternoon, much less make it up to Truchas.

(On another day, however, they did get to Maria's grandmother's ranchería and were welcomed by her long-lost tíos and primos and taken out to the camposanto to visit the graves of her hispano and mestizo ancestors of the last four hundred years.

This gratifying visit would lead Maria that following autumn—having always felt innately displaced in California, especially in that monstrous metropolis of the angels where she was raised—to say an overdue goodbye to Helena and start a new life on her own, in what she felt to be through blood ties, her true native homeland.

And it was a very sad parting, indeed. Maria left behind the two Greek cats, which tended to get neurotic the farther away they got from their familiar turf, but she did take along Xochitl, the Aztec migrant cat, who on the other hand adapted very well to whatever climate.

She left Helena everything else, too—oh, guilt was a

bottomless well—packing her clothes, books on the healing arts—only the ones with the little cat sticker inside that read "Ex Libris: Maria," of course—and the CD player—which was rightfully hers, or at least would be in two more payments.

So this account which leads us temporarily astray from our story is about all kinds of beginnings and endings but mostly, like all accounts, about what goes on in the middle. Maria, tarot reader and pseudo-poet, herself would have said—and many metiches who later made it their business to know who she was, agreed—that even this existence of ours has no start and no finish but is the continuance of a journey on an endless, unpaved road.

But a lot can happen even in between the middle of things, not the least trying the patience of a good ear, and since "brevity is the noble soul of wit," like ese Hamlet said, I will do my best from here on to keep this story to the telling of the events of that day.)

Just as Helena and Maria got off the main highway, Helena caught sight of a pickup tailing her close enough so that, thinking that what he wanted was to pass up her well-worn VW Bug, she moved aside to let him do just that. At first, she didn't say nothing out loud when he insisted on staying behind since she was unfamiliar with the road and wasn't sure if they were even going the right way.

In the meantime, Maria, snacking on the novelty blue corn chips, made California-consciousness talk about the wide-open spaces and snow-peaked black mountains that penetrated the white-clouded and azure sky, and pondered over the significance of the occasional wooden cross dug along the road or atop a hill, or the hand-painted little sign that read "Pig for Rent," or the big official billboard that read: "Future Site of the Monument of Governor Juan de Oñate, Conquistador and Colonizer of New Mexico" (which really set her off). She was meanwhile completely oblivious to the fact that there were only two vehicles on that sandy road and that while there was no explanation for it, the larger one had become the predator of the small one.

Then Helena, not only because of her tough survival skills from growing up in a mega-metropolis but just because it wasn't in her to cower under bullying circumstances, stepped on the gas and began doing her darndest to leave that pickup in the dust. But let's face it, a VW Bug, even Maria's restored and freshly painted one with the brand-new engine, was no Fiat and the guy with the sports cap driving the pickup (which was no Fiat neither but had the distinct advantage in horsepower) caught up to kiss her bumper no matter how fast she accelerated.

Finally turning around when they were purposely bumped by the tailing pickup, Maria put down the bag of blue corn chips and map, pulled off her shades, and asked, "What's going on?" Surely there was enough room on the road for him to pass them up since it was obvious that Helena kept yielding the road to him. But each time she pulled over, he slowed and stayed right behind her.

Then they felt a jolt when the pickup bumped their car with a meanness that meant to knock them off the road. "Agh!" Maria gasped, but Helena, lockjawed, with a tense fixed look in her eyes, only shifted to high gear and giving it all she had, pushed the gas pedal to the floor.

Again, she pulled over to let the son-of-a-gun pass and again, instead of going on with his business on that empty side of the road, he deliberately took aim at the VW and attempted to side-swipe it. "What's going on?" Maria repeated but not expecting an answer no more, since it was already obvious that Helena was doing all she could to get away from the pickup with no time to think about why she was doing it.

Side-swiping the Bug at the speed that both of the vehicles were going nearly knocked it over, but after getting her bearings, Helena was back on the road again. The pickup, having pulled over just ahead, was waiting for them and as Helena passed him up, he stepped on the gas and belligerently stayed close behind.

If belligerence was his only problem Helena could have coped with the chase, especially when she caught sight of a gas station down the road and thought for a second that they were saved, but no, the worst was yet to come. As he came up behind them again, measuring his vehicle with hers, she looked directly at her opponent, wanting a good look at the "asshole," she thought, only to be horrified to see that aside from his cynical grin he had a rifle pointed right at her.

"HIT THE DECK!" she yelled at Maria who, never having heard that expression before except maybe somewhere in an old World War Two–era movie, nevertheless did just that. Helena, too, slumped as far as she could down in her seat just as they heard a blast fired and the truck peeled rubber and passed them up. He didn't stay ahead of them very long, neither, but waited for them to catch up and pass him up again and just as they were nearing the gas station he pulled up behind them.

Helena drove up to a pump and when the attendant came around she told him to fill it up, check the oil, and wipe the windows while he was at it, too, please, hoping they might kill enough time so that the pickup-back-road terrorist would give up and just go on his way. But before she could hand the key to her gas cap to the attendant, the pickup drove right up to the other side of the pump. Everyone else seemed to freeze at that moment when the guy jumped out of his truck and started to walk directly toward the VW.

Helena got her bearings and rolled up her window. The guy (and once she got a good look at him did not look like much more than a two-legged fly in well-worn Laredo boots) held his denim jacket open with a hand in his pants pocket to reveal a gun he had stuck inside the belt of his jeans.

Helena heard a little squeal from Maria but didn't turn to look at her, keeping her eyes instead pinned on the guy's eyes and he, in turn, glaring at her. "What d'you want around here, bitch? Come to make some trouble?" he shouted at Helena through the glass.

Helena turned and glanced for a moment at Maria, as if Maria could possibly give her some clue as to what his problem was. Maybe it was all a question of mistaken identity, Helena thought. Two women with spiked hair and camping gear strapped to the top of their car were probably not from around there, but they were not being mistaken for someone's ex-girlfriend come back to avenge him, were they? And yet the guy was standing face-to-face with her with a gun in his belt and acting like it was she who was a threat to him.

"Me?" Helena shouted. "Me?" was all that Helena could get herself to shout back. The man with the gun didn't say nothing else, not even to Helena's third "Me?" but instead with an exaggerated stride that was supposed to let her know how disgusted he was by her he went off toward the store. Helena didn't roll down her window and the attendant made no move to get the gas cap key from her neither. Instead, he pretended to suddenly remember a tire he was patching up when they had driven up and went back to it.

"Let's just get some gas and go on to find my grandmother's ranch," Maria said. "I'm sure this guy is just high on something. He'll probably leave us alone now."

Helena stared at Maria and yet another thread in their once perfectly seamed union ripped without a sound, but before she could say anything, a woman stepped out of the store with a big loud barking dog and shouted at the attendant: "We're out of gas! Tell 'em we ain't got no gas left!" Maria and Helena exchanged glances and then looked over at the attendant, who had been instructed to relay a message to them as if they had not heard it loud and clear themselves.

"Sorry! No gas, ma'am!" he shouted with an apologetic grin, without leaving his tire. Helena immediately put the VW in reverse, turned it around, and sped off. Once on the road, she responded to Maria's suggestion that they continue on to Truchas. "What do you mean—'let's just go on'?" she yelled. "Didn't you see the gun that guy had?" Maria, who was not good at handling Helena's temper, kept silent.

But they were no more than a quarter of a mile down the road when again Helena caught sight of the pickup following them. Instead of heading in the original direction as they had planned she had started back toward Santa Fe with every intention of staying as far away from that guy's stomping grounds as she could. "Now, what does this fucker want?" she said, banging the steering wheel with the palm of her hand. He wasn't big. She would have been glad to jump out and take him on, but the memory of a rifle pointed directly at her on the road kept her from doing anything but pushing hard on the gas pedal. She could see in the rearview mirror that he was still getting a big kick out of scaring her. Finally, after a couple of miles or so, he pulled off the road and sped off back in the direction from which they had just come.

"Man! And I thought L.A. freeways were dangerous!" Helena said, relieved to see that they were rid of him at last. Innocent people were shot at by snipers on freeways in big cities but it was too much for Helena to see that even on these sleepy roads, people could fear for their lives. And that furthermore, dudes were just dudes no matter where you went, even in the sacred land of the Anasazi.

Then Helena remembered something her older brother who had been with the LAPD for more than fifteen years told her once. Back in the '70s, he said, there was a small town somewhere up north in New Mexico that he and his fellow cops used to refer to as the Narc Capital of the United States. Helena couldn't remember the name of the town her brother had referred to. "Hmm," she said aloud. "What do you know about your ancestral village, anyway?" Helena asked Maria after she had finally calmed down and was driving at normal speed.

"Not much," Maria replied. "Like I told you before, I've never kept in touch with my relatives in Truchas."

"Hmm," Helena said again. She thought to herself that it was possible that she was completely off base with her hunch that that crazy dude threatened to kill them because he suspected they were narcs. But then again, her guess made her feel better than to simply conclude that he was just nuts and had chosen them at random to stalk.

Maria, on the other hand, had a very different feeling about that experience that day. Her veins ran with the blood and dust of that land and she stayed quiet all the way back to Santa Fe thinking only about what she had seen in that slender man's dark eyes. She had foreseen a time in her future alone when Helena, brave and fast-acting warrior woman that she was, would not be there to warn: "HIT THE DECK!"

Yes, Maria saw in that fly's eyes a time when she would surely need a warning most.

9

Sofia, Who Would Never Again Let Her Husband Have the Last Word, Announces to the Amazement of Her Familia and Vecinos Her Decision to Run for la Mayor of Tome

It was exactly two days after her fifty-third birthday, while Sofi was putting another load into the washer out in the enclosed back porch, shooing away the moscas and saying to herself things like, "If that Domingo doesn't fix the screen door this week, *I'm* gonna have to do it myself; then I'll throw his butt out for sure; what do I want him for then anyhow?" and things like that, just before the old wringer went out with a big shake and clank (not too surprising considering its age) and she said aloud, "God damn . . . !", quickly pulling out her scapular from inside her white blouse and kissing it to heaven, that she decided she was going to run for la mayor of Tome and make some changes around there . . .

She called up her comadre, the one who lived down the road, with the ten good acres of bean and chile crops, and asked her to come over. She had big news, she said.

Her comadre, meanwhile, thought that Sofi had called to ask for her Singer back and she didn't want to tell Sofi that after she got her dress for the fiesta at Our Lady of Belen made, she had decided to do her 'jita's new baby's baptismal dress and the silver metallic thread got jammed up somewhere in all that spooling and, well, something happened to the machine, so it wasn't working no more.

The comadre (whose name it is best not to reveal here for this reason as well as some others that we shall soon see) had been after her husband about it. He was pretty good at fixing things, mostly things that were big and wide and not very complicated, like the roof or a viga fence, but he sometimes got something to work again in the house. God knows everything they owned had had its day already, so his efforts came in handy, but truthfully, he was no real handyman. Of course, she could take the old Singer, which as far as she could tell had had its day too, to a repair shop in Albuquerque, but all that meant money that they just wouldn't have until after they were able to harvest the beans and chile.

So she was glad that la comadre Sofi did not mention the Singer when she called. In fact, Sofi seemed a little absentminded about things like that lately, you know? Like she actually forgot to charge the comadre last month for her purchases at the carnecería. For years, the comadre had been buying every week from la Sofi and because times were sometimes a little harder than others and they were comadres and one never knows when she'll need her troca jumped some cold early morning and the compadre down the road never minds too much being woken up to give it a jump, or you might find your comadre's grown daughter with the child's mind wandering down by the acequia barefoot in the snow, so you run to tell her where she is and things like that that happen between neighbors all the time, it all evens out.

So Sofi let such matters as immediate payment for the hamburger for the fried pies and chopped lamb for the green-chile stew go until the end of the month, and once in a while also "forgot" to charge for a week's purchases. But she had never let the charge for the whole month go. So, what favor could the comadre from down the road offer to merit that kind of pardon?

But no, Sofi did not mention the bill. She hadn't asked for her sewing machine back, neither. So the comadre changed her chanclas and put on her black going-out shoes that used to be her Sunday Mass shoes before they got so worn. She didn't know why she was putting them on just to run down to her comadre Sofi's where she had visited a million times, but something in Sofi's voice on el telefón gave her the impression that the visit was going to be formal.

Maybe it was her business-like tone or maybe it was just the fact that Sofi had never called her on el telefón before. But then, how could she? The comadre had just installed her line when her youngest went to the Army, but before that she had never seen a need for it. Besides, who could afford it? So using el telefón alone made the comadre feel like Sofi must be having an emergency.

The comadre pulled up in front of the house and rapped on the front screen door. Dogs started barking near and far. Then the peacocks that Mr. Charles was mating or breeding, or whatever he called his business, woke up too, and started letting out those strange cat-in-heat sounding calls that they'd been making for weeks. (She didn't know the new neighbor's last name and since she didn't know him hardly at all, she didn't feel right saying just "Charles" to him, even though that was how he had introduced himself to her one afternoon. Just like that. Just like an Anglo to be so forward with a woman!)

The comadre got goosebumps. All the animals around were really going crazy. Then she pressed her nose against the screen and caught a glimpse of La Loca running to her room to hide. Sofi came out from around back where she had been hanging up clothes on the line—soaked and half-washed as they were.

As soon as the comadre got into the house, she asked Sofi what was so important that Sofi had got her away from her quehaceres just to tell her. The comadre wasn't really doing no chores when Sofi called; she just wanted to heighten the drama of the "emergency call" for when she repeated the story later to the other comadres.

"Come on in, comadre," Sofi said, still sounding mysterious and full of importance all of a sudden, like a changed person actually, since the comadre had never known anyone more self-sacrificing and modest than la pobre Sofi. Especially when you considered all those years she had worked to support her four girls without no help from no one and with that . . . *man* having abandoned her just like that when the girls were so small.

You know, la pobre Sofi had never had one moment of fun all those years while she was alone, no birthday or New Year's Eve fiestas, no Christmas posadas. She did not attend one wedding reception, baptismal party, First Holy Communion, Confirmation, or high school graduation fiestas neither. No quinceañeras for none of the girls' fifteenth birthdays. Nada. Well, she hardly had been able to attend even a velorio or a funeral for that matter, although she always tried, out of respect for the defuncto's family. But everyone understood. She was alone with four children. What could people expect?

And just about the time her girls were teenagers, la comadre still remembered so clearly how that nice-looking Eusebio from up north, Mora or Las Vegas or someplace, who had spent a year coaching at the high school, had been so taken with Sofia. All of Sofi's comadres were sure that he made excuses to go to Sofi's Carne Buena Carnecería. After all, he was always eating out. More than likely he didn't even know how to cook!

But there he was twice a week buying lamb chops or murcia (which he probably threw at the neighbors' dogs on the way home), just to get a chance to chat with la Sofi. Sofia, with those funny-colored eyes that were not green or gray or brown but something in between that changed with the light, and with that pretty brown skin to contrast with them!

No, Sofi never did let herself have a good time. Of course, who could blame her, with that strange child of hers with that peculiar affliction of being allergic to people? She couldn't go nowhere and no one could ever visit very long at her house. Well, la abandonada Sofi did her best, turning out her girls however she could under the conditions and tests that God put on her. So it was no surprise that none of her daughters had been able to get married by the Church.

It was tragic how the oldest one (although not very surprising since she had always been high-strung—no, high-strung was not the right word, a mitotera, a troublemaker about politics, as if she knew so much) had got herself missing in Saudi Arabia. Her name was mentioned on the ten o'clock news almost every night. But now since the whole war business was over, people seemed to be losing interest, and in the meantime, Sofi's girl was still missing. Maybe she was killed out there. The comadre made the sign of the cross at the thought.

If Sofi's eldest 'jita and her baby 'jita had been tragic victims of life—one who never left home and the other who had strayed too far—there was still a little bit of hope for the two middle daughters. Although, let's face it, La Armitaña—la comadre quickly dropped the "santa" from that daughter's new "title" after la Caridad had neglected to go out and bless her crops—had always been a little pathetic.

For instance, here you had a case of a pretty girl who really had no business leading the kind of life she had been living before, going to bars all the time, letting any pelao who felt like it have his way with her. Everybody still remembered the very shameful start she had, getting pregnant from that mocoso, Memo, and all that embarrassing business for la pobre Sofi—without a man to put a stop to such things.

And ese Memo shamefully running around behind Caridad's back like he did when they had just gotten married and she was expecting. He really should have been more of a man and just settled down to support his new familia instead of running away to the Army or wherever it was he'd gone off to. La Caridad, obviously, had taken it real hard, being young and in love and all and ended up ruining her life because of that whole disgraceful mess.

Then, nobody, not even the priest at Mass, had been able to explain how Caridad had recovered from the massive injuries she suffered from that horrible attack. Bueno, gracias a Dios, nomás. But just when everybody was getting over that shock, Caridad, who had become known as kind of a, well, puta, went off to doña Felicia to become a curandera!

Well, maybe all that had some sense to it, after all. Since God's hand was definitely involved in Caridad's recovery, it must've been for a reason. In any case, ever since she came back from living in a cave, there was something really changed about her. You couldn't put your finger on it except to say that men were now the last thing on Caridad's mind . . . and that really was a milagro, the comadre thought.

The other one, la Gritona—who worked at the bank and was always wearing those little belted dresses with the big bows tied at the collar and always had on pumps that matched the exact color of the dress, with the shoes always the same, two-and-a-half-inch heels, plain—was dying to get married. She couldn't stand that she had been dumped practically at the altar and that she had become the brunt of every joke made by all her Anglo friends at the bank. She'd probably get married with the first you-know-what who would let himself be caught.

And regarding all these unkind reflections that the comadre was having that night while she was sitting in Sofi's kitchen waiting for her to make her very surprising announcement, in a few months she would be satisfied to find that her hunch about Fe was right: indeed Fe would marry a you-know-what, or more precisely, Casimiro, her myopic cousin.

Casimiro de Nambe was no longer of Nambe (although still Fe's cousin), since he had been raised in Phoenix because his father had moved the family there years ago to start a cement business. Or was it making swimming pools for the ricos?

In any case, the family broke away from a two-hundred-and-fifty-year tradition of sheepherding. But in la comadre's mind, once a sheepherder, always a sheepherder, and although Casimiro, Jr., had gone to the university there in Arizona and got his degree in accounting (the first in his family to ever go to college), he still looked like a sheepherder from northern New Mexico: thin, small, with thick black eyebrows and mustache, wearing tight denims, a big cattleman hat, and snakeskin Tony Lama botas. ¡Hijo! What a show-off.

Sofi poured the comadre a cup of coffee from the pot on the stove. With Domingo back, there was coffee made all hours of the day; it was his only addiction, he said. He had to have a cup in his hand all the time—half a cup, grounds, cold, no matter even when he was going to bed.

"Here's my idea," Sofi said, sitting down, with a hand on her comadre's arm, certain that her plan was going to excite her friend as much as it did her. "I have decided to run for mayor . . . !"

La comadre stared at Sofi, not comprehending. "Mayor?" She blinked.

Sofi nodded enthusiastically. "Yes, comadre, mayor of Tome!"

Now the comadre really didn't get it. She especially didn't get it because Tome never had no mayor. She didn't know much about those kinds of government things (the one and only time she had gone out to vote in fact was for Kennedy in 1960), but could one just decide to become a mayor of an area? After all, Tome wasn't even an incorporated village like Los Lunas or Belen. *That* much she knew!

Then why stop at mayor? Why not elect herself la juez de paz or la comandante of Tome as they had had in the old days? Why not be Queen of Tome for that matter? Who would care as long as she didn't try to tell no one what to do.

La comadre frowned. As the reader might well imagine, she was among those doubting Tomasas who were never convinced of the things Sofi and her family were capable of doing. "I don't know, Sofi," she said, staring into her cup. She couldn't bear to look at Sofi in the eyes, now that she thought the poor woman had lost her mind, which surely had to do with all the worrying about her daughter disappearing so far away in the Arabian desert . . .

Sofi, undaunted, jumped out of her chair. "Ay, comadre!" she said, running her fingers through the front of her hair, which was still mostly black. "You have always been like this, ever since we were girls!"

"Me?" the comadre said, pointing to herself. "Like what? How have I always been? *You're* the one who's always . . ."

"Always what?" Sofi asked.

"Always had a lot of . . . imagination," the comadre answered timidly, looking back into her cup.

"Imagination? I don't know what that means, but I can tell you this. I have been living in Tome all my life and I have only seen it get worse and worse off and it's about time somebody goes out and tries to do something about it! And maybe I don't know nothing about those kinds of things, but I'm sure willing to work for community improvement!"

" 'Community improvement'? And what does that mean? You are starting to sound like your daughter, the revolutionary!" The comadre stopped herself. She had not meant to bring up la Esperanza at such a bad time, especially not in that way either, although everyone had always known what a mitotera that troublemaker girl was. "Anyway, there has never been no mayor of Tome!"

"¿A'ca'o qué, comadre?" Sofi said, hands on her hips, ready to take anyone on. And here she thought that the comadre would be excited about her news, ready to help out, considering she hadn't had a decent crop in three years! That kind of attitude was just the reason why things never got better around there.

"¿A'ca'o qué? ¿A'ca'o qué? What d'you mean, a'ca'o qué, comadre? You can't just decide one day, like today, that you are going to be mayor of a place and that's that, and everyone's gonna listen to you and say, 'Yes, Mayor Sofi, just command us'!"

"It's not 'imagination' that I've always had, comadre, it's *faith!* Faith has kept me going," Sofi said, truly exasperated with the fact that la comadre had not taken to her idea as she had anticipated. "But *you* . . . *you* have always been a . . . a . . . !"

"A ¿qué? Tell me! What have I always been, Sofi?" la comadre demanded, ready to get up and leave right then and there if she didn't like what that crazy comadre of hers had to say about her.

"A conformist!" Sofi said, folding her arms and staring point-blank into her comadre's eyes.

"A conformist? A conformist?" la comadre said, looking like she was about to hyperventilate. Then she got hold of herself and turned to Sofi, "And what does *that* mean?"

"That's what my 'jita la Esperanza used to call people who just didn't give a damn about nothing! And that's why, she said, we all go on living so poor and forgotten!" Sofi responded.

"Well, what ARE we supposed to do, comadre? All we have ever known is this life, living off our land, that just gets más smaller y smaller. You know that my familia once had three hundred acres to farm and now all I got left of my father's hard work—and his father's and his father's—is casi nada, just a measly ten acres now, nomás, comadre! Barely enough for my family to live on!"

"And I have even less," Sofi said, sad to remember that even the tiny bit she had inherited had been sold out of Domingo's recklessness.

"And now we have los gringos coming here and breeding peacocks . . . ," la comadre complained. "Now, I ask you, what can you do with peacocks? Do these New Yorkers eat them, like in fancy restaurants or something?"

There was really only one person in the vicinity who was breeding peacocks, but the point for the comadre was that he did not have to earn his living from raising the birds, much less use them for food. He was an outsider and there were a lot of outsiders moving in, buying up land that had belonged to original families, who were being forced to give it up because they just couldn't live off of it no more, and the taxes were too high, and the children went off to Albuquerque or even farther away to work, or out of state to college, or out of the country with the Army, instead of staying home to work on the rancherías. The truth was that most people had not been able to live off their land for the better part of the last fifty years. Outsiders in the past had overused the land so that in some cases it was no good for raising crops or grazing livestock no more.

Sofi looked at her comadre, seeing that maybe there was a

chance to win the conformist over, after all. (And if she had *this* one on her side, the rest would be easy, since this comadre was the biggest mitotera among all her neighbors, which was why Sofi had picked her to be her campaign manager.) But for the life of her, Sofi couldn't figure out what she was talking about with these peacocks. She decided to ask her. If they were going to work together on her campaign, they may as well understand each other. "What peacocks, comadre?"

"Down the road, on the other side of the acequia, comadre! Haven't you heard them? Haven't you met ese Mr. Charles, with the reddish beard? I think he's a *sculpture* or something. He's got all kinds of junk all over his land, rusty parts of old cars, hasta los bones of all kinds of carcasses . . . ! He's breeding esos birds. Haven't you heard them?"

There were so many new people moving in and abouts Tome in recent years, most of them gringos, that Sofi hadn't noticed no "Mr. Charles." Then she started to remember a very strange-sounding loud birdcall early in the mornings lately and she said, "Oh, yeah! I know what you mean! Yes, that's just what I'm talking about! Here we have peacock breeders taking over our land, and we have to sell it to them because we need the money and they got the money to buy it, and we end up without no livelihood to depend on no more. You're one of the lucky ones, comadre!"

"I know I am, Sofi! And still, look how hard it is for us! But what would you as mayor suggest for us to do?" la comadre asked.

"Well, I hadn't thought that far yet," Sofi answered. "I was hoping that as my campaign manager and as a member of one of the original land grant families around here, you might help me with some ideas, comadre!"

Yes, the comadre was starting to like the thought of being able to engender some new spirit back into Tome, land of her ancestors. They were both sitting quietly lost in their imaginations about what they would or could do for their vecinos with Sofi as la mayor when Domingo walked in to refill his cup with coffee. He stopped and stared at the women, who didn't seem to notice him.

"¡Buenas noches, comadre! ¿Como 'sta el compadre?" he said as a way of announcing himself. The comadre snapped out of her daydream. She had nothing personal against Domingo, but she didn't think too much of a man who would walk out on his familia like he had and then just decide to waltz back in twenty years later—and *waltz* he did, since everyone saw how Sofi and he danced that whole night gazing into eyes other's eyes shamelessly, at the fiesta in Belen . . . !

"My husband is fine, thank you," she said, cordially. "We're just sitting here making plans for Sofia's campaign to run for mayor!" She said this with a little tone of cockiness. Maybe el Domingo didn't appreciate the woman he had but others did—or might, depending on what Sofi had in mind as mayor.

Domingo stared at the comadre and then at Sofi, very much the same way that the comadre had looked at Sofi when she had first announced her plan to her. "What is she talking about?" he finally asked Sofi. He didn't know whether to be concerned or to laugh.

"That's true, Domingo. I am running for mayor . . ."

"Mayor of Albuquerque? Are you serious?" Domingo asked, just on the verge of laughing. His wife couldn't be serious! What did she know of politics? And anyway, everyone knew you couldn't run a campaign without money.

"Don't be ridiculous!" la comadre responded before Sofi got the chance. "How can Sofia run for la mayor of Albuquerque!"

"Then mayor of what?" Domingo asked, truly dumbfounded by the whole conversation. He figured at this point that the women had maybe found that bottle of homemade pisto he had stashed in the tool cabinet in the back porch . . .

But no, they were sober and what was worse, serious, and the "best" of the news was yet to come when Sofi looked him straight in the eye and said, "I am running for mayor of Tome, of course! And furthermore, *I* will be la mayor of Tome! I swear on my parents' grave—may they rest in peace—even if it's the last thing I ever do!"

Domingo decided not to laugh. It was clear by now that no matter what he did to convince Sofia that he was sorry for everything and that he wanted to leave the past behind them, she was never going to completely forgive him. But she did not have to go so far as to mock him there with her comadre by saying such absurd things. What were they trying to prove anyway by making fun of him?

But Sofia continued, and he realized that their point was not to try to put him in his place but that they were very serious indeed. "You know, Domingo," Sofia said solemnly, "our 'jita, Esperanza, always tried to tell me about how we needed to go out and fight for our rights. She always talked about things like working to change the 'system.' I never paid no attention to her then, always worried about the carnecería, the house, the girls . . . But now I see her point for the first time. I don't really know how to explain myself right yet, but I see that the only way things are going to get better around here, is if *we*, all of us together, try to do something about it . . . The washing machine, the screen door, the stall for the horses, one of the freezers at the carnecería has been out for months . . ."

"Your sewing machine . . . ," the comadre added. Sofi stopped for a moment and looked at her comadre but decided not to question her about the Singer right then. It was important to keep her alliance with her comadre campaign manager in the public eye, but she made a note to find out about it later.

"So it sounds like you're going to run for mayor of this house, not of Tome . . ." Domingo tried not to sound worried about that small prospect, but he knew that under the circumstances, with everybody but La Loca gone, Sofi being the mayor of the house would mean that he would be the only one around to be delegated every task that occurred to her. Things could get out of hand. "Well, you know I been planning on fixing all those things, honey. It's just that sometimes a man can't find enough time in a day for all that he has to do!"

Sofi did not want to bring out their dirty laundry in front of the comadre, knowing that that would just spread like wildfire all over in no time, and that too would be hurtful to her campaign. Apparently having an instinct for politico protocol she chose to be discreet about her business with Domingo just as she had just been with her new campaign manager about the sewing machine.

Unfortunately the little eye exchange between Domingo and Sofia did not go unnoticed by the gossip comadre who raised an eyebrow about it. Being a bean farmer she muttered an old dicho meant for Domingo under her breath, "Semos como los frijoles, unos pa' 'riba y otros pa' 'bajo . . ." We are like beans boiling, some are going up and some are going down.

Both Domingo and Sofia heard it clearly and gave her a deserved dirty look, so the comadre decided to say no more and got up to fill her coffee with a loud sigh, letting Domingo know by that, that for her part she only wished he would get out of the kitchen so they could go on making their campaign plans.

But Domingo, who usually wasn't of the temperament to get into tangles with neighbors, especially not his women neighbors, and who almost always tried to make light of a tense scene by coming up with a joke, at this moment did not find nothing funny with what was going on. His wife was obviously experiencing some psychological breakdown because of all the pressure she'd been under: Esperanza missing in Saudi Arabia, probably kidnapped or worse, the accounts at the butcher shop not adding up and the business going down, one thing or another needing repair, La Loca spending more and more time wandering down by the ditch so that he had to check in on her in the evenings since she sometimes spent the whole night outside . . .

So, from someplace very deep inside him the idea of this metiche noseybody comadre coming around to brainwash his wife was more than he could take. Maybe it wasn't the woman's idea for Sofia to run for mayor of Tome, nobody in their right mind would think to convince nobody of something like that. But here she was, egging Sofia on, probably with the idea of convincing Sofi to run Domingo out of the house! And then all of a sudden he said, "¡En boca cerrada no entra mosca!" In a closed mouth no fly goes in. Domingo blurted out this dicho in return, not looking at the comadre, but just kind of saying it, as she had uttered hers.

Of course, the metiche caught that it was intended for her and knew that in so many words she had been told to shut her trap. But why should she? she thought. La pobre Sofi needed someone to stick up for her now and then! Sofi's metiche comadre stopped at the stove. Her eyes were wide and her mouth did not shut up as Domingo's dicho suggested but on the contrary dropped wide open; and in fact, she looked as if she had just swallowed a fly.

Then she thought of another old dicho, also a favorite of her father's—may he rest in peace—and this time, turning about-face, she looked Domingo right in the eye. This was no indirecta but said directly at that scoundrel: "¡Bocado sin hueso!" By this dicho, she was implying Domingo to be a freeloader.

"¡El mal vecino ve lo que entra y no lo que sale!" A bad neighbor sees what goes in but not what goes out. Zas! Domingo, who had a few dichos handy himself, came right back with one for the metiche.

But she was just as quick to the draw. "¡A quien mala fama tiene, ni acompañes ni quieras bien!" He who has a bad reputation, do not accompany nor love too dearly.

"¡Cuerpo de tentación y cara de arrepentimiento!" Tempting body and face of regret!

"¡Seras payaso, pero a mi no me entretienes!" You may be a clown, but you don't entertain *me!*"

"STOP! Parale right now!" Sofi screamed at both her husband and her campaign manager comadre. "¡Chingao! The way you two are fighting you're gonna end up in bed together!" And that was no dicho, but actually sounded so wise, it stopped Domingo and the comadre in their tracks.

The comadre bit her bottom lip, astounded at Sofi's accusation. And yet, she was the one who started the personal innuendos with the dicho that said that people who have a bad reputation should not be accompanied nor loved very well.

Domingo had surprised himself, too, at the way he had gone for the comadre's throat, who until that very hour, he had hardly ever noticed and here he was telling her things like she had a tempting body but a regretful face! He looked at Sofi with an expression that was both apologetic and frustrated and left the room. A second later the women heard the front screen door slam, followed by his truck pulling fast out of the driveway, and the whole night passed before Sofi saw Domingo again.

"I'm sorry," the campaign manager comadre apologized quickly to Sofi. "That's okay," Sofi responded, "we have a lot of planning to do, so let's just throw those little hairs into the sea and go on with our work."

And that is what they did.

Now, to rescue an area as economically depressed as Sofi's and her comadre's would truly have taken more than the desires and dreams of a self-proclaimed mayor and her campaign manager–assistant—metiche comadre. So the two earnest women started their campaign by going around for months talking to neighbors, to fellow parishioners, people at the schools, at the local Y, and other such places to get ideas and help; and little by little, people began to respond to Sofi's "campaign," which they did not see as a mayoral one so much as one to rescue Tome.

There were many community-based meetings in which debates as to what ideas would lend themselves best toward some form of economic self-sufficiency for their area before some people came up with a plan that eventually mobilized everyone into action. It would take YEARS of diligence and determination beyond this telling to meet their goals but Sofi's vecinos finally embarked on an ambitious project, which was to start a sheep-grazing wool-weaving enterprise, "Los Ganados y Lana Cooperative," modeled after the one started by the group up north that had also saved its community from destitution.

Every single step of launching off the cooperative took a lot of effort, a lot of time, and mostly a lot of not only changing everyone's minds about why not to do it but also changing their whole way of thinking so that they *could* do it. At first, people were really nervous and for good reason. To begin with, the government had no money to lend them, so they were on their own. But finally it became a debate of either everyone doing it all together or nobody doing anything at all.

Neighbors who had inherited land from homesteading ancestors that was no longer farmed or used for nothing, mostly due to poverty, were persuaded to sell or barter it off for services in shares to those skilled neighbors who hadn't. By bartering, people were able to get their run-down farm equipment, homes, home appliances, cars, and trucks fixed.

Skilled as ranchers or not, many began working in some way for the cooperative—by learning an aspect of the business of sheep grazing, wool scouring, weaving, administration, and selling the wool products. Unemployment had been at an all-time high in the first years of the enterprise so there was no shortage of volunteers.

The second year after the start of the sheep-grazing enterprise a core group of twelve women began the wool-weaving cooperative. Eventually, the business created and sustained the livelihoods of more than two dozen women. As cooperative owners of their wool-weaving business they had paying jobs they could count on and were proud of and the mothers among them didn't worry so much about their babies and childcare because they could bring their 'jitos to work.

For some of the women, the greatest asset that came with the weaving cooperative was the arrangement they made with the local junior college. Due to the wide range of skills they learned from running their own business, those who were interested could work for college credit and potentially earn an associate's degree in business or in fine arts. And no years of cleaning the houses of los ricos or serving tables in restaurants could ever get them that!

What the Ganados sheep-grazing part of the business also found out was that there was a growing demand for their hormone-free meat.

Building this cooperative caused untold challenges for Sofi's vecinos. The first year was especially hard on them when they lost many of their sheep to a series of catastrophes, first to an electrical storm and later repeated attacks by coyotes. But they carried on, although by trial and error at first, because above all, to stay on their land, to work it as their families had for many generations, was the desire of everyone who joined in and became everyone's dream.

Some neighbors began planting organic vegetables. In this way, most people had inexpensive access to pesticide-free food, not to mention just having vegetables to can for their familias.

The Ganados y Lana Cooperative took so much of Sofi's time that she soon decided to sell her Carne Buena Meat Market in shares to her neighbors and they developed a food co-op. In this way, too, the less fortunate neighbors and even the not so unfortunate neighbors, like el Mr. Charles Peacock who took over the management of the food co-op, could live on more substantial diets than what they had previously relied on from the overpriced and sprayed produce of the huge supermarket down at Los Lunas Shopping Center.

Years later, once Los Ganados y Lana was fairly secure, they also established a low-interest loan fund for their members, so that those who were motivated and willing could start up their own business.

Still others, inspired by the diligence, ingenuity, and communal spirit of Sofi's vecinos, began to work on the drug problem that had found its way into the local schools and into their immediate vicinities, by forming a kind of hard-nosed drug SWAT team. And while the problem was not completely obliterated it would not be a lie to say that some lives had been saved because of the SWAT team's own diligence, ingenuity, and communal spirit.

As time went on the morale of Tome had gone up and most of Sofi's neighbors were interested in contributing in some way to their community's improvement. And although the local residents learned early on, or perhaps some always knew that they could not realistically go to Sofi—who had indisputably started it all—with all their problems, the title of La Mayor Sofi did catch on informally, out of respect.

La Mayor Sofia, in the meantime, had gotten most of her own things that needed fixing around her house done through bartering, including the Singer. Needless to say, this put Domingo ill at ease, knowing that without contributing nothing worth mentioning to Sofi's household, he would sooner or later be reproached in some way for his habitual dawdling. Nor was he ever able to find his niche in the Ganados y Lana Cooperative and nowhere else neither.

So, without saying much one morning except a few words to La Loca, who didn't acknowledge them anyway, he packed a bag and set out to Chimayo to resume the project of building la Caridad's little adobe. Caridad had returned to doña Felicia's trailer complex and never asked about her unfinished house in Chimayo because that's the way la Caridad was, but Domingo had promised it to her and despite the fact that he had pilfered a good portion of the lottery winnings that were supposed to go to the builders, he still had enough money left to buy the materials needed.

He himself would complete it, he decided. He would install the plumbing—using a manual, finding a claw-footed tub in Dixon, a sink with brass faucets in Española. The mud plastering would not have to be done alone, since there was always a helping hand available for a cold beer in exchange, and this way, using his own perseverance, ingenuity, and more or less communal spirit he would finish his 'jita's house.

In six months the project would be done and having shown his true mettle, Domingo would *ask* her this time—not la Silly Sofi, but la Mayor Sofia of Tome—if he could come back home.

10

Wherein Sofia Discovers La Loca's Playmate by the Acequia Has an Uncanny Resemblance to the Legendary Llorona; the Ectoplasmic Return of Sofi's Eldest Daughter; Fe Falls in Love Again; and Some Culinary Advice from La Loca

By midday on a certain afternoon in June it reached 98 degrees, but a minute after it was best to stop counting. La Loca, finding no relief from the heat in the house, swamp cooler going full blast or not, would seek at least a little comfort from the shade of a cottonwood near the acequia that ran by her mother's house. Sometimes one of the dogs or a horse, tongue hanging to the ground and not feeling so great about the heat either, went along to keep her company.

Lately, on its own accord, however, a strange bird with a tremendous turquoise blue tail that opened at whim like the Spanish fan her mother used to cool herself when sitting on the front porch had found its way to her shady spot. She hid when its owner came looking for it, saying things to the bird with the big fantail like "There you are, you bad bird!" and "Your wife's been looking all over for you!"

Later, overhearing her mother and a comadre talking about the big fantailed bird, she learned that it was called "peacock." The comadre had said "pavo real," which meant it wasn't just any kind of strange bird, but one born of royalty. And it was indeed the most splendid thing on two claw feet that Loca had ever seen, this noble bird.

Loca tried to make friends with it. She imitated the peacock's walk and tried to make peacock talk, but it didn't go along with any of her playfulness, not because it was stupid like a chicken or ornery like a rooster either. The peacock, Loca concluded, was just not an imitator. Or maybe it was just too preoccupied with being on the run from its owner to let itself be amused by Loca.

The acequia was as far as Loca had ever drifted from home, and her place to play and hide since she had learned to walk. Consequently, she knew and loved everything about it. She knew its quiet nature in summer, its coolness in spring; and she didn't mind it in winter when the muddy water was frozen most of the time. It was her own place to be—until the invasion of the peacock, which seemed to have the same sense of proprietorship toward the acequia as she.

Sometimes a vecino would catch sight of La Loca down there and think she was lost. Most people around mistook the fact that she showed no apparent social skills to mean she was a simpleton. None of them realized just how aware Loca was of her surroundings and of all the things that went on outside and away from Sofi's house. And not only that, but how effective she could be in handling circumstances that were beyond most people's patience, not to mention ability.

She had grown up in a world of women who went out into

the bigger world and came back disappointed, disillusioned, devastated, and eventually not at all. She did not regret not being part of that society, never having found any use for it. At home she had everything she needed. Her mother's care and love, her sisters, who, each in their own way, had shown their affection and concern for her, and she, in turn, for them. Even the man who came to stay—who her mom said was her dad who had left when she was a baby before she died, who really smelled of hell, entertained her with card games and cheap magician's tricks that to Loca were nevertheless extraordinary—even he, in his own way, brought her contentment, and thus she fit him into her world.

Although she did not love her sister Caridad best, she loved her sweetest. Caridad, unlike don Domingo, who couldn't hide it no matter how much aftershave he used, did not smell of hell no more. Instead, her hands and breath smelled now of laurel and sage. Her eyes and voice smelled very sad but always soothing, like a lullaby with no words. But Loca never said nothing about it to no one, how much she liked her sister's presence more and more, because above all she knew that nothing that exquisite could last in the vulgarity of the big world very long.

Loca, far from being una inocente as some of her all too simpleminded neighbors assumed, among many other things was an expert horsewoman. She had trained all the horses since she was tall enough to climb up and ride on her own. Her favorite was a beautiful black-with-gray Arabian that she had helped its mother give light to, that was her best friend. She called it Gato Negro.

"Why the heck would you call a horse a cat?" don Domingo had asked her when he first heard Loca calling it over.

"I'm not calling Gato Negro a cat," Loca said, lovingly

stroking its salt-and-pepper mane while feeding it carrots.

"You named that horse Gato . . ." Domingo laughed, as exasperated by Loca as by the other strange and wondrous women in his home that he had missed for twenty years. He would never figure out how they all came to be that way.

"I named it Gato Negro. I never said it was a cat," Loca said with that kind of precocious tone of hers that sometimes was charming and sometimes really grated on her familia's ñervos. Her father gave up and walked off. Gato Negro was mostly black and had that fixed look of cats when they are readying for an attack or think they are going to be attacked and ready themselves. Calling it Gato Negro didn't mean nothing more than that, obviously, because horses are not attack animals. Everyone knew that.

"Where's Loca, Ma__?" Fe called as she came in on one of those hot afternoons when Loca was down by the ditch. On Wednesdays Fe got out work at the savings and loan at 3 P.M. and sometimes stopped by to see her mother, who was home on some days now that there were community volunteers at the shop.

Shortly after her "recovery" la Fe had moved out. She took a little apartment with a roommate, a gringa who also worked at the bank. Her mother had not wanted her to leave home just like that, because she was not quite her organized self after the blowout with her Tom, but Sofia understood that la Fe was trying very hard to learn something from it by becoming more independent, so she didn't try to stop her third daughter from leaving.

Caridad left. Esperanza left. Then la Fe left, Fe's departure being premeditated and uneventful. She simply had responded to a notice on the bulletin board in the employee's lounge: NON-SMOKING FEMALE LOOKING FOR SAME IN ROOMMATE TO SHARE EXPENSES. WALKING DISTANCE FROM THE SAVINGS AND

LOAN OF TOME. On the first of the month, Fe moved a few personal belongings into the two-bedroom apartment and she was settled.

Sofi thought it was kind of weird but Fe did not recall any of the specifics that immediately followed receiving Tom's Dear Juana letter. Fe thought she had only dreamt herself open-mouthed, eyes bulging, as if she had gotten trapped in that ghost mine her grandfather, Cresencio, used to tell her about when she was a child.

Her father Domingo's father, abuelo Cresencio, was about ten years of age when he herded sheep for a rich family in Tome. One day he discovered an entrance to a mine shaft. He found a shovel, pickax, and other miner's tools. He took off his red handkerchief from around his neck and placed it at the entrance, with a stone on top of it to mark the place because until that day to the boy's knowledge nothing had been known of such mine shaft. That night little Cresencio reported it to don Toribio, whom he worked for, and the next day they both went to find the mine. But though they searched all around the area where he thought the mine entrance was, they found nothing.

"Juan Soldado is guarding the gold mine," abuelo Cresencio would whisper to the girls. "Who's Juan Soldado, 'buelo?" Esperanza spoke up, being the oldest and therefore not supposed to be afraid.

"Juan Soldado was a Spanish soldier and that was his gold mine. He was trapped in there, killed. ¡Ay, esos gachupines! They were really greedy. So even though Juan Soldado died he didn't want no one to find *his* gold. So he has kept the entrance a mystery.

"Many, many people have seen it over the years, like I did, but when they go back with help, prepared to go in, it's gone."

Fe had gotten lost in the Juan Soldado gold mine of her head. In the darkness of that mine, she called to Tom, hearing only her own echo reverberating back, with never no reply from her beloved, who surely, she thought with great conviction, was also lost in there. She wove in and out of those moments in which she suspected that Tom was just as lost as she was, more so, maybe, because Tom, true love that he was, she never thought to be too smart.

At other times (and these were the most unbearable) Tom did not even exist, had probably never existed, and in fact, was probably local folklore, like Juan Soldado. And in what we may rightly call her darkest moments, like Juan Soldado, fiercely protecting the discovery of his gold mine, Fe suspected that Tom had purposely made the path to his miserly heart disappear so that she would never find it again.

In the internal caverns of her mind in which Fe had gotten lost, she could not accept lost love. She once had Tom's devotion and would find it again, if it took a hundred years. Even if she had to search through slimy darkness forever, she would get the Tom that had loved her to materialize again as her bridegroom, in that tuxedo he had picked out to rent for their wedding. He would write her another neatly printed note to undo that last one: "Honey, I'm sorry. Forgive me. Just take me back and I'll make it all up to you."

She wrote that imaginary note over and over in her head when that image of herself with her eyes bulging and her mouth wide open came to her and she could hear from somewhere far, far away the spine-chilling cry of an agonized woman . . . And all this can only be said to be a glimpse of what the stubborn Fe must have gone through during her "illness," which to her was remembered as that, an illness, while to the rest of the household behind her back it was the time referred to as *El Big Grito.*

"What's Loca do__ out __?" Fe said to her mother, who had just come in through the kitchen. Sofia went over to the window and stood next to Fe to see what she meant. They could see that Loca was down by the acequia, and although they could not see her very well, it appeared very much to them that she was going rapidly in circles around the cottonwood tree. Loca was wearing a pair of cutoff jeans and a T-shirt and was barefoot, as always. Round and round at a dizzying rate she went, looking down at the ground, and apparently distressed.

"Agh! Oh Mom, stop __!" Fe groaned, thanking God that no one else could see Loca making a complete fool of herself—like usual.

"That's enough, Fe," Sofia said to la Gritona. "Maybe your sister lost something out there . . ."

"Mom! She loo____ a hamster____wheel!"

Sofia gave Fe a dirty look and ran out to call Loca from the front porch. "¡'Jita! ¿Qué te pasa? Come on in! You're getting sunstroke!"

But Loca didn't stop, she just kept going round and round, until Sofia ran down to get her. Once Sofia was next to Loca she saw that Loca was not just upset, but looked terrified. Her red-toasted dirty cheeks were tear-stained and Loca threw her arms around her mother, glad to be rescued from her never-ending rotation. "Come on in, 'jita," Sofia told her daughter and arm-in-arm they walked back up to the house.

Once they were in and Sofia sat Loca down to calm her, Fe, with her usual lack of compassion for her sister, began to badger her. "You __ you're a woman now, __ you?" Fe added, "The charm's worn __. All that eccentric behav__ __ yours! And __ don't __ wear any sho__? You got __ with not ____ __ __ go to school. Well, ____ ____ pretty smart __ you back __, but how ____ ____ gonna keep up __ act, Loca?"

Loca looked at Fe as if she didn't have the slightest idea what Fe was saying to her, but in fact it was because she didn't understand *why* Fe was saying what she was saying to her.

Sofia squinted her eyes at Fe, who at that moment in her

mother's opinion had earned the name la Gritona more than ever. "I told you earlier, Fe, that's enough! You have no place to talk about a 'crazy woman' here! *You* were the one out of your mind when your boyfriend broke up with you! As if he were the first man to ever get cold feet with a woman! You were lucky he showed his true colors and left you *before* the wedding! If it wasn't for your little sister, I would have had to put you in some kind of hospital—something which I could not afford! *She* is the one who fed you, who washed you, who combed your hair and kept you from getting bed sores! ¡Sí! Bed sores! What do you think of that?"

Fe winced.

"Your sister la Caridad was half dead at that time," Sofi went on, feeling pretty good about it, too, since a scolding was overdue for la Fe. "Heaven knows I had my hands full, and if it wasn't for this pobre criatura here who EVERYBODY looks down on and tries to make out as retarded, no matter that she's smarter than most people I know, I don't know what I would have done with *you!*

"I don't never wanna hear you talk to her that way again. This is her home. Yours too, but you chose to leave it and are a visitor here now. So you respect her when you come here, you hear me, Fe?" Sofia stood squarely facing Fe, waiting for that daughter, who since birth acted like she had come as a direct descendant of Queen Isabella, to dare reply.

Meanwhile Fe could only blink back a few tears at her mother's challenge. Her mom had really changed in the past year. She had never raised her voice like that to any of her daughters, but since becoming La Mayor of the Village Council, even if it wasn't official (nor was the village council, for that matter, since Tome was not incorporated), there was just no stopping Fe's mom from ever speaking her mind no more.

Light-skinned Fe (although she was not nearly as white as

she thought she was) was redder than a radish from her mother's scolding. No one had never said nothing to her about what she was like during that long blackout between the letter from Tom and the night she felt like she had broken a fever and found herself holding her sister, Caridad.

She thought that they had both had the same awful sickness together, like the Asian flu or something like that, and that that was why they had been laid up in the same room. Even the fact that she had come out of it with damaged vocal cords she dismissed as a result of her illness, which she thought must have been terrible indeed since no one at home ever wanted to talk about it, so that eventually she herself had to give it a name.

People at work didn't seem to want to talk about it, either. Some looked embarrassed even to say hello to her after her long absence. But if anyone did ask what it was that she had had, proud Fe did not seem embarrassed at all. She would stand squarely and with more conviction than ever about her irreproachable self-image and answer: "Adult measles."

"Mama!" Loca began to cry again.

"Tell me, 'jita, what upset you so much out there? Is it one of the animals? Did one of the animals fall into the ditch?"

Loca shook her head and continued sobbing. Finally she answered, "*She* came to tell me that la Esperanza is died, Mama!"

"Dead," Fe corrected, which got her another stern glance from her mother. Obviously, Fe didn't take nothing Loca said very seriously, even such a horrendous announcement as the death of her sister, who had been missing in the Persian Gulf for months and months. The nearest to an answer that the family had ever been given by the military was that Esperanza and her colleagues were surely kidnapped when they got too close to enemy lines.

"What lady? 'Jita, tell me! Was there someone out there

that came to look for me, from the Army or something?" Sofi asked in a panic.

"No, she came to see me. She always comes to see me. I don't know her name, the lady with the long white dress . . . ," Loca said. She timidly looked past her mother at Fe, waiting for Fe to scold her for talking "nonsense," even nonsense that was the truth since Loca did not know how to lie and what might be attributed to "imagination" in others, in Loca's case was nothing short of what had happened, like it or not.

Sofia swallowed hard. She felt a lump form in her throat, but with a little gesture of her chin let Loca know she should go on. "I didn't see her for a long time, but she came a little while ago and told me that Esperanza won't never be coming back because she got killed over there. Tor . . . tured, she said."

"Who told you this terrible thing, 'jita? Tell me, who is she?" Sofi begged, grabbing Loca's shoulders. But she only upset Loca more with her reaction and Loca started sobbing again.

And so that's how Sofi first learned that her eldest daughter had indeed been killed. Although the official letter was delivered by two Army privates a week later it gave no details. Esperanza had been disappeared for months, long after the great but brief war was over. Everyone in the country knew this because it had been on the news. In the official letter the Army said that through sources which it could not reveal, it had confirmed that Esperanza and her colleagues were all dead.

Esperanza died an American hero, the letter said. Even though she had been a civilian, the Army had interceded, and eventually Sofi was taken to Washington, D.C., to receive a medal posthumously awarded to her daughter.

The people in Washington, D.C., knew a lot more than

anyone else ever would about what had happened to Esperanza and the other reporters she was with, and even though the Army officials claimed to know for a fact that she was dead they also claimed to not be able to locate her body so as to send it home.

Sofia and Domingo had gone to Washington, D.C., three times to talk to officials, thanks to their neighbors who helped raise the money for each trip. First they were sent to one office, then to another. Everyone in Washington seemed sympathetic to them, but no one had an answer. Each time Esperanza's parents returned more frustrated and sadder than when they left. Although in their hearts they never gave up yearning to locate their daughter's body, without no one important enough on their side to help them do it, Esperanza's missing body remained a mystery.

What still remains at hand here, however, is *who* was the mysterious lady who came to tell La Loca about her sister?

A woman whom everyone knows, who has existed under many names, who has cried over the loss of thousands but who was finally relegated to a kind of "boogy-woman," to scare children into behaving themselves, into not straying too far from their mothers' watchful eyes.

But no one had ever told Loca the legend of La Llorona. The Weeping Woman astral-traveled all throughout old Mexico, into the United States, and really anywhere her people lived, wailing, in search of her children whom she drowned so as to run off with her lover. For that God punished her forever on earth.

La Llorona was usually sighted at night near bodies of water calling to them. The idea of a wailing woman suffering throughout eternity because of God's punishment never appealed to Sofia, so she would not have repeated it to her daughters. Furthermore, the Church taught that when people die every soul must wait for the Final Day of Judgment, so why did the Llorona get her punishment meted out so soon? Sofia used to ask herself this when her father first told her this scary bedtime story when she was a little girl. Unlike her sister, Sofia was not afraid to go to the río alone to swim; she didn't mind the acequia running close to her home, neither. She didn't believe in La Llorona, in other words. "Ay! God's gonna punish you for that!" her sister warned her.

The land was old and the stories were older. Just like a country changed its name, so did the names of their legends change. Once, La Llorona may have been Matlaciuatl, the goddess of the Mexica who was said to prey upon men like a vampire! Or she might have been Ciuapipiltin, the goddess in flowing robes who stole babies from their cradles and left in their place an obsidian blade, or Cihuacoatl, the patron of women who died in childbirth, who all wailed and wept and moaned in the night air. These women descended to earth on certain days which were dedicated to them to appear at crossroads, and they were fatal to children.

Her mother's mother had been from old Mexico and Sofi knew a little about the antiquity of this tale, but mostly she just knew what her father had told her, that La Llorona was a bad woman who had left her husband and home, drowned her babies to run off and have a sinful life, and God punished her for eternity, and she refused to repeat this nightmare to her daughters.

Sofia had not left her children, much less drowned them to run off with nobody. On the contrary, she had been left to raise them by herself. And all her life, there had always been at least one woman around like her, left alone, abandoned, divorced, or widowed, to raise her children, and none of them had ever tried to kill their babies.

Sure, she did hear of something like that once, in the newspaper or maybe it was on the radio, and not to make any excuse for such a woman, the mother was only human and anyone is capable at some point when pushed into a corner like a rat to devour her babies in order to save them, so to speak.

Sofia didn't like to think of these things, and that's why she didn't want to think of La Llorona. But how was it that Loca had heard of her?

"She has been coming to see me since I was little, Mom," Loca said, as if in response to Sofia's thoughts. "And she told me today that Esperanza is died. She wanted you to know, Esperanza wants you to know."

Then, as if a baseball bat had just struck her across the back and taken the wind out of her, Sofi stumbled over to the couch and fell on it. Fe tried to revive her mother, and then just held her until she came to and when she did, it hit Fe, too, that her sister was dead and all three women began to wail and moan like Cihuacoatls, holding each other and grieving over the loss of Sofi's oldest child.

So some time passed, months in fact, understandably, before Fe gave the news that she had come over with that afternoon, which was that she thought she was in love again, and was fairly certain that setting a wedding date was not far off for her and her cousin, Casey. In the meantime, having moved out on her own and knowing now that soon she would have her own home and she hoped her own familia, it had dawned on her that with regards to cooking, she did not know so much as how to boil a pot of chicos.

Even if Loca was not someone she would for any other reason go to for instruction about nothing, it was Loca whom she had gone to see that afternoon specifically, to ask her for cooking classes. But all of this, as I said, was postponed, indeed, nearly forgotten after Esperanza's family got the message she had sent to them via La Llorona, Chicana international astral-traveler.

Who better but La Llorona could the spirit of Esperanza have found, come to think of it, if not a woman who had been given a bad rap by every generation of her people since the beginning of time and yet, to Esperanza's spirit-mind, La Llorona in the beginning (before men got in the way of it all) may have been nothing short of a loving mother goddess. So it was she whom Esperanza sent to deliver the news to her dear mother in Tome, knowing by then that La Llorona was on a first-name basis with her little sister who had always hung out by the acequia. And everyone knows, if you want to find La Llorona, go hang out down by the río, or its nearest equivalent, especially when no one else is around. At night.

Which was where, after that, that Esperanza was also occasionally seen. Yes, seen, not only by La Loca, but also by Domingo who saw her from the front window, although he didn't dare go out and call to his transparent daughter. The first time he saw Esperanza down by the acequia conversing with Loca and another equally dubious figure in a long white dress, his fingers, holding the venetian blinds apart at eye level, froze, and Sofi found him a half-hour later, as still as a statue in that position and dry-mouthed.

Sofi also saw Esperanza down there. And once, although she had thought at first it was a dream, Esperanza came and lay down next to her mother, cuddled up as she had when she was a little girl and had had a nightmare and went to be near her mother for comfort.

And of course, la Caridad over in the trailer complex in the South Valley by then was having long discussions, even if mostly one-sided, with Esperanza about the war, about the president's misguided policies, about how the public was being fooled about a lot of the things that were going on behind that whole war business, how people could get some results by taking such measures as refusing to pay taxes. But Caridad really didn't understand politics and she had a hard time following her sister, so Caridad usually just nodded her head so as not to offend Esperanza by acting as if she didn't care.

They talked while Caridad "meditated" in her room. Doña Felicia, from the doorway, only saw Caridad's lips move occasionally while her eyes were fixed on a jar of water. "Why doesn't your sister come to talk to me?" doña Felicia asked Caridad one morning over breakfast. "What a know-it-all that sister of yours was . . . and still is! Dios sabra, how much I could tell her about all the wars and injustices I witnessed!"

Not only did Caridad have a certain don, a faculty, as a vaso (or as they called her in Santa Fe, a channeler), but La Loca too, and no one could argue this, had some natural gifts as well that were nearly as impressive. For instance, who had taught her to train a horse? Granted, there did appear to be an intuitive connection between La Loca and all animals, but still, none of the other women in her family, not even her mother, rode as well as Loca did.

And who the heck had taught her to play fiddle?

Then there were the things she knew about women's bodies. She had never delivered a human baby, but she knew all about a woman's pregnancy cycle. There wasn't even a medical book around for Loca to have learned from the pictures—since she didn't read very well and didn't like to. And it was she who took charge back in the days when Caridad had her untimely pregnancies . . .

Among other domestic talents that Loca cultivated, such as embroidery, coming out with the most beautiful pillowcases and ruanas as Crismas presents, Loca had become a one hundred percent manita cook. Well, she not only did the kitchen stuff, but all of it. Since she was a child, she was the one who helped her mother slaughter a pig for a matanza, skin it, disembowel it, and roast it outdoors.

She was also the one who helped her mother at the end of every summer with the canning. Together they jarred corn, chiles, peaches, currants, squash, and tomatoes and put them to boil in a big pot on a wood-burning stove Sofi's mother had left outside many years before just for that purpose, since it would get so hot.

Since Loca did not go to school and did not have to do homework nor get up in the morning, ironing pleats into uniforms and looking for a clean white blouse and a pair of socks that matched like her other sisters had to, she worked hard until sunset with her mother and slept in in the mornings.

Above all, Loca knew how to cook. She was, in fact, a better cook than her own mom, even though she learned most of what she knew from Sofi, who had learned what she knew from her own mother and so on. Every now and then, it happens that a child actually surpasses the knowledge and the knack for doing some things that a parent has shown her and this was the case with Loca.

You've got to give credit where credit is due. And Fe eventually did take culinary instructions from her otherwise antisocial and (perpetually held up for scrutiny) kid sister.

Three of La Loca's Favorite Recipes Just to Whet Your Appetite

"If you want to be a good cook," Loca started out in a solemn tone with her sister (who Loca was sure must have found it pretty hard not only to admit that she didn't know how to do *everything* perfectly but that furthermore, Loca could do at least one thing even better than her), "you have to first learn to be patient." Loca believed in doing things from scratch.

Most meals contained corn so it was necessary first to prepare the nistal by boiling it in lime water until the skin peeled off. Then it was washed two or three times; if you wanted to be an especially meticulous preparer of corn, you would follow with the ever-so-tedious task of "despiquando" the little black off the corn with a penknife, so that if you were going to make tamales, they would come out nice and white and smooth.

Since Loca had nothing but time on her hands, once she took care of the animals, she often did do this for which she eventually won the reputation at Crismas time of making the best tamales all throughout Valencia County. And above all, *everyone* loved her blue corn tamales, which took even more work since that corn required grinding on a stone metate.

"Now, another big secret to our cooking is in the chili sauce, naturally," Loca told her sister the next time Fe came to take a lesson. Loca had actually kind of taken on a bit of an attitude with these cooking classes and Fe wasn't sure if she cared for that dash or two of cockiness that Loca was blending in with her teaching.

The best, or at least the tastier, chili sauce was made from whole, dried pepper, not from the chili powder, although the second alternative was pretty good and a lot faster, especially if a person didn't have the time or the *patience* to make it from scratch.

After carefully selecting your chiles (since Sofia grew her own, Loca had the advantage of being able to do this and not have to worry about going to the market for her chiles) you removed the stems and seeds and scraped off the veins. Next, you crumbled them in a puela, any good iron skillet, and covered them with water. You let them soak for a few minutes, and then worked them with your hands until all the meaty pulp was dissolved. Next, you strained it through a colander and poured it into a bigger puela containing pork lard, a little flour slightly browned, a cup of meat stock, a grated garlic clove, salt, and just a pinch of dry oregano.

Now you were ready to make La Loca Santa's carne adovada: For two days you would soak pork meat in the above sauce (only you would put a lot more garlic in), and on the third day you cut up the meat in small pieces and would fry it.

Another dish that was a must to learn for Fe, especially after she found out that it was Casimiro's favorite meal, was posole. First, she was told by La Loca, she must prepare the corn as she had been taught to make nistal for tamales, but she should not grind it! For every pound of stew pork, one cup of the whole nistal corn was boiled until half done, and then the meat was added and enough water to cover everything. Then you just let it cook until tender. Meanwhile, you added salt, chopped onion, and two whole red chiles—with the stems and seeds removed, of course, Fe!

Then, one afternoon, the two sisters and mother made a batch of biscochitos which are really customary mostly at las Crismas, but are also a delight at weddings and other types of fiestas. Biscochitos are Spanish cookies or Mexican cookies, depending on who you talk to. Doña Felicia, for instance, would tell you they were dreamt up by Mexican nuns to please some Church official, like mole. Sofia, on the other hand, was told by her grandmother that the recipe came from Spain. In any case, they are made from rich pie pastry dough, to which you add baking powder, sugar to sweeten, and—here's the trick, there's always a trick, you know, Fe—a bit of clean aniz seed. Next, you roll it out on the board to about a third of an inch thick. (Loca would not say a third of an inch, of course, but for our purposes here, I am adding specific measurements myself.)

Then you cut it into long strips about *two-thirds* inches wide, and then across into *two-inch* lengths. Finally, you cut little narrow strips about *an inch* long on the sides, pull along, and roll back each strip into a curlicue shape; dip in sugar and bake. (Doña Felicia would tell you here that in Old Méjico, these cookies were also cut into heart and star shapes!)

And while they kneaded and baked they all talked as if

they were old comadres and laughed at the flour that got on their noses and the dough that somehow stuck itself to their hair, and that was when Fe first really talked about her new and quickly serious romance.

"Why is it that I didn't know that my brother-in-law's son was back here?"

Fe shrugged her shoulders. Her concentration was on getting the dough to form a perfect curlicue. Her mother persisted, "Didn't Casimiro like Phoenix? He was practically raised there. Are you two planning on moving back there together, 'jita?"

"Mom, we haven't discussed ____ that far," Fe said, wiping her brow with the back of her sleeve since her hands were sticky with masa. "Casey said __ h__ a fall__ out ____ ____ father and did not __ to work for __ anymore, so __ decided to come __ here. He __ other family __, too, __ know."

"Yes, I know that," Sofi said, "and now that I think about it, your father was always considered the black sheep of the family, so I can see why they didn't keep in touch with us after Loca's funeral. It was nice that they showed up, at least my cuñada with a couple of her kids did, even if her husband didn't. Now, I remember! That little Casimiro was busying pinching you the whole time Father Jerome was giving his sermon! Do you remember, Fe?" Sofi was saying all this rather joyfully, because, of course, she was trying to be joyful about Fe's new relationship and without thinking she said to La Loca, "Remember, 'jita?"

Loca did not answer but instead put a cookie sheet with a batch of biscochitos into the oven and Fe gave her mother a hard nudge, moving her lips so that only her mother could get the message: Loca was dead then. Remember, Mama? Sofi "got it" and immediately felt bad for having been so insensitive to her 'jita Loca.

"So how was it that he found you?" Sofi asked Fe.

"Well, he __ came into __ bank one day __ open__ __ new account and there I was. __ there he was. And __ rest __ history . . . we liv__ happily __ __ter!" Fe said.

And if __ that ____ been true.

11

The Marriage of Sofia's Faithful Daughter to Her Cousin, Casimiro, Descendant of Sheepherders and Promising Accountant, Who, by All Accounts, Was Her True Fated Love; and of Her Death, Which Lingers Among Us All Heavier than Air

It was that month in the "Land of Enchantment" when it smelled of roasted chiles everywhere. Fresh red ristras and sometimes green ones were hung on the vigas of the portales throughout—all along dusty roads, in front of shops and restaurants to welcome visitors and to ward off enemies. Propane-run chile roasters were hand-rotated by bagboys in front of local supermarkets and everyone who didn't grow their own lined up to get their chiles, women were packing them up, whole, dried, and in sauces, to send off to homesick boys stationed in Panama and to wayfaring relatives in Wyoming and Washington, D.C., but mostly to feed their familias right there and to freeze for the winter.

That chile-roasting month was also the month that la Fe chose to be wed—yes, married at last—not to the shriveled-hearted wimp who had been her first novio, but to her very own cousin, Casimiro.

But above all, when the pungent, nostalgic aroma of roasting chiles filled the air again in following years, that month would always be remembered by everyone who had known her as the one in which la Fe died right after her first anniversary.

But not, however, before Fe got the long-dreamed-of automatic dishwasher, microwave, Cuisinart, and the VCR, not for wedding presents (since nobody seemed to have gotten none of her hints . . . either that, or they just couldn't afford them), but which she had bought herself with her own hard-earned money from all the bonuses she earned at her new job.

And it was that job that killed her.

A year from the time of her wedding, everything ended, dreams and nightmares alike, for that daughter of Sofi who had all her life sought to escape her mother's depressing home—with its smell of animal urine and hot animal breath and its couch and cobijas that itched with ticks and fleas; where the coming and goings of the vecinos had become routine because of her mom's mayoral calling (which, by the way, sent La Loca into permanent exile, in the roperos and under the bed for hours, or off riding Gato Negro, or down by the acequia with her peacock-friend and sometimes to places nobody knew about); and where her prodigal dad, though generally a sweetheart, was always hard up for cash, talking Fe into writing him a check or giving up her watch, high school graduation ring, whatever she had on her to get him out of some urgent debt. Despite all this and more, Fe found herself wanting to go nowhere else but back to her mom and La Loca and even to the animals to die just before her twenty-seventh birthday. Sofia's chaotic home became a sanctuary from the even more incomprehensible world that Fe encountered that last year of her pathetic life.

And meanwhile, most of the people that surrounded Fe didn't understand what was slowly killing them, too, or didn't want to think about it, or if they did, didn't know what to do about it anyway and went on like that, despite dead cows in the pasture, or sick sheep, and that one week late in winter when people woke up each morning to find it raining starlings. Little birds dropped dead in mid-flight, hitting like Superball hail on roofs, collecting in yards and streets, and falling on your head if you didn't look out. Unlike their abuelos and vis-abuelos who thought that although life was hard in the "Land of Enchantment" it had its rewards, the reality was that everyone was now caught in what had become: The Land of Entrapment.

But that month the year before, when everybody was chile roasting and when esa Fe was still having bridal dreams of everlasting happiness, she did not plan a wedding like the one she wanted when she was engaged to you-know-who, the convenience store manager, who was still managing the store off I-25, when the local paper ran an engagement photo of pretty Fe in the arms of her new fiancé and cousin, Casey the Accountant, announcing their imminent marriage.

He got to see it, too—you-know-who—as Fe would have been so glad to hear, thanks or no thanks (depending on which of the two you talked to) to his cashier who had been with him for years and therefore remembered that ex-fiancée of his who she had always thought was wound up too tight.

What's-his-name was busy working on the Big Slurpy machine that had been giving out more slurp than flavor all day. The repairman had not showed up after three calls in to his beeper. Meanwhile our efficient and dedicated convenience store manager was losing business, so Tom had decided to tackle the job himself when Luella looked up from the Daily she was reading between customers and said,

"Well, look at this, Tom. Your ex-girlfriend's getting married this Saturday!" And then added, not being able to resist a dig at her uptight boss, "You invited?"

Tom left the machine to see if in fact what his less-than-brilliant cashier was talking about was true. Sure as sure, there she was, once his Fe, still lovely, hair perfectly styled, next to a guy that the paper was saying had graduated from the University of Arizona and who was going to be her husband, and meanwhile the Big Slurpy machine was letting loose all the cherry syrup and ice slush on the floor, so that la Luella did not get much pleasure out of Tom's miserable expression since he sent her to the back room for the mop to clean it up while he took over the register.

He said nothing about it but rang up six-packs and the Sunday edition of the Daily in total silence, and when Luella finished the KP-type assignment, he went back to working on the Big Slurpy machine. The rest of the day he almost did not speak at all and Luella kept out of his way, all too glad when her shift was over and she could take off to the more pleasant atmosphere of her trailer home, with the teething twins and her pain-in-the-ass old man.

Luella didn't bring it up no more but she knew and Tom knew. It was over. It was official. It was in the paper. Not even in the dreams he used to have about Fe after crying himself to sleep on most Saturday nights, after a double shift at the store and a few whiskeys at a poker game with friends, would Fe ever be his again.

Back in Tome, meanwhile, Tom couldn't have been further from Fe's mind. And considering what she suffered over that joke of a fiancé, Sofi couldn't have been happier for her daughter, except that, of course, marrying one's first cousin was not always the most prudent choice. On the other hand, plenty of manitos up north where Casimiro was from had traditionally married their cousins. It was almost a custom in some villages. It must be fate actually, Sofi resigned herself, after giving some thought to how Fe and Casey came together again. She finally decided that since it was Fe's life, the only thing left to do was to wish her happiness and healthy babies.

As opposed to the Fe that had belonged to Tom, this Fe, in some ways, was not as much of a snob toward her sisters since her "illness" and Esperanza's being given a posthumous medal as a national hero, and La Loca teaching her how to cook, and Caridad becoming a channeler—so that if she could have had them all in her wedding party—in formals—perhaps she would have.

But where was Fe to get an escort for a transparent sister (and I am not speaking metaphorically here); and would she in her life ever get to see her little sister Loca *touching* any human being (besides her mom), much less walking down the aisle on the arms of a man? As for Caridad, she never changed out of those white tunics that doña Felicia made for her to enhance her vaso role. Somehow, Fe concluded, more or less objectively she thought, none of these sisters was pastel chiffon material. Not solid taffeta neither. And forget gold lamé.

Well, maybe gold lamé.

But Fe decided to forgo the whole idea of bridesmaids altogether because of another little problem that had to do with her fiancé-primo, Casimiro. Casimiro, as everyone well knew, descended from an old, prestigious sheepherding family. In the last half a century, however, like most large cattle and sheep ranchers in the territory, his familia lost its profits, gave up big chunks of land, and finally moved on to other lines of work. That was how Casey ended up studying accounting. His father relocated the family to start a cement business in Phoenix with his brother, and Casey, as the oldest, took up a career that would be helpful to them.

That was all fine and well, and actually to Fe, pretty wonderful. It sure impressed more people at the bank than a fiancé who managed a convenience store–gas station. Casey was a hard worker and made a decent income. They both wanted to buy a home as soon as they could, and anyone could see that the cousins were made for each other.

But over seven generations of sheepherding had invariably gotten into Casey's blood, so that even though nobody would ever admit it, and it was hard to actually prove—since Casey was such a soft-spoken man to begin with—Fe was certain that her fiancé had somehow acquired the odd affliction of bleating.

It was like this: Sometimes he'd be working in his office at night and if she was around (not to imply that she stayed over before the wedding or nothing) and thought that maybe he'd like a cup of oshá, knowing how much he suffered from indigestion, just outside his door she'd hear a soft but distinct ba-aaa sound. Maybe it's his heartburn, she'd say to herself, or maybe he's just tired, as if bleating were the natural sound men made when yawning, or burping for that matter.

But eventually, she began to notice him doing this on the street, in actual broad daylight, in public, although not quite in front of her, since he was always maybe two or three feet ahead of her whenever it would happen, in the Broadway picking out new underwear, let's say, when out of modesty, Fe was intentionally staying behind a bit. She was sure she heard a bleat. She'd look around quickly to see if anyone else had heard it, too. But as it happened, nobody else was ever near enough to hear it, if, in fact, that's what it was.

After a few months, there was no doubt that her fiancé had this inbred peculiarity that couldn't be helped, as I said, after three hundred years of sheepherding and a long line of ancestors spending lifetimes of long, cold winters tending their herds.

She was so embarrassed, however, that she could not even speak to her mom about it. Instead, she announced to her family and friends (without even consulting with el Casey, whose psyche she already knew was also affected by the many generations of males in isolation so he would not object to a private affair) that theirs was to be as simple and as intimate a wedding as they could possibly arrange. And she was right, of course.

After Fe's Big Day, which consisted of little more than the Mass and a chile enchilada and posole dinner in the church hall for the immediate members of the groom's family (none of whom she was worried about with regards to Casey's "problem" because by then she figured that it was, if not a genetic, a family idiosyncrasy) and those of the bride who more or less attended. Her parents were present. Loca watched the ceremony from outside the church, peering in through the open door. Caridad was not physically present but "channeled" in her aura. And Esperanza was seen there by some, but not by everybody.

After dinner, for those who stayed, there was some dancing to the live music of Los Hermanos de Chilili. Despite a roomful of introverted bleating in-laws, the six-member Western Tex-Mex band was just something she refused to forsake. Although Fe had no use for musicians, she had had a secret crush on the youngest brother of the Chililis, who played the accordian, since high school. Some of her friends back then had been lucky enough to have quinceañeras and hired the brothers from Chilili to play for their balls. But Fe's mom had not been able to afford a coming-out party for any of the girls (although Fe was the only one disappointed about that fact), so Fe had to wait for her own wedding to have that foot-stomping, gold-tooth-flashing accordian player with the cleft chin sing just for her, although by then he was already long married and had gained a few unflattering pounds around the middle.

Fe and Casey settled into a three-bedroom, two-car-garage tract home in Rio Rancho with option to buy. They furnished it all new, sold Fe's car and bought a brand-new sedan model, right out of the showroom, for the occasions when they went out together to nice places like the Four Seasons Hotel to dance on Saturday nights.

Outside of marriage itself, perhaps the biggest change that Fe undertook at that time was that she also left her job at the savings and loan in Tome where she had worked since high school.

Well, Fe considered herself the steady and dedicated worker type, always giving her one hundred percent to the job, even when she was passed up twice for promotion at the bank and remained in New Accounts without so much as a prospect to get a real raise, neither. What she was finally told was that although the company did not want to discriminate against her new "handicap," her irregular speech really did not lend itself to working with the public. "What do __ mean, handi__ ?" she asked the manager, but was only advised to go to speech therapy and that was that.

Nobody had complained before to Fe about not understanding her, at least not to her face. Her mom and sisters always understood her. Her dad did not seem to care one way or the other whenever he misinterpreted something she said. And Casey, well, Casey never said nothing about her speech, because to Casey, Fe was about as perfect a wife as a man could get.

Then a girl (she wasn't really a girl, this is just how Fe referred to most of her female co-workers) who had once worked at the bank told Fe that they were hiring assemblers at Acme International. Acme was a big new company and though the work was, let's face it, shit, the "girl" told Fe, the pay was real good. "Hell, you make twice what you do at the bank. And depending on how good a worker you are, you keep getting raises!"

What she did not tell Fe, because she herself had not put two and two together yet, was that in addition to the raises she was getting nausea and headaches that increased in severity by the day. What she also did not tell Fe, because those bonuses were helping her catch up on her bills—or maybe it was the migraines clogging up her sense of reason, was that many of the women she worked with at Acme International were also having similar symptoms.

They all went to complain to the nurse at some point or another, it's not like the money was *that* good that they couldn't tell that they were feeling almost too lousy to make it through the shift. And the nurse gave them each ibuprofen tablets, advice about pre-menopause and the dropping of estrogen levels in women over thirty, and pretty much that it was just about being a woman and had nothing to do with working with chemicals.

But Fe was not over thirty and had had a clean bill of health at her pre-wedding gyn exam. She hadn't had no babies yet but she and Casey were looking forward to a big familia. "Let's have all boys," she said, thinking about the lot of girls her mother had had. Then remembering Casey's bleating and his shepherd's blood, she said, "Well, let's just see. Maybe we'll get girls. That would be okay, too. Hopefully, they'll take after me." And Casey said nothing, as usual, but smiled, because to him, like I said, his Fe was perfect.

Meanwhile, Fe was intent on moving up quick at Acme International, therefore from the start she took on every gritty job available, just to prove to the company what a good worker she was. But also, as her friend had told her, people were in fact given raises on the sheer basis of "utilization and efficiency." Yep, that's exactly how a supervisor put it to her one day, probably quoting out of the employee's manual or something, "utilization and efficiency."

And even though it really wasn't too clear what "utilization" meant, we know that nobody could be quite as efficient about anything as Fe was. Like even when she lost her mind because Tom had broken up with her, she did it without a second's hesitation; and just as quickly snapped out of it, even if it was a year later.

So in a few months Fe was promoted from assembler to materials dispatcher trainee. Some of the women who worked there did not have a high school diploma like Fe, several spoke Spanish, Tewa, Tiwa, or some other pueblo dialect as a first language, and none (except her friend) had had the prestigious experience of having been a white-collar worker before. Also, most had children already and the children wore them out before and after work so that they did not have their all to give to Acme International, as did Fe.

Casey usually drove her to work and picked her up and it was Casey who liked to cook dinner most evenings. Casey was in love. And just like newlyweds, every evening was a special night for them anyway, so sometimes it was pizza on a weeknight, sometimes they went to the Chinese carryout on Central Avenue on the way home. And it was going to be like that until Fe started getting pregnant as far as either of them were concerned, so Fe made the most of it and put her full concentration on the job.

In fact, before she got promoted to materials dispatcher trainee she was pregnant, but she did not know it until she miscarried. After she came back to work, having taken a few days off to recover, she told some of the women whom she usually had lunch with. "Well, at least you can still have babies," one woman told her. "I had a hysterectomy last summer." Before Fe could say nothing, although she didn't know what to say to that anyway, two of the other women said the same thing.

"You know," one of those women said, "my mom had her last baby when she was forty-four! She was still working out in the fields at that time and there she was as big as a house with my kid sister Concepción! My oldest sister was already married then and pregnant at the same time. And now, I'm just barely going on thirty and I already can't have no more kids."

"Well, at least you have little Joshua," another woman said to console her, referring to the first one's only child.

"Yeah. But too bad I ain't got the man that helped produce him . . ." And everyone kept quiet then, just went on eating their bologna and Kraft cheese subs from out of the vending machines, because really, what could anyone say to *that*?

There did seem to be something eerie and full of coincidences about it all to Fe's mind, but she kept working right through the headaches that by then were part of her daily routine.

Every morning for the first six months this is what she did. She went to a little desk that was called a "station," which gave it a kind of an official feeling, although all it was was a little desk. She had the same station every day. Another woman probably used it in the night shift, but Fe liked to think of it as her own, like the desk she had had at the bank (although not as nice) and that she never let nobody get near.

All the stations were situated in an open manufacturing area. Every morning each worker was given a pan about the size of a square foot which was filled with some nasty smelling chemical or other that would clean what Fe was told were parts for high-tech weapons.

Acme International was in the business of subcontracting these jobs from larger companies that had direct contracts with the Pentagon. They "cleaned up" the parts that in and of themselves did not seem all that dangerous, sent them back to the contracting company, and that company in turn took the parts and put them all together. As far as Fe could figure out that's how weapons for the military came to be made, manufactured like anything else in factories by people like herself, plastic and metal, undecipherable shapes, pieces and bits, down assembly lines and one day, somewhere, they were all put together and went off to be used for what they were made to do.

Very important work, when you thought about it.

Being so good at utilization and efficiency, the queen of it, you could say, there at Acme International, she was on to bigger jobs and better pay in no time. She worked hard no matter what, even though, for instance, she did not like the last cleaning job she was given. It's not like she had complained about it or nothing, but three months of working in a dark cubicle could get to anybody. The results of working with a chemical that actually glowed in the dark and therefore you could work with it in the dark, with special gloves and cap (and why you did, as a supervisor explained, was to be able to detect if any fingerprints or hair got on the parts) was this red ring around her nose and breath that smelled suspiciously of glue.

Well, the odor of all those chemicals in that open area as well as throughout the whole plant was enough to make anyone nauseated at first, but after about an hour of being there every morning, you would swear there was no smell at all. So Fe had no idea that her body had actually absorbed the smell until one evening Casey asked her, tactfully of course, if she was not doing something on her lunch hour that she shouldn't.

"What ____ that mean?" she asked, tired and understandably irritable, since having deadly chemicals in your pores will do that to you. Then he explained. In the last few weeks her breath was emitting a kind of sweet but peculiar smell . . . like glue. Casey knew that teenagers liked those kinds of kicks but had never taken Fe for one into cheap thrills. Fe ran to the bathroom and immediately washed out her mouth with Listerine, but just like with

Casey's bleats, the Listerine was not going to wash out what her lungs and liver and kidneys had already absorbed.

So one morning, as a kind of reward for her being such a utilizing and efficient worker, she was the first one that one of the main supervisors came to ask if she wanted to take on an especially tough job. It seems they had hundreds of a certain piece that had not been able to get cleaned through the "car wash," which was their way of referring to the assembly line. Nothing else available to them had worked on those troublesome parts either, but they had just gotten something "new" in and were pretty sure it would work.

But Fe was by then feeling a little less enthusiastic about her new job since the breath thing and the nose ring and the damn headaches that would not go away one thousand ibuprofen capsules later, so she asked the rotating foreman on the floor, who was not rotating of course, but was called that because foremen as a rule rotated regularly from one department to another, to please be so kind as to tell her what was in that brown bottle with no label that he was proposing for her to clean those big parts with.

"Ether," he responded, nonchalantly, handing her the first of ten of those twenty-pound pieces that she would clean that day. "Ether," he said, as in what was used to anesthetize patients when undergoing operations. Ether put you out. So Fe asked if that would happen to her. "Oh, no," said ese rotating foreman, with a bit of a smile as if as usual a subordinate was asking a stupid question, "you can't get put out by just inhaling it like that. Yeah, it'll make you sleepy, but that's all."

Then, Fe was told the next thing that she didn't find entirely on the up-and-up, and that was that she was going to have to carry each of these heavy parts downstairs to the basement and work in isolation. "Because of ether?" she asked. Yep, came the response. They did not want no one else in contact with it. So down she went. Down to the basement, first carrying the parts to be cleaned that day, one by one and then a big brown bottle of harmless, sleepytime ether to keep filling the pan with. She lifted and dunked the parts two or three times until finally she got the job done. Spic and span, right out of the ether pan. Nothing harmful about this. All in a day's work, she told herself all day. Yawning all the time never killed nobody was another thing she kept telling herself, down there alone.

After the first day of what she called Ether Hell, she got used to the constant lethargy and just went with it. She was getting better bonuses, too. It was a lot of work, though, even for someone like Fe, so she was really earning them. When another girl was put on the same job for a few days, she went right back to the assembly line because she couldn't handle the smell or having to lug those burdensome parts down all day, neither.

Not that Fe liked it any better, nor did she like the sorry excuse for a vent at the far end of the wall. That first day she put her hanky up next to it and it just dropped to the floor. She wasn't given no mask by any of the useless and ineffectual rotating foremen, so she helped herself to the kind used upstairs, and though she realized that in fact, it did no good, she still wore it because at least symbolically it made her feel better. She also used the usual orange gloves that they had upstairs, and not only did the chemical eat them up, it dissolved her manicure, not only the lacquer but the nails themselves!

"¡Hijola!" Fe said, and a few other choice words she did not hesitate to utter out loud, since she was alone all day and all and the only time anyone else came down was when a supervisor would stop by just for a minute or two to inspect her progress in cleaning those troublesome parts. After she lost most of her fingernails, she was given some "special" gloves for working with ether, they told her. But they could not come up with a mask that helped none, and three months went by and that's just how it was.

In the beginning, since the chemical she was working with was supposedly harmless, at the end of the day she poured what she had left down the drain, like they did upstairs. One morning one of the supervisors found out and bawled her out. He instructed her then, like she was stupid instead of having only been following the order she'd been given by all the other supervisors, that from then on she should just let what was left in the pan evaporate rather than pour it down the drain. If it was so harmless, Fe did not understand why it couldn't be poured out as the other chemicals were, but she gritted her teeth, said she would do as he said and after he left, she cried from rage since nobody had ever raised his voice to her like that before.

And at the end of the three months she was done and she got another raise.

She considered herself a kind of specialty person at Acme International, and as a matter of fact that is exactly what she was called officially. So, just like a specialty person, reserved for only the toughest jobs, after she was done she returned to being a materials dispatcher trainee to wait out the next big assignment.

But the next big assignment did not come. Instead came two men from the U.S. Attorney General's Office directly to Fe one day and told her that she was going to get a subpoena.

"A subpoena?" Fe repeated, eyes wide and blinking at the two men in suits and ties and looking so official-like and very intimidating, having stopped production just to come to tell Fe this. "Did I do some __ bad?" she asked.

They did not answer whether she had done nothing bad, but instead told her that Acme International was going to assign a counselor on her behalf and that furthermore she shouldn't say nothing about it to no one, not even to any of the rotating foremen or the supervisors. "If anyone has problems with our coming to talk with you, have them call us," one said, and then they left like a couple of gumshoes out of "Dragnet."

There was nobody to ask about it at Acme International since Fe was told by the federal government that she must not talk about her subpoena to no one. In the next few weeks, Fe was so upset, she could hardly keep up with her quotas much less earn any bonuses. Meanwhile the red ring around the nose, glue breath, big dried spots on her legs, and one constant fire drill going on in her head were doing nothing for her once-a-fairy-tale life with Casey.

"Mom," she went to Sofi one night after work, "I'm gonna lose my career and I do __ __ know why!"

"Well, 'jita, I don't really think you could call that job a career . . ."

"Yeah? Easy for you to say, *My Mom the Mayor!* __ since you be__ the may__ of Tome, __ like your daughter's fut__, aren't __ impor__ to you no more!"

"Watch how you talk to your mom," don Domingo interjected, only to get a dirty look from Fe.

"That's not true," Sofi told Fe. "It's only that I care more about you than about no career! Look at you! Look how upset you are over all this! And what's that you keep popping into your mouth, anyway?"

"Rolaids," Fe said. "For my ______."

"She takes them for indigestion all the time, tía, like candy," Casey told Sofia, seizing the opportunity to perhaps make his aunt an ally in this mysterious struggle he was having with Fe and her loyalty to Acme International. Something was definitely not right with his Fe no more, as much as it broke his heart to admit it. Sofia and he exchanged glances.

Casey thought for a moment he heard something swoosh a little over by the window, like the kind of sneaky movements a resident mouse makes, and then realized, seeing not a mouse but Loca's bare feet sticking out from beneath the drapes, that she was keeping out of sight but making sure she was in earshot range.

"Tomorrow morning you are taking Fe to the hospital for a full checkup and then we are going to see a lawyer!" Sofia told Casey.

And that's what they did.

And that is when they found out that Fe had cancer. She had cancer on the outside and all over the inside and there was no stopping it by then. But what they also found out was that before she started at Acme International, she already had skin cancer. And because she already had melanoma, what they found out from the lawyer they retained was that she would not be able to sue Acme International for the other cancer she had undoubtedly gotten from her chemical joyride at Acme International, which was eating her insides like acid and which no amount of Rolaids would have ever helped.

The rest of this story is hard to relate.

Because after Fe died, she did not resurrect as La Loca did at age three. She also did not return ectoplasmically like her tenacious earth-bound sister Esperanza. Very shortly after that first prognosis, Fe just died. And when someone dies that plain dead, it is hard to talk about.

Fe was given a Mass in Tome by Father Jerome who said her cremation was approved of by the Church (and paid for by Acme International) because at the time of her death there was so little left of Fe to be buried anyway.

And how that came to be had a lot to do with the "torture," as Fe came to refer to the medical treatment she received by the staff at the hospital. First they went about removing the cancerous moles on her legs and arms and eventually, chest and back and then whole body, so that Fe's flesh almost all at once was scarred all over. Having her whole body surgically scraped was agony enough, but then to add to this, the stress of the mysterious subpoena would cause these scars to swell from hives, and then Fe could not even walk, much less go to work—which she still did whenever she felt well enough because of all the payments due on all the things that she and Casey had bought on credit.

The next stupefying "mistake" made by the medical staff was when feeding a catheter through her collarbone, which was supposed to supply chemotherapy down somewhere, the guideline traveled up to her head instead. They thought they removed it when she left the hospital, but they hadn't. And until it was discovered because of an infection it caused and was finally pulled out, Fe went around feeling for seventy-one days and seventy-two nights like her brain wanted to pop out of her skull and nobody could figure out why, and they only kept insisting that it was all due to stress.

In the meantime, the FBI had come back a few times to talk to Fe. They said the reason that Acme International would have to get her a lawyer was that the chemical that she had used to clean those infamous big heavy parts in the basement was illegal; and since it was Fe alone who had used it, it was all her fault, the use of what was so obviously by then not ether (as Fe said to the FBI she had been told), but something that had already been banned in New Mexico and some other states but not in the state which was where Acme had gotten it from.

Fe didn't understand none of it. Especially what she did not understand was how the Attorney General's Office could be so concerned about who was to blame for the illegal use of a chemical but it was not the least bit concerned about her who was dying in front of their eyes because of having been in contact with it.

But that's really as far as Fe got with all that drama, because after a whole lot of anxiety and not even working no more at Acme (having been put on some kind of strange probation with no pay), everything was dropped, just as quickly and unexplainedly as it had started.

Fe's lawyer told her to get the data sheet from the company on the actual chemical that she had used on those parts and for which she was almost subpoenaed by the government for using. This took a lot of determination on Fe's end, calling and coming by and each rotating foreman hiding and telling the girls to tell Fe he was out to lunch, until she finally left a message for the supervisor in charge of rotating foremen that she knew that they knew that the FBI was on her case, so not to give her no more crap about that chemical having been ether or *she* with her lawyer would sue each little rotating ass there, and if she felt like it, she'd give every name of everyone who had ever so much as been in charge of when she could take a coffee break to the FBI. (Fe, as you can guess, was no longer in the mood to play Acme's star worker.)

Finally, the next time she went by, the rotating foreman of the week let her read it, although he would not let her take it away with her or photocopy it for her lawyer. So Fe sat down, patched up and in perpetual pain, with the manual in the foreman's partitioned-off station, which he called his office. And she began to read, not Fe the manicured, made-up bride of a few months before but a Fe without even the nice insides she had when she had started at Acme International, about the chemical she more than once dumped down the drain at the end of her day, which went into the sewage system and worked its way to people's septic tanks, vegetable gardens, kitchen taps, and sun-made tea.

The chemical must always be sealed, "reclaimed" is what the manual said. It should not be left to evaporate, it said too, because in fact it was (and this last part really got to Fe) *heavier than air*.

And if she had been supposedly letting it evaporate all those months she worked down there by herself, but it was heavier than air, then where had it gone? "It ____ wasn't ____ rushing out __ the room!" Fe jumped up, and screamed at the foreman—who in any case was nobody in charge of her life no more, but a cholo who did not know enough to open up a manual so as to properly inform a girl who had only wanted to make some points with the company and earn bonuses to buy her house, make car payments, have a baby, in other words, have a life like people do on T.V.

"It didn't go ____ the roof, and it ____ didn't go __ through that excuse __ a vent without no hood down __, neither!

"SO WHERE __ IT GO?" she yelled, grabbing by his Pendleton collar with her scarred hands that good-for-nothing former foreman that all the girls there thought was so cute (but not nearly as cute as *he* thought he was) and who at that moment to Fe only had the face of a grim reaper with a goatee. "WHERE DID __ GO, PENDE__, SON-__-A- . . ." She screamed again, "IF NOT IN __ ME?"

And that's when Fe, looking around suddenly, noticed it all for the first time and let go of the guy, who was just looking sorry at her, but who could say if he really was? The whole plant had been completely remodeled in the short time since she had been let go, down to the replaced sheetrock. And all the stations, not just the foreman's, which used to be open to everybody and everything, were partitioned off. Nobody and nothing able to know what was going on around them no more. And everybody, meanwhile, was working in silence as usual.

12

Of the Hideous Crime of Francisco el Penitente, and His Pathetic Calls Heard Throughout the Countryside as His Body Dangled from a Piñon like a Crow-Picked Pear; and the End of Caridad and Her Beloved Emerald, Which We Nevertheless Will Refrain from Calling Tragic

"I don't get it," Loretta sighed, shaking her head and walking out of the kitchen. Francisco el Penitente, or Franky as she had always called him, did not look up from his breakfast of blue corn atole and a side dish of huevos and posole. She was not objecting to the food, which she had prepared herself. It was good and what her husband, Franky's uncle, had had that morning. No, it was that Loretta caught Franky doing something real strange to his food that made her walk out.

Well, face it, she said to herself, putting on

her gardening gloves and going out to do some work on the vegetable garden, Franky *always* was kind of strange; but mixing up ashes from the fireplace into his food was a new one for the record. That was too much. Still, she knew darn well what he was up to. But what could she say? She had married into that family over a quarter of a century before and knew well enough that it would do no good to laugh nor cry about what she saw the men in her husband's family do in the name of God.

Francisco finished eating his tasteless ashen breakfast and went out to start on a bulto of San Isidro commissioned by a nearby rancher. He was the patron saint of farmers, and to not revere him could bring a farmer the worst punishment of all: bad neighbors. A farmer could survive droughts and bad crops, but not an ill-willed neighbor.

Francisco el Penitente Santero had not spoken a word in days, having decided to "enter himself" like an "Apostolic Serpent," shedding his old skin to dress his nakedness with mortification and repentance, as the good Saint Bonaventure had taught in his doctrines for the novice friars who had descended upon the landlocked territory of Francisco's kingdom three centuries before.

And as Caridad became more and more fixed in his consciousness, worse than any of the pine splinters that stayed lodged in his palms, Francisco el Penitente became more determined to exorcise her out at whatever price to his body and soul. "More bitter than death I find the woman who is a hunter's trap, whose heart is a snare and whose hands are prison bonds," Francisco el Penitente recited. "He who is pleasing to God will escape her, but the sinner will be entrapped by her." He moved his lips, quoting chapter and verse from Ecclesiastes, but did not let a sound come out of his mouth.

And yet, despite this determination to rid Caridad the Hunter's Trap out of his mind, he was not convinced that his obsession with Caridad La Armitaña Santa was at all of the carnal kind. If not for fear of committing heresy, he would venture to say that he looked upon her as one looked upon Mary. In Francisco's eyes, Caridad had proven herself to be all that was chaste and humble with that year of self-imposed ascetic life in a cave.

Even the first time he saw her he was taken aback by the glow her body emanated. Despite the beating of the sun on his brow and the cross that bent his bare back on that Good Friday he knew that it was not delirium. One less faithful might have dismissed what he saw as a mirage caused by the pain he had chosen to endure emulating the passion of Christ. But Francisco el Penitente knew what he saw in Caridad was nothing short of a blessing, an unmerited reward for the physical suffering he was imposing on himself as penance.

When he saw the quiet young woman trailing behind his godmother he already knew who Caridad was. Everyone knew the family of La Loca Santa of Tome. Despite what anyone wanted to say or not about the elusive youngest daughter, she could not be of this world, having returned from the dead before a hundred witnesses.

He remembered because doña Felicia and he had been there in front of the church. Doña Felicia had heard of the child's tragedy, and while she did not know the family personally, it was her custom to join with the mourners of her community. And when little Franky, who was really not that little by then, saw the child fly up to the church roof, man! What he wouldn't have given to know the secret of that trick! To the boy it was a trick, the way all children view the magical, which to them falls within the realm of possibility.

Francisco ignored his tío's wife in the garden pampering her calabasas, which were sure to win her first prize again at the state fair because no one in the whole state grew calabasas as big and as tasty and rich in color as Loretta's, and furthermore, without any kind of pesticides. (To say that Loretta and three of her children posed sitting on top of her grand-prize-winning calabasa last year would tell it all. No, it wasn't true what the envious calabasa contestants said about Loretta's gardening methods: "She injects them with Miracle-Gro, judge!" "She has a brujo come and do a ritual on her garden, judge! No normal calabasa could get that big!" They were very wrong, these poor excuses for gardeners and farmers, for Loretta's green thumb secret was as old as agriculture itself but had been forgotten so long that anyone knowing it would have suspected witchery, and that was that Loretta planted and harvested according to the *moon's* cycles, not the sun's. But how Loretta came upon this ancient wisdom is another secret, and yet another story.)

Francisco el Penitente went to his favorite place to work beneath an old cedar, where, while he meditated on the saving of his soul—repeating throughout the day the sign of the cross, the Credo, the Pater Noster, the Ave Maria, the Salve Regina, committing to memory the fourteen articles of the faith, and the commandments of God, reciting the list of the mortal and venial sins, the cardinal virtues, the works of mercy, and the powers of the soul and its enemies, namely, the world, the devil who lurked behind each shrub and tree and the treacherous flesh—he soothed himself with the scent of cedar and kept out of the scorching sun.

And yet he remained mortally contemptible. Who had told him that he deserved relief from the sun or to entice his lustful nostrils with the scent of cedar? Ah, ese pobre Franky of such human frailty had a long way to go before he could dare be so vain as to imitate even imperfectly the life of the saint for whom he was named.

Meanwhile, tío Pedro was across the field mending the corral with his friend, Sullivan, who had come over from Isleta Pueblo to give him a hand. "Has your nephew taken to talkin' to 'imself?" Sullivan asked, who seemed to have laser-beam vision and had observed from the half-mile between where they were working and where Francisco was carving that his lips were moving. Sullivan pulled out a worn bandanna from his back pocket and wiped his brow.

Pedro didn't stop to look up at Francisco because he already knew. For some time now it had gotten harder and harder to have even a simple conversation with el Franky. He didn't even bother to answer direct questions no more. All the man did was work on his santos and pray. Yes, it was good to pray while working on the bultos, but Francisco was even moving his lips like that in his sleep!

To make it worse, the guy never went home no more, neither! Pedro had always let his nephew know he had a room there whenever he needed but, after a few days of intense work on a bulto or a retablo, Francisco used to insist on his going back to the little studio he kept in the "student ghetto" near the university. But something was welling up inside him like a fever, something that was going to have to give way soon, otherwise everybody was going to explode: him, Loretta, and el Franky for sure.

"I think he needs a woman," Pedro said and surprised himself to have said it, since he had never really wanted to think about that nonexistent side of his nephew's life. After all, a man *was* entitled to some privacy, ¿qué no? But there, he had said it. Loretta had been saying it about Francisco, the youngest of their morada, for years. "When's Franky gonna find himself a girlfriend?" "When's Franky gonna get married?" And now, unless Francisco decided to become a monk, his tío Pedro had the same thought. It was time for his nephew and fellow penitente in the morada to do something with his life. In other words, get himself a woman. There. He had said it and having done so, straddled himself on top of the fence and continued to work.

Sullivan grinned, still staring over at Francisco el Penitente, and dropped his tools. Before Pedro could stop him he saw Sullivan making a beeline for Francisco, hearing him call from the distance to Francisco already, "Hey, bro'! What's up?"

Francisco looked up, startled out of his religious reverie, and found himself smiling sublimely at his uncle's approaching friend, as if he were an apparition rather than a gritty cowhand. Sullivan sat down on a tree stump, lighting up a Camel and making like he was just taking a little break and not there to get personal or nothing. So Francisco went back to his work, feeling relaxed about Sullivan's presence yet asking himself if that feeling was, like the shade of the cedar, too self-indulgent.

Seeing that Francisco was working on a bulto of San Ysidro, Sullivan began an offkey Pueblo song that was dedicated to the saint:

When the Lord punishes us
With a poor harvest,
With your generous coat
You protect us from the rest

Meanwhile, he was giving Francisco a thorough appraisal, with a sly sideways squint. Well, Francisco was no Mr. America, but there was no obvious reason why some lady out there shouldn't take a fancy to him. Unless of course, something happened to him in Vietnam that nobody wanted to talk about. "Been to any dances lately?" he asked abruptly. Francisco shook his head and did not look up from his work.

"Was a real good one at the Fairgrounds in Albuquerque last week, lots of pretty ladies there," Sullivan went on.

Francisco stopped for a moment. "Aren't you married now, Sullivan?" he said, breaking his three-day silence without ceremony.

"Yeah. So?"

"God is going to strike you dead if you commit adultery. You know that, don't you?" Francisco heard himself say.

"No, you got it wrong, man," Sullivan said. Sullivan was one of those people—*souls*, let's say—whom it would take a whole lot and then some to really bring him down. "If lightning struck my body dead, I'd become a Cloud Spirit, sacred and nurturing to this Earth and to my people. So, I wouldn't mind that at all," he informed Francisco, who only stared at him harder.

Both men were silent. Sullivan watched a fly dancing around Francisco's face, landing on his nose and forehead, nose and forehead, which for some reason Francisco didn't seem to acknowledge. Sullivan resisted the urge to slap it off. Instead, he took an unnecessarily deep drag from his cigarette, looking kind of Marlboro Man-ish, profound like, or at least trying to look profound, and turned away.

Pedro, whom Sullivan had abandoned in the middle of their task, continued without so much as looking up at Sullivan and Francisco to see how they were getting along on the touchy subject that he surely knew Sullivan had gone over to bring up.

"Sullivan," Francisco said after a long minute, as if it were the first time he had pronounced that name and, indeed, it was the first time he had. "How'd you get to be called Sullivan? After some explorer?" Francisco started to help himself to one of Sullivan's Camels but to his satisfaction triumphed over the temptation and drew back his hand.

"Nope," Sullivan grinned. He wasn't bashful about grinning, a thing he liked to do a lot, despite the fact that he had only a few teeth left and those that he showed were a definite yellow.

"Wasn't there a musical composer, Gilbert y Sullivan? Or was that two guys? Did your mother like music, man?"

"Nope. She liked television," Sullivan said, with a bigger grin. "We were the first family in the pueblo to get a T.V.

And it was my grandma. She named me after the 'Ed Sullivan Show.' Ain't that a hoot?"

He felt he had gotten Francisco's attention by then, so he decided to get down to business, "You need to get yourself a woman, Frank." Sullivan was not a man to mince words. The more he knew he was agitating Francisco el Penitente, Cross-Bearer, Fandango Flagellant, the more witch hopper Sullivan the Weedchopper became.

Francisco shook his head and resumed his work more diligently, peeling wood shavings with his knife as if he were skinning a pig. "I'm waiting for a sign," he confessed without looking up.

"Hey, man, the only sign you're gonna get is that *bulto* in your pants!" Sullivan laughed.

"Don't be blasphemous!" Francisco's ears were red. The veins on his neck bulged and Sullivan wondered if this was about to be one of those days when the best you could say about it was that at least you got in one good punch.

"Hey, man! You ain't no saint and I ain't your temastiano bell-ringer! So cut the crap! I knew you back when you were in high school, man. You used to have every girl around here crazy about you! What happened to you came from 'Nam and from smoking too much weed, that's all! So cut the shit! I was just trying to give you some manly advice this morning, that's all." Sullivan almost stopped grinning—about as mad as Sullivan ever got—as he stood, kicking up a little dust while walking back to Francisco's uncle.

Francisco, in the meantime, responded to Sullivan's cockiness by singing an alabada. He had the best voice of all the brothers in the morada, reverberant but slightly flat, which nevertheless lent itself to the lament of the alabada and reached Sullivan's ears as he approached Pedro.

Él que nace desgraciado
desde la cuna comienza

desde la cuna comienza
a vivir martirizado.

Pedro and Sullivan shook their heads at each other, and way far away, they heard Loretta's voice, "Shut up, Franky! You're upsetting the hens!"

Then, it got worse. Since Caridad had returned to her traila at doña Felicia's, she had become more despondent than ever. And Francisco—who, the more he prayed, the more raveled as tumbleweed he got about her—was further disconcerted that he couldn't get Caridad to so much as acknowledge his presence.

Always remembering that encounter between his penitente brothers and Caridad, Francisco did not dare approach her directly, for fear that she held a grudge against him for trying to force her out of her cave. Grown men had not been able even to budge her, so why should he, despite all the yearning in his heart, expect to persuade her to even glance his way?

Francisco felt himself powerless to his desire—which he nonetheless tried to justify by equating it with his spiritual calling. So he got it into his head that even if the Hunter's Trap did not seem to notice him, it would bring his torment some relief if he could at least stay close to her. So, figuring that nobody would ever be wise to him, he did just that.

It was a tedious exercise and if the truth be known, boring most of the time, since Caridad hardly left her trailer and on most days the furthest she traveled was the few yards between her trailer and doña Felicia's. Yet Francisco was a relentless devotee and he did not complain, even to himself, of the endless hours he spent on the hard ground behind the agaves and hedgehog cactus surrounding doña Felicia's trailer complex.

Doing nothing but keeping in proximity to his beloved, he meanwhile made friends with the little lizards that squirmed up his legs, surely mistaking them (because his limbs would inevitably go numb after a few hours in the same position) for trees, and with the cicadas and beetles and other lowly things that crawled about.

On the other hand, the crows who swooped down to rescue an occasional lit cigarette butt Francisco had flung out in the distance and flew up to perch on the telephone wires to smoke were most unwelcomed, since they above all threatened to give his hideout away. Anyone looking up at a row of crows puffing away at cigarette butts would only be inclined to look down to see who was supplying them.

However, on one afternoon Francisco had the unquestionable and fortuitous sign that he was where he should be behind the thorny shrubs, sagehorn, and palo verde, when he witnessed a pair of hummingbirds making their nest just over the ledge above Caridad's door; and hummingbirds, as everyone knows—unlike those scoundrel hustling crows that have no redeeming value—are an omen of true love.

That evening he went home, that is, to his tío Pedro's ranch, in ecstasy, and as he mixed ashes into his pork stew, causing Loretta to grit her teeth and his uncle to fix his gaze into his own bowl, so distressed was he over his young penitente brother's obsession with dulling his sensory perceptions, he recited aloud the Hail Mary. The agitating part being that he didn't just say "Hail Mary," but "HAIL Mary, FULL of grace," like that, like he wanted to break out in a gospel song or something, or like there was a private joke going on there between himself and Whomever, which really annoyed Loretta until she finally slammed the salt shaker down on the table and snapped Francisco el Penitente out of it.

"Where are you off to?" Pedro asked Francisco one evening shortly after that. Francisco had not been out anywhere after sunset since he had moved in. Well, let's face it, he *had* moved in. He only had one set of clothes, which were on him, of course: black jeans, black shirt, black belt, black boots, black hat, black coat, black everything in other words, not because he was a poet or trying to be stylish, neither. It was just in his long-ago Andalusian blood. His brother, James, the off-and-on jailbird, had always dressed that way, too. So had Pedro's father, come to think of it.

And besides his clothes he brought his few books, *The Soul's Journey into God*, which he had gotten out of the public library up north in the village of Las Vegas a few months ago and was never going to return, not because he was a thief but because he could not stop reading it over and over, a very fragile copy of *Cartilla y doctrina espiritual para la crianza y educación de los novicios que toman el hábito en la orden de N.P.S. Francisco*, which had belonged to his great-grandfather, original founder of his morada, and a copy of *Legends and Writings of Saint Clare of Assisi* that had belonged to his mother's sister, Sister Clara of the Society of Our Lady of the Most Holy Trinity. His tía, Sister Clara, was still alive but had taken a lifetime vow of silence so he had never kept in touch with her. The only time he had ever seen her was at his mother's funeral, which was when she had given him the book, just slipped it to him without saying nothing, of course.

Besides these books, his only other possessions were a bottle of Old Spice aftershave someone in his family—probably Loretta—had given to him last Christmas, a spiral notebook, three new Bic pens, and the original cassette recording of the Jimi Hendrix Experience that he had bought on his first leave from Fort Bliss over twenty years ago. All these things he had with him, so Pedro knew that el Franky had moved in.

"Out," is all Francisco el Penitente responded.

Great! Pedro thought to himself, although he did not reveal his joy, while thinking that just maybe Francisco was going to get himself a life! Then his wife said aloud (because you get to know a person after living with them for the better part of three decades and what one thinks the other will usually say), "Great. Maybe Franky's gonna get himself a life."

But how could Loretta know or even tío Pedro, who believed he had some understanding of Francisco's ways, but who ultimately would not win any prizes for being a good judge of character, that this was not the beginning of a life but the beginning of the end of one?

That night, Francisco went to Caridad's to keep vigil outside and was unsettled when he saw that her truck was gone. He waited behind the usual shrubbery, his own truck parked down the road and out of sight, until she finally came home, which was just about dawn. This upset him more than sleeping on the cold ground and waking up with more of God's creatures creeping all over him than he cared to shake off as he stumbled down the road back to his troquita.

The next afternoon when he was vigilant at his post nearby Caridad's trailer, he did not leave at sunset but instead stayed on until, as he suspected, she came out and jumped into her truck.

He ran to his pickup and caught up with her as she made her way through the South Valley and finally parked her truck right across the road from a little stucco house, but did not get out. There were people in the house, he knew that by the lights and the truck and VW Bug parked in the driveway. But you couldn't see in, at least not from where he was parked, which was a ways down so that Caridad wouldn't see him. But nobody came out and she did not ever get out of her truck.

The next night was the same thing. And the night after that and so on. Except on weekends. Everybody seemed to take the weekends off from their sleuthish behavior, or so he concluded because Caridad did not leave her trailer all weekend. So just for the heck of it, he went by the little stucco house and one of the vehicles was gone all weekend and the driveway light stayed on during the day which pretty much proved to him that the tenants were away.

But on Monday it all started up again. Everyone resuming their posts, and by Tuesday, instead of following Caridad to the little stucco house, Francisco just met her there at the usual time, so to speak.

When he had gone to the stucco house and suspected nobody was around, he had taken the liberty to get out of his truck to see if he could find out who lived there. On the mailbox were the names of two women. It was all a great mystery to Francisco el Penitente and he decided he couldn't continue not knowing why his sweeter-than-the-nectar-from-a-trumpet-vine Caridad spent every night in vigilance there, so he went to ask doña Felicia, who, being the one who seemed to know Caridad best, most assuredly would know something.

Of course he was going to be tactful. The last thing he wanted his nina Felicia to suspect of him was that he was in love with Caridad, not because it wasn't true, but because it wasn't true. At least, he wasn't in love in the base human sense of the word. But after a couple of doña Felicia's fried papita tacos with green chile, he found himself just blurting out the question that had brought him to visit his godmother: "Who are Maria and Esmeralda, nina?"

Doña Felicia stopped and looked up, scanning the brown rain spots on the ceiling, like a Serbian fortune-teller searching a coffee demitasse, as if somehow the answer were there. "Esmeralda . . . and Maria . . . ¡Ah, sí!"

"Who are they, nina?" Francisco asked again, aware that he felt himself tense waiting for the response. He had caught a glimpse of these women that very morning. They both looked Indian maybe, or of mixed blood, or maybe hispanas. He had been out there waiting in hopes of seeing them and that is what happened as they both left the house together, he guessed on their way to their jobs. They were holding hands and laughing and gave each other a little peck on the cheek, before one got into the truck and the other in the VW.

Who were they and why did Caridad keep vigil in front of their house every night, all night? And why, oh why, could he not let it all rest, and go home and sleep himself, instead of watching Caridad watch the stucco house sunset to sunrise?

"Esmeralda is kind of a friend of Caridad's," doña Felicia said, as if carefully selecting the words to reveal this information that was obviously so important to Francisco. But the truth was that doña Felicia was just not really sure who Maria and Esmeralda were. She remembered the names right away. She knew they came by to see her and Caridad. Maria had chronic neck pains and came for sobasos, which doña Felicia administered. They both seemed to have enormous regard for Caridad, but as with most people, Caridad recoiled and had hardly ever spoke to them. But it was the one named Esmeralda who doña Felicia got the impression had made the initial contact with Caridad, although Caridad never did explain to doña Felicia how she came to meet them.

"Esmeralda?" Francisco el Penitente uttered with difficulty, as if pronouncing a word foreign to him.

"Sí, mon cher. Pretty, isn't it?"

"Does she come to see Caridad often?" he asked, blinking hard like he was maybe going to cry then and there.

"They have both been here together maybe about three, or four, five times. I give Maria a sobaso and Esmeralda waits for her in Caridad's traila. But you know how shy Caridad is! She gives the young woman a cup of tea and then goes and hides in her bedroom. At least, that's what *I* think, since I asked la Esmeralda once how Caridad was when she had not come out all that day, and she said, 'I'm not sure, señora—she didn't speak to me.' "

Francisco lowered his head. He left shortly after that and knew he could not ever let himself set eyes on Caridad again. This is just the way that Francisco el Penitente's mind was going, kind of haywire, all the while thinking he was making sagacious connections when he wasn't even plugged in.

Doña Felicia watched him from her front window when he left. "Ay, ay, ay!" she said to herself like a little moan, and crossed herself. Her godson was thinner than usual, and in those black clothes he always wore he looked more and more like a zopilote, about ready to fly up and circle above dying prey. She saw him hesitate outside Caridad's door before he made his way to his truck, and then he took off, peeling rubber down the road like a no-'count teenager.

Meanwhile, Caridad's own obsession was, of course, Woman-on-the-wall-later-attendant-at-Ojo-Caliente, who inadvertently had caught Caridad's snarelike heart and who finally got a name. But Caridad barely let herself pronounce it, much less love Esmeralda openly for many reasons. First, because as she found out that very day at the mineral baths, Esmeralda already loved someone and her name was Maria.

But also, everyone and everything that Caridad had ever given her heart to had gone away. There hadn't been but two instances, Memo and Corazón, but two were enough. Then, of course, she had lost both her sister Fe and her older sister Esperanza, in a way.

Esperanza only in a way, because everyone knew Esperanza, stubborn as she had always been, was still around. She was not only around to La Loca, appearing occasionally by the acequia, and to other people, like Sofia and doña Felicia in their dreams, but she really talked pretty plainly to Caridad. So it was hard for Caridad to miss her older sister, having become closer to her after death than in life.

But Fe, who had stroked Caridad's brow so tenderly on that night of restoration when she had returned to the living after her encounter with the malgora, was really dead. And you couldn't bring back something that was so dead no matter how much you sat on your ankles before your candles and incense and prayed for a word, a sign, no matter what you did.

No, she would not take a risk and let beautiful Esmeralda die, too, just because of her apparently fatal touch. Doña Felicia was always teasing Caridad about becoming more and more like her sister Loca, afraid of people, but maybe La Loca was on to something all along.

So, every night Caridad, whose sleeping patterns tended to extremes—either she did not sleep at all, or she slept for days and even weeks at a time, usually before or right after making a prophecy—pacified her yearning by simply keeping an eye on the little home of Maria and Esmeralda. It's not like she thought anything bad was going to happen to them. She didn't keep her vigil because of that. It just made her feel good to be close by, the way Francisco el Penitente felt good being close by to her. Yes, she had always known that he was there. How could she not feel his own nearby yearning for the impossible, which was so akin to her own?

As for Esmeralda, she continued to see Caridad like the long-lost cousin she thought her to be at first. You might say she had a natural love for Caridad, which grew immediately once she found out that Caridad was kind of a medicine woman. The words "medicine woman" never came from Caridad's lips, of course. Esmeralda knew that Caridad was still too young to understand her gifts so she didn't mind when Caridad shied away from her when she went to visit while Maria got massaged by doña Felicia.

Caridad always let her into her little trailer without saying more than "Hi. How you doin'?" She gave Esmeralda a good tea, cota or something like that, and a little piece of sweet bread if she had it, also without saying much.

The two women never said much to each other, although undoubtedly they were communicating on a level less pedestrian than mere words. In any case, Caridad never knew some things about Esmeralda that Francisco el Penitente very soon made it his business to find out, like the fact that she was a trained social worker and had also been working as the assistant director of the new rape crisis center in Albuquerque for the last few months.

If Caridad did not speak to her, it comforted Esmeralda nevertheless, just to sit at her little wooden kitchen table, knowing that Caridad was in the next room praying for her, because although Caridad never said it, surely that is what she was up to in her little bedroom with the incense burning.

Praying for Esmeralda but not knowing why, and maybe Esmeralda could have figured it out for herself if only Caridad had ever said what was on her mind, but nobody was talking to nobody about nothing and everybody meanwhile was in a constant state of the willies, feeling like they were being followed all the time, because of course, they all were. So when Francisco did make it apparent he had followed Esmeralda to her employment one day, instead of being on guard and taking all the advice she gave to the women who came to the center, Esmeralda the Assistant Director of the Rape Crisis Center stopped to talk with Francisco el Penitente to find out once and for all what was going on.

The tall man in black who said he was doña Felicia's godson had parked himself all day right in front of her office. Esmeralda had noticed him at lunch when she came out to get a carne adovada burrito from the vending truck parked right outside and saw this shadow-like man perched on the hood of his truck, a bunch of cigarette butts scattered all around him on the ground indicating to her that he had been there awhile, and unwrapping an aluminum-foiled burrito of his own. He didn't say nothing to her then, but they exchanged long hard glances before Esmeralda went back in.

After work, Esmeralda saw him still out there, more cigarette butts around him and drinking out of a large coffee thermos. That's when she went right up to the truck, but he was the one who started the talking. He asked her a few questions about Caridad, and she knew right away that he had a thing for her but she couldn't understand why he was talking to her about it, much less how it was that he came to her place of employment in the first place, and before she knew it, Francisco had abducted her.

Yes, abducted her, right in front of the rape crisis center. Most of the volunteers and staff on her shift were gone, had driven off in their cars and trucks or walked down the street to the bus stop, so there was not one witness when he, skinny as he was, malnourished as he was, delirious with living mostly on prayer and cigarettes, got her into his truck.

Not physically, you understand. He would never have won that struggle since Esmeralda was no kind of wimpy woman. Her brown belt in judo and her first-place trophy from the Southwest Women in the Martial Arts Annual Competition would surely have caused her to make a neat stack of toothpicks out of that scarecrow of a man. No, it wasn't with muscular force but with the power of words that he was able to drive away with her. But what those words were, nobody will ever know.

"We'll call the police," Maria said to Esmeralda that night when Francisco dropped her off in front of her house. Maria had been pacing the living room, smoking a joint, half out of her mind that Esmeralda had not called to say she would be late and suspecting the worst, and the worst was what had happened. Well, maybe not the worst, that would have meant that Francisco el Penitente would have left off a dead body.

Maria had never seen Francisco el Penitente. She had not had even a glance to guess what he was capable of or not capable of. She only knew that Esmeralda should not have trusted him. Or maybe Esmeralda hadn't trusted him, maybe he had pulled her into his truck biting and screaming. Esmeralda said nothing or did nothing but look up at her occasionally with an expression on her face that also said nada.

So Maria did not try to stop Esmeralda from going that day, even though her heart wanted to fold itself over, she just gave Esmeralda a little peck and with a "See you later, honey, I'll wait for you guys to have dinner, okay?" she just watched Caridad's old truck go off down the road toward I-40.

Then Maria threw her lead pipe protector back under the seat, saying to herself that she was on her way to get a massage, but really because she already knew that she would not see Esmeralda again and she wanted to be at doña Felicia's so that she could say what she had to say when it was time to say it.

It was as dry as always at Acoma Pueblo that afternoon as Caridad and Esmeralda made their way up to Sky City, the oldest city in all of the Americas that has had constant habitation. They were allowed to drive up because Esmeralda's grandmother lived there. Esmeralda's baby sister would one day inherit the little adobe which her grandmother had helped rebuild as only a thousand-year-old house would need to be, and which Esmeralda's baby sister also was having to mud-plaster those days.

Although the baby sister was not there that day when the two women arrived, her little son was, playing outside with a bike that had no foot pedals. After being introduced to the grandmother, Caridad waited for Esmeralda outside the door, to gave Esmeralda some privacy to talk, as she figured that was what she went to do.

Caridad, meanwhile, had been aware of Francisco's truck behind them—it had become like a constant companion to her own for months—as they drove up to Acoma. He could not come up the mesa in his truck like they had in theirs, however, because outsiders were not allowed to drive up uninvited.

She looked around. It wasn't easy to hide up there. As far as she could see there was only one puny tree under which an old station wagon was parked—the only vehicle that would probably not get baked by the sun that day. The Sky City tour bus was pulled up in front of the big church. There was a little tour group being led by a young woman. Caridad squinted to see if Francisco was among them, but didn't spot him, shadow that he was and more elusive than a strand of hair.

There were just some things even a clairvoyant couldn't see, couldn't put her ultra-perceptive finger on, so to speak. Caridad had prayed for clarity. She stared for hours into a clear jar as doña Felicia had instructed her to do when she was having such difficulties. She went into trances with sweetgrass, and still there was something opaque when it came to Francisco.

She had even consulted with a famous channeler who was living in Santa Fe, an Anglo woman from New York who claimed to speak to a two-thousand-year-old spirit, but neither the New Yorker nor the two-thousand-year-old spirit had ever heard of Francisco el Penitente. In fact, neither of them even knew what a penitente was. "Where did you say you were from?" Caridad asked the channeler.

"Which one of us?" the channeler asked.

"Either one," Caridad said.

"Long Island and Egypt, respectively," the woman answered in a kind of strange stereophonic-sounding voice. Caridad winced. She didn't know very much about either of those two places, but she was pretty much convinced then and there that she had just wasted seventy-five hard-earned dollars and went back home to consult with her own inner voices.

And still, there was no clue as to what Francisco's motives were, which is why, as she sat there that day, shooing away the flies, having a piece of bread that Esmeralda's little nephew offered her fresh from the grandmother's orno and some sunflower seeds from a basket that the grandmother had left out there for her as well, something hit her like a terrible lightning bolt when she unintentionally overheard Esmeralda and her grandmother talking just inside the open doorway. And all she could say to herself at that moment, being the humble clairvoyant that she was, was "How could I be so blind?"

And if only it had been a real lightning bolt and not just an expression—perhaps it would have turned our Caridad into a Cloud Spirit as most certainly would happen to Sullivan from Isleta one summer day. But no, this expression was only to show how hard it all hit Caridad, all in an instant. And when Caridad heard what she heard, she could do nothing more than bring her knees up to her chest, and fold herself into a Chinese magic box, her wet weeping face hidden inside.

"What is it?" Esmeralda asked when she heard Caridad's loud sobs and came out to see, but Caridad could not answer. So Esmeralda scooted down and simply held Caridad, trying to comfort her. "There, there," she said, not just a little choked up herself from what she had been recounting to her old grandmother.

Then, as if bad dreams once having been entered are the inevitable long road to hell itself, Esmeralda looked up and uttered "Oh my God," because she recognized among the small group with the guide a tall, lean, lonely coyote trying to camouflage himself as a tourist. And while we know that Esmeralda was not afraid because she just was not, we don't know why she did what she did next. She started to run.

And behind her came running Caridad, screaming, "Stop!" and the boy too, saying, "Auntie, where're you goin', Auntie?" Until his little voice faded, and Esmeralda was flying, flying off the mesa like a broken-winged moth and holding tight to her hand was Caridad, more kite than woman billowing through midair.

Tsichtinako was calling! Esmeralda's grandmother holding tight to her little grandson's hand heard and nodded. The Pueblo tour guide heard, cocking her ear as if trying to make out the words. The priest at the church, who happened to be performing baptisms that morning, ran out and put his hands to his temples. Two or three dogs began to bark. The Acoma people heard it and knew it was the voice of the Invisible One who had nourished the first two humans, who were also both female, although no one had heard it in a long time and some had never heard it before. But all still knew who It was.

Meanwhile, Francisco had seen Esmeralda and Caridad as they ran and watched paralyzed as together they leapt into the air. After getting his bearings, he went to the edge of the mesa along with the other tourists in Sky City, some in disbelief, others shouting and crying in panic, and one or two just walking over slowly to take a peek at the results down below out of curiosity. But much to all their surprise, there were no morbid remains of splintered bodies tossed to the ground, down, down, like bad pottery or glass or old bread. There weren't even whole bodies lying peaceful. There was nothing.

Just the spirit deity Tsichtinako calling loudly with a voice like wind, guiding the two women back, not out toward the sun's rays or up to the clouds but down, deep within the soft, moist dark earth where Esmeralda and Caridad would be safe and live forever.

Tío Pedro and Loretta would not know for a long time the whole story. But doña Felicia knew it that same night because Maria told her what she knew when the police got to Caridad's trailer and then later more police came to see doña

Felicia to tell her that her godson was found that evening, just after sunset, at the far end of his uncle's land, dangling sorrowful-like like a crow-picked pear from a tall piñon, which was how someone had first put it and how it was remembered after that.

He was discovered by his uncle Pedro, who had been relaxing watching a video of Charles Bronson with his wife Loretta and his friend Sullivan, after a hard day of trying to set up a windmill on the ranch, when suddenly Sullivan said, "Sh-hh, shhh! Did you hear that?" Loretta quickly hit the pause button on the remote control, then all three together heard it, a tenor lament, resonating distinctly, carried across the corn fields, Loretta's moon-harvested squash garden, the corral and thick night air and right through the screen door: "Caridad!" they heard Francisco's voice, low and mournful. "Caridad!"

And then there was only the dissonant choir of the cicadas.

13

The Final Farewell of Don Domingo, sin a Big mitote; and an Encounter with un Doctor Invisible, or Better Known in These Parts as a Psychic Surgeon, Who, in Any Case, Has No Cure for Death

After Fe's cremation, her father took up an old habit from his youth and got involved in the cockfights organized by compadres in the South Valley every Saturday night since Domingo was at least ten years old, which was when he first started betting. On Sundays don Domingo went to Mass with Sofia—which was not an old habit—but like the increased cockfight fever, had also resulted perhaps as a way to alleviate the pain of Fe's brutal death.

Not that the deaths of Esperanza and Caridad were less brutal for el don Domingo to think about. The abduction and death in the desert of one and the jumping off a mesa like an Acapulco cliff diver with no ocean below of the other were hideous memories of the departures of their two eldest daughters for both don Domingo y la Mayor Sofia. But Fe's death somehow hit them hardest, not because they had favored that daughter, but because they had personally fought the wasting away of Fe's life and spirit and lost.

The sheep-raising wool-weaving co-op was doing well for the unofficial village of Tome, and so was the Tome Food Co-op (formerly Sofi's Carne Buena Carnecería), and Sofia, at least with regards to her own livelihood, experienced a brief period of economic balance for the first time in her adult life. But this, unfortunately, did not last too long.

Sofia's dry and thirsty land by its very nature was a land of ingenious undertakings; and while its early Spanish transplants learned irrigation methods from the indigenous residents to sustain crops and graze animals, and how to make do with raw materials, talk with the sky, and honor mountains and streams, and despite all their relentless faith together, the sheer daily toil, the centuries going by, the world changing around them, it never got no easier.

Meanwhile, Domingo's bets got bigger and bigger and then came the day, very soon—since it don't take a gambler running a high fever much time to lose all his jolas and then dip into yours if he can—when Sofia had enough and said "¡Ya!" Again . . .

All of a sudden, like a palo hitting her over the head, she remembered—oh so clearly! "Like if it was only yesterday, comadre!" she said aloud.

As her memory came back to her, Sofi la Mayor now relayed the whole story to her comadre, doña Rita de Belen, one morning at the food co-op, how back in those early days Domingo was little by little betting away the land she had inherited from her father, and finally she couldn't take no more and gave him his walking papers. Just like that, she said, "Go, hombre, before you leave us all out on the street!" Yes! It had been Sofia who had made Domingo leave.

Believe it or not, comadre.

But for twenty years, everyone (starting with Sofia herself) had forgotten that one little detail, calling her la "Pobre Sofi" y la "Abandonada," and that was pretty bad because there was almost nothing more pitiful to her than to be called an abandoned woman.

And what brought her to send Domingo out of her life once again was the day she realized he had given up the deed to the house. He couldn't give up the butcher shop (which he probably would have, given the chance), because she had sold it already in shares to the community and it no longer belonged just to Sofi.

But the house, that home of mud and straw and stucco and in some places brick—which had been her mother's and father's and her grandparents', for that matter, and in which she and her sister had been born and raised—that house had belonged to *her.* The law, however, based on "community property," stated that the house also belonged to her legal husband who remained, even after twenty years of being la Abandonada, Domingo.

One day, that very same woman, who, not just a few vecinos whispered, should never have let that so-and-so and such-and-such come back to begin with, was notified by the bank that her home, along with one measly acre next to her property which she had not given up to the Tome collective so as to keep Loca's horses, was being transferred over to a certain Judge *Julano.*

Immediately Sofia knew what had happened and found it, well, let's just say it, plain dishonest that Domingo lost such a bet to a *judge,* a servant of the people, for heaven's sake! Sofia was not going to take it lying down, neither. So she got up one morning and went down to see the peacock raiser, who, among other things, was a lawyer by profession. Since he had turned out to be a good vecino, Sofi didn't really think of him as no lawyer but more like gente, so she felt she could trust him, and through his efforts she finally got the judge to return her calls.

Yes, indeed, Judge Julano had won the house at a cockfight "fair and square," the judge told Sofi in that way that legal-type people always talk to people who are not, giving off that feeling that they got the law on their side, whether or not they do.

"But how can it be fair and square, when those gallo fights are illegal!" Sofi cried in exasperation.

"Well, señora, lo siento muncho," the juez apologized like the big hypocrite that he was. "But it's no less fair than not putting your husband and the rest of those guys running that operation in jail, now is it?"

Knowing that Domingo's options weren't many and not really wanting to see him suffer in prison, with his rheumatism and his bad days—after losing the girls one after the next worked itself into his joints and if he wasn't out gambling, he was just sitting there all demoralized in his Lazy Boy in front of the television watching telenovelas, and predictions by *Walter*, the Puerto Rican mystic, or talk shows like Cara a Cara, where they brought on experts on devil worship in East Los Angeles or discussed marital infidelity or one really weird time where they had the mother of a woman whose dead seventeen-year-old virgin daughter was exhumed and raped by the camposanto caretakers in Miami (¡Hijola!) and fifteen-minute cooking programs sponsored by Goya Foods—Sofi quietly let the matter go, along with her beloved ranchería, which were all one and the same thing, of course.

The judge found it in his heart, however, having no need for the house, to let la Sofi continue to reside in her own home after she agreed to pay him a modest rent, something no one in that house had ever done before since her grandparents had built it with their own hands.

"What do you think?" she asked her comadre. "No more

land and to top it all off, I am renting property built by my own abuelos!"

"I know what you mean, comadre," empathized la Rita of Belen. "Me too. You know that my great-great-grandparents were the direct grantees of a land grant from King Felipe II, the very land *I* grew up on as a child. Except that what I grew up on was barely enough to plant a little corn, some calabasas, chiles, nomás, and graze a few goats and sheep to keep us alive.

"First the gringos took most of our land away when they took over the territory from Mexico—right after Mexico had taken it from Spain and like my vis-abuelo used to say, 'Ni no' habiamo' dado cuenta,' it all happened so fast! Then, little by little, my familia had to give it up 'cause they couldn't afford it no more, losing business on their churros and cattle.

"Now all I have is my casita, too. Now that my kids are grown and had to leave the ranchería to find work elsewhere, I don't worry so much. It's just me and my husband, you know. And we manage on the little we get from our pension, I guess."

Sofia patted her comadre's hand. La Rita was a gifted weaver and the cooperative owed her a lot for her beautiful rugs that she sold on behalf of everybody. The two tired women smiled sadly at each other and kept stacking little cans of tomato sauce on the shelves as precisely and patiently as if they were knotting loops on the loom frame for a cobija.

Everyone had troubles. At least neither Sofi nor la doña Rita were on food stamps. But Sofia didn't want to remind her comadre that when it came to retirement time for herself, Sofia would no longer even have the satisfaction of knowing that she would die in her own home. And that really was the final straw for her.

So, without exchanging two words about her decision with Domingo who surely must have seen it coming anyway,

Sofia had her peacock-raising lawyer serve the papers she figured were twenty years overdue, and told him to leave.

But back then, to be excommunicated was more fearful to Sofia than the thought of destitution; not to mention that her mother was still alive then, and her mother had been like the Church's conscience incarnated to her daughter. If anything ever brought the fear of God to Sofi even more than the thought of being excommunicated it was her mother's disapproval, so divorce had been out of the question.

Sofi had devoted her life to being a good daughter, a good wife, and a good mother, or at least had given it all a hell of a good try, and now she asked herself—"¿Y pa' qué? ¡Chingao!" She said this aloud and then crossed herself. Now there was no mother to honor, no father to respect, no 'jitas to sacrifice for, no rancho to maintain, and no land left to work. Nothing to look out for no more, except for la Loquita, her eternal baby.

If the butcher shop no longer belonged solely to Sofi, it was also not Sofi's sole worry to keep it going. Since she didn't have no land left to graze her own livestock, it was beyond her means to run a butcher shop. After all, you sure couldn't run no meat market with a few measly chickens and an occasional pig to slaughter!

After Domingo received the divorce papers, he left without making any big mitote about it. Why be a bigger hypocrite than the Judge Julano, and act like he was sorry and would never do it again?

Sofia's heart did not allow her to just put him out on the street, however. So, Domingo, with her permission, went to live in the adobe in Chimayo which he had built with his own hands for Caridad, but which she never got to live in, pobrecita. Sofi let him stay there for approximately the same amount of rent she was having to pay el Judge Julano. So, in terms of the sad rent business, and as far as any of Sofi's comadres could tell, Sofia looked like she at least came out even. But, you and I both know that without a steady job and with Domingo's steady gambling, on most months nobody could hardly call it even between them.

In her divorce settlement, Sofi had taken Caridad's little one-room house, thinking that at least after her death Loca would have a place to go. And Domingo, knowing himself all too well, agreed, so he signed his share over to Loca. And that was that.

But Loca was not destined to live in that little one-room round adobe, neither.

After each daughter's death, Sofi noticed that Loca was a little more off-center than usual. Loca spent more and more time down by the acequia, ignoring the animals, hardly playing her fiddle, losing interest in life, it seemed, and when her father was gone, she adapted his mindless habit of indiscriminate T.V. watching.

And though no one would have ever thought of the television as any kind of psychic vehicle, one Sunday evening while Loca was staring at one of those "news magazine" shows, Sofi got a premonition from it, and with a deep sigh, resigned herself to the fact that she was going to die alone.

"Look, Mom, come 'ere," Loca had called on that occasion to Sofi, who was doing her income taxes at the dining room table when Loca saw something that had caught her attention.

The report was about a woman named Vicka from a place called Medjugorje who had experienced a vision of the Virgin Mary years ago when she was a teenager. "Listen! Listen!" Loca interrupted when Sofi started to ask something. Vicka was telling the reporter that not long ago, the Virgin Mary had taken her on a "tour" of heaven, hell, and purgatory.

"Pos, ¡chingao!" Sofi said under her breath and forgot to

kiss her scapular for cursing, she was so taken aback to hear of another case similar to her daughter's. The woman went on and explained what she had seen, but as she did, Loca began to frown. Vicka explained that her "tour" with the Virgin had taken no more than twenty minutes because that's all it had required. She told her story to the news anchor just as she repeated it almost daily in her native land to the faithful throngs that journeyed from all over the world to see her and to pray at the spot where the Virgin first appeared.

Hell, she said, was a fiery pit of men and women turning into beasts and blaspheming God, purgatory was simply ashes (kind of an aperitif of hell, Sofi figured by the brief description), and heaven, well, heaven was a happy place, where people floated on clouds with little angels on their shoulders, dressed in yellow, pink, and gray cloaks (which apparently was heaven's color scheme, according to Vicka). And oh yes, she added, one final important fact about the permanent residents of heaven: everyone in heaven was thirty-three years old, forever.

Sofi looked at her daughter for some kind of verification when the commercial came on. But with her usual taciturn manner, Loca got up without a word, picked up her fiddle, and started out the screen door. So like that chiple daughter to make no comment and just walk off, Sofi thought with disappointment, but did not stop her.

Instead, as she watched Loca from the window going down to the acequia where she laid her fiddle down and sat against the cottonwood just staring out at nothing, Sofi took notice that her daughter was losing weight because her jeans were really getting baggy at the butt (baggier than usual since she hardly had a butt to begin with), and that the label in the back had been deliberately cut out, leaving an indecent tear.

There was so much Sofi did not know about the whys of Loca, despite the fact that since the age of three when she had died and been "resurrected" at her funeral Mass, Loca had never left home and her mother was the sole person whom she ever let get near her. Loca went only as far as the stalls and riding the horses along the acequia and walking down to the acequia on foot. That was it.

She had never been to school. She had never been to a dance. She never went to Mass. (At first this, above all, had concerned Sofi due to pressure from el Father Jerome, but no coaxing, no threats about punishment neither here nor in the afterlife bothered Loca, who, when the priest told her on the phone that if she did not honor the Lord's day in His Home she would surely burn in hell, said, "I've already been there." And then, much to Sofi's embarrassment, certainly having learned this expression from that other malcriada daughter Esperanza, Loca added, "And actually, it's overrated".)

She did not take her First Holy Communion as each sister in her turn did, nor the Holy Sacrament of Confirmation. Not because Father Jerome would not have accommodated Loca's particular affliction by offering some form of private instruction but because Loca had flatly refused it. Loca would have been walking a very thin line to getting excommunicated herself, insisting that *she* could tell Father Jerome a thing or two about the wishes of God, but Father Jerome took pity on her and finally dismissed Loca as a person who was really not responsible for her mind.

To her sisters, the saddest part of all was that Loca had never had a social life. Her limber horse-riding body had never so much as felt the inside of a dress, much less of a bra! No, Loca had done none of the things young ladies did or at least desired to do.

She had become proficient in cooking and sewing but only to help her mother and sisters at home. She was the caretaker of the animals and had done excellent training with the horses since she was barely five or six years old.

And though no one had given her a single lesson, and surely no one in that household could even carry a tune, nobody played the fiddle like Loca—the very one that had belonged to her abuelo and which she found as a child in her mother's armoire.

So it may be said she had a full life. Maybe not one reserved for a lady, but then, neither had the rest of the women in her family.

"How come those jeans fit you that way ¿y qué pasó with the label and back pocket?" Sofi finally asked out of exasperation one day, seeing Loca's jeans getting looser. Since Loca wore the same jeans until they could almost walk themselves over to the washer, a week after she first noticed them on Loca, Loca still had them on. She even slept in the same clothes, but since she slept half the time in the stall with the horses instead of in her bed, it was just as well.

"They were la Caridad's. She was bigger 'an me, remember?" Loca replied to the first part of Sofi's two-part interrogation. To the second, she said, "I saw on the T.V. that some people in a factory are boycotting the company that makes these jeans . . ."

Before Sofi could say nothing about Loca's sudden social consciousness, Loca went on. "You know. Mom. Una factory that is unfair to its workers, just like where le Fe worked at. The woman on the T.V. that was saying it reminded me of la Esperanza, like the way she took the microphone off the lady that was asking her the questions."

Sofia stared at her daughter in amazement, although that might sound hard to believe after everything Sofi had experienced with her youngest. But it made sense that even if Loca never left her home and seemed to have no use for society, some of her own sisters' experiences had affected her. "So is that why you ripped off the label? 'Cause you were mad about your sisters?" Sofi asked, underestimating La Loca at that moment like everybody else always did.

"Uh-uh. They said on the T.V. that if you already have a pair of those jeans, then tear off the label to protest. They said it would make people ask why."

"But *who* ever sees your jeans?" Sofi asked.

"You, Mom. You asked. You'll tell somebody, ¿qué no?" Loca answered and of course she was right since that very evening—in her tireless quest to convince the world (or perhaps herself) that her daughter was not a "pobre criatura" as she was so often called behind her back, but in her own way a very responsible young woman—Sofi proudly relayed the boycott information via the jean story about Loca at a meeting she was attending at the local high school about the noise pollution coming from nearby Kirtland Air Force Base.

But the boycotted jeans got baggier before they got dirty enough for Loca to discard and Sofi, more concerned about Loca's health than the boycotted jeans, called in the family doctor.

Doctor Tolentino was one of those old-fashioned general-family-practice-type doctors, the kind people only find in rural areas nowadays, and not always there no more, really, since women in labor in such places can be helicoptered to hospitals during snowstorms, and very sick people don't die peacefully at home no more but are forced to a strange bed in a hospital, days and even weeks before their time.

Well, all that aside, Doctor Tolentino had been practicing in the Rio Abajo region since before Lorenzo of Isleta Pueblo's time, Lorenzo, looking around ninety or so, being the oldest person living in the area that comes to mind. Doctor Tolentino not only delivered all of Sofi's girls at home but delivered Sofi herself in that same house. So with all that familiarity (or maybe because Loca didn't have it in her no more), Loca did not refuse to see him.

Doctor Tolentino came over with his Anglo wife the same

day that Sofi called him. Now, Doctor Tolentino was not native to the area, but because his wife, the daughter of a Protestant missionary who had settled in Tome a *long* time ago, insisted on staying there, he had made it his home away from home, which was, as a matter of fact, actually in the Philippines.

Both Doctor Tolentino and his gringa wife spoke very good Spanish, better than anybody around there, for that matter (but then, they had studied theirs in college back East, which was where they'd met), so all the local familias had always accepted them and saw them as belonging there.

Now besides this, nobody knew much else about el Doctor Tolentino and la Mrs. Doctor. They did not even know if the Tolentinos had ever had children, for example. It appeared not, since no children were ever seen, nor mentioned for that matter. They did not know what kind of food they ate at home, neither. Like, did they eat chili and did la Mrs. Doctor ever make posole for el Doctor Tolentino? Although they never turned away little gifts of food that were offered to them in addition to or in lieu of payments for home visits.

Although nobody ever saw him, nobody knew for sure if el doctor ever went to Mass (even if the Protestant wife didn't). Nobody knew these very personal things and nobody asked. People were just glad to have such a good doctor and assistant who never complained about being called at any time of the day or night and who would be there administering flu shots and bandages as quickly as their 1953 deluxe station wagon would get them there.

It is true, however, that by the time he came to see Loca, whom he had not seen since the day her mother gave light to her, his eyes were not what they used to be. And there was something particularly disturbing about that cough of his, especially since he smoked those smelly cigars all the time. But aside from these frailities, Doctor Tolentino looked as able as back when he had come to tell Sofi's strong father three decades ago he'd better take it easy if he didn't want to push his heart too much, a piece of good advice that unfortunately Sofi's stubborn, proud father did not heed.

Now, Loca had never been sick before, and aside from when she suffered that abrupt death she never got no other medical attention. Since el Doctor Tolentino was out on a ranch that night delivering a breach birth, Sofi had rushed her infant to the local clinic where a young intern nobody knew had pronounced Loca's death.

Surprisingly, as the girls were growing up, Loca was the one daughter who missed all the childhood diseases and all the colds and flus that the others passed on to each other so generously, quickly driving poor Sofi to exhaustion tending to them night and day until each one recovered.

Even if she had gotten sick, she would never have let no one get near to examine her. But now, as she admitted to Sofi, aside from the sudden unexplainable weight loss, Loca also had a sore throat all the time, not to mention that she couldn't stay awake or do nothing no more. She just plain did not seem to care much about nothing, so that, as I said before, she did not have it in her to refuse to see el Doctor Tolentino and la Mrs. Doctor, with her oh-so-very-wrinkly-white-powdered-smiling-all-the-time face.

When they were done with their brief examination of Loca in her room, Doctor Tolentino lit his cigar in the living room and asked Sofi to sit down. La Mrs. Doctor sat down next to Sofi and took her hand. "Señora Sofi, hija," Dr. Tolentino said, almost as if it pained him to speak, and then as if something else had just occurred to him, he looked around and asked, "Where is your husband? Didn't I hear that Domingo was back home?"

"We're divorced now," Sofi answered, not wanting to beat around the bush about it. Besides, no longer thinking that her marriage or divorce was anybody's business, she wanted to get to the point about Loca's health, "Doctor, is my daughter just depressed? You know, losing the girls, as we have . . ."

"No, she is not just depressed," Mrs. Doctor said. "Although understandably, Sofi, I'm sure she must be heartbroken about losing her sisters . . . as we all are, you know."

Sofi lowered her head and prepared herself now for the worst. She fixed her gaze on the pattern of her leopard-print leggings. Ever since she started working out at the jazzercise class at the local Y, partly out of a desire to tone up and partly just to get some nervous energy out of her system that she no longer knew what to do with, she had taken to wearing spandex. ("¡Ay, comadre!" her comadres teased her. "Who do you think you are, anyway, una teenager?" Sofi ignored them because deep down she knew they all wished they had her naturally petite figure.)

"Your daughter is *very* ill," Doctor Tolentino finally declared, taking a deep breath. He waited a few seconds to see if Sofi was ready to hear the rest, and seeing her more or less composed, went on, "Only about twenty percent of my terminally ill patients survive my efforts, señora Sofi, but I am willing to try if you and she want me to . . ."

"What are you saying? Speak clearly, please, doctor! What is my daughter . . . *ill* from? What does she have?"

"Have you heard of the human immunodeficiency virus, Sofi?" Mrs. Doctor asked.

Sofi stared at the wife and then at the doctor. Of course she had. And she only knew two things about it: that there was no known cure for this frightening epidemic and . . . there was no way that Loca could have gotten it. But Doctor Tolentino was a doctor so he couldn't be wrong and she said nothing. Yet to herself she said, tomorrow we will call doña

Felicia, and then we'll go to the hospital for tests, and then . . .

"Sofi," the doctor stopped her thoughts. "Before you do anything else regarding your daughter's condition, do you have enough trust in me to try my own last efforts? I can't promise anything, Sofi, but if you have faith, we can all try. She is your only surviving child y me duele mucho to think of you losing her too . . . We could talk it over with her father about it first, if you prefer."

Sofi shook her head but did not look up from her fluorescent pants. "You know I am a great devotee of our Lord, Su Hijo y La Virgen, doctor, and I resign myself to Their Will. I've known you all my life and I trust in your knowledge."

"In this case, Sofia, you must put your faith in the Holy Spirit. I cannot and will not promise you your daughter's recovery. If it is God's will, there is nothing anyone can do for her . . ."

"But pray, dear," La Mrs. Doctor added, with a little smile which la Sofi noticed cracked a little of the powder along the cheeks.

The doctor, whom Sofi found out only then, always having been too polite to ask anything personal about him, had been born at the foot of a place called Mount Banahaw, and though he had followed in the footsteps of his own father's profession, and like his father attended Northwestern University Medical School in the coldest city in the world, it was from his mother that he learned the tratamiento he gave Loca that night.

"We are now in the age of the Spirit," Doctor Tolentino spoke, using the same confident tone that in years past he used for advice as to how to alleviate Esperanza's sprained knee, Fe's skin rashes, or Caridad's ovary problems. "If we do not have faith altogether, there is no hope for any of us—es decir, en todo el mundo. So we will begin the treatment by praying together."

Doctor Tolentino kneeled at the side of Loca's bed where she lay as still as she had as an infant in her little coffin, when she had looked to her sisters like una Crismas wrapped doll. He took her hand in his, in his other hand he held his wife's, and Sofi held his wife's hand and Loca's, all connected, in other words. Then they closed their eyes and prayed an Our Father.

Without no explanations as to what he planned to do, he and his wife started to work on Loca. Out of his black bag la Mrs. Doctor took out a vial of holy oil and some cotton balls in a plastic bag. Doctor Tolentino rubbed the holy oil on Loca's exposed tummy. Sofi continued to hold her hand. With his hands over her stomach, Doctor Tolentino asked Loca to breathe deeply, which she did. There was a popping sound, then Sofi fainted.

La Mrs. Doctor had soaked a handful of cotton balls with holy oil and squeezed them over Loca's tummy. Doctor Tolentino dipped a cotton ball in a pan of warm water and as he dripped the water on Loca's stomach with his right hand, his left hand made an opening through her flesh and disappeared right up to the wrist inside her stomach.

They did not stop their psychic surgery to tend to Sofi, and Loca did not seem to notice that her mother had fainted, so fascinated was she to see the doctor's hand disappear into her body. She felt no pain, although she did find it hard to breathe deeply, as the doctor was telling her to do while the right hand also went inside her stomach, the opening maintained by the left one. In a few seconds he pulled out his right hand holding a bloody coagulation which he held up for Loca's appraisal, explaining that it was a blood clot and then dropping it into the bowl of water his wife held out for him.

He continued this treatment two more times, maintaining

his left "material" hand in the opening, while the right "spirit" hand sought out the maladies. He next pulled out some cystic fibroids and finally a tumor that had lodged itself to one of Loca's ovaries.

By this point Sofi had recovered and though she steadily held Loca's hand, it was apparent that the hand-holding was more for her benefit than for La Loca's, who, though she looked more glazy-eyed than usual, appeared very calm about the whole procedure.

When the doctor finally removed his left hand, la Mrs. Doctor wiped up the slender line of blood that was left on the red mark across Loca's belly as the only sign that any surgery had been performed.

He wiped his hands on a towel and lit his cigar stub. "How do you feel, hija?" He asked Loca. Loca grimaced for the first time, sensitive to the smoke, or maybe it was the fact that her people allergies were reactivating and she was finally responding to the presence of the doctor and la Mrs. Doctor. Either way, La Loca wasn't the same Loca no more and she only said politely, "I'm okay. Just a little tired, nomás, like always," and then sat up.

Since the "Amen" when they had prayed together, Sofi had not uttered a word. But gradually, as she saw that her daughter was indeed "okay," she convinced herself for the moment that what she witnessed was nothing more than a hallucination. Then, as if Doctor Tolentino had stuck his hand into her head and pulled out her thoughts he warned, "Don't forget your faith, señora . . ."

But as el Doctor Tolentino had told Sofi before his tratamiento, there was no guarantee of saving Loca from AIDS, because this was still a time in which the cure was as mystifying to all of society as was the disease. Even as wise a doctor as el Doctor Tolentino knew that although sometimes a disease could be stopped, death ultimately could not be.

14

Doña Felicia Calls in the Troops Who Herein Reveal a Handful of Their Own Tried and Proven Remedios; and Some Mixed Medical Advice Is Offered to the Beloved Doctor Tolentino

Doña Felicia also went to curar La Loquita, as she affectionately called her, alternating with Dr. Tolentino's visitas. We say curar when a woman has an abortion or gives birth, which is to say, she is "alleviated." In this case, too, doña Felicia knew and Sofi knew and, above all, La Loca knew that there was no cure forthcoming—not just for her AIDS but for the utter loneliness she felt, for her sisters who had been, along with Sofia and the animals, the meaning of her life.

Doctor Tolentino came about as near modern medical treatment as Sofi got for La Loca's AIDS. The atrocities that Loca saw Fe suffer in her last days on the Acme International Medical Group Plan were enough to keep her far away from anyone wearing anything that even looked like a smock as long as she lived.

Anyway, Loca would never have agreed to go to a hospital, no matter what. If she had ever been pregnant, she certainly would have been capable of delivering her own baby, probably in the stalls on soft hay, where she had delivered the colts, or down by the acequia, squatting, arms tight around the cottonwood, with no one around. And she surely did not want to die in a hospital which was what she figured hospitals were really for.

But Sofi was relieved that in Loca's final months, she did permit some outside treatment for herself—not by just anybody of course, but like by Dr. Tolentino the Filipino Psychic Surgeon and his wrinkly-white-smiling-face la Mrs. Doctor, and la doña Felicia, whom she liked and had never minded near her so that she had even had a sobaso or two from her back when Caridad first went to live with her.

Although Loca was not going to let every curandera in the region of Rio Abajo come to see her, she occasionally agreed to make exceptions for a few besides doña Felicia who, hearing about La Loca Santa's terrible enfermedad, came on their own to give her a sobaso or a limpia, the results of such tratamientos, as we know, depending as much on the power of the hands that issued them as on the treatments themselves.

It had been over twenty years since the child had become famous for her resurrection at the church at Tome. Although she had never wanted to see no one after her mother brought her back home so the stories of her miracles could not be verified by no one (La Loca was no Niño Fidencio, that's for sure), many still believed in her. A great wave of sadness, like a dry ocean tide, went over the whole region when the news spread that La Loquita Santa was dying again. ¡A-yyy!

And when she did die, young and old, poor and not-so-very-poor, Catholic or whatever, believers and non-believers alike, "Indian" and "Spanish," a few gringos and some others, even non-human (since it was never no secret that all her life animals were closer to La Loca than people) came to that second funeral. Perhaps some—especially those who had missed it the first time—had hoped to see her rise again. And yet there were still others who believed that her true powers would be revealed after her final death.

Someone did a sketch of La Loca Santa as she was seen on Gato Negro at the Way of the Cross Procession that memorable Holy Friday (which we will also see in the following account) in her sister's blue robe and reproduced it, except that in the drawing it flowed and looked more like el San Martín Caballero's Roman robe than a chenille bathrobe. A factory in San Antonio quickly caught on and made up votive candles with a picture of La Loca Santa on a horse to petition help from her as the new emissary to heaven. "Patrona de todas las criaturas"—Patron of all of God's creatures, animal and human alike—the little ribbon design at the bottom of her picture read. On the back was a special prayer to La Loca and instructions for those who wanted to dedicate a novena to her.

Altars were quickly adorned with the Santita's picture and candles and requests and flowers and although no one really knew what kind of food she liked best, the rumor was biscochitos, so there was usually a little plate of wedding cookies as an offering to her on the altars of the really devoted.

Doña Felicia, meanwhile, while Loca was still among the living, fearing that all her years, nay, her good century of practice had not done her an ounce of good in the face of this hideous disease, put aside pride regarding her knowledge and relented to try every tratamiento known to the Rio Abajo curanderas, medicas from the montes, yerberas from the llanos, brujas de las sierras, gias from the pueblos—and men of that same profession, too, for that matter.

So, tablespoon after tablespoon of this solution and that oil went into Loca's mouth, and Loca, becoming increasingly apathetic, just opened up and swallowed without so much as a grimace after a while. Aceite de comer cooking oil mixed with hot water and sugar for La Loca's sore throat. No, no, said Teresa of Isleta, a drop or two of kerosene in a teaspoon of sugar for the throat. Poleo water for mouth sores!

Garlic tea for the stomach and intestines. "What are you talking about?" said doña Berna. "Everybody knows corn water cleans out the kidneys." "Not water from the boiled corn but from the corn silk!" another insisted. And yet another recommended only mesquite water for kidney and urinary problems—and don't waste your time with nothing else!

Well, all of these healers had lived in the Rio Abajo region, that is, in Los Lunas, Belen, Tome, on the Isleta Pueblo, from Alameda to Socorro, all around on their own little no-name rancherías, and up in the Manzano Mountains away from everybody for a very long time, not to mention that most had learned their remedios from grandmothers who had learned from grandmothers. And all who had lived on that tierra of thistle and tumbleweed knew that every cactus and thorn had a purpose and reason, once put into a pot to boil.

Failing that, there was little that an aspirin wouldn't take away overnight to make you new and strong the next morning when the rooster crowed and it was time to start all over, aches and pains and all.

There were other remedies born of sheer ingenuity, and not growing out of the earth, but still in a farfetched way related, so that if you felt bad enough, you'd try it, like that of doña Fermina. Doña Fermina swore by her "estampas de tabaco" remedy. Although they were getting harder to find, the revenue stamps used to seal tobacco can lids—the canceled ones, naturally—placed at the temples were a sure cure for severe headaches.

And speaking of severe, doña Severa, la sobadora de Belen, insisted on doña Felicia's giving Loca a lard-and-salt rubdown. "You cover her whole body with the manteca y sal to bring down her fevers," doña Severa insisted. "And give her te de inmortal!" Immortal tea was commonly used for women in labor but also for all fevers and all kinds of headaches, and not just for women either—so why not?

Oshá, which flourishes in the Manzano Mountains just east of Tome, as many a sheepherder discovered ages ago, practically became a staple in Sofi's household, used alternately as a spice, medicinal tea, suppository, and enema. Oshá de la Sierra was a general all-purpose plant, and Teresa of Isleta added that it could also be used to treat sores.

Although la doña Felicia did not recommend it, more than one of her colleagues suggested a drop of mercury for Loca's severe stomachaches—but only a drop, since everyone knew how dangerous mercury was. "But that's exactly why it works!" doña Severa insisted.

Doña Severa was particularly proficient at curing "suspensión," an ailment unknown to gringos and which has no translation. In so many words, the main symptom is constipation as a result of shock. The cause is the big colon of the stomach being suspended out of place. The treatment was delicate, but doña Severa was very adept at manipulating the colon back into place through the rectum.

Doña Severa prepared her own suppositories, too. The pildoras were made from ground Oshá, Yerba Buena, Trementina soap, Piloncillo, all mixed with bile—cow bile, sheep bile, even chicken bile worked. The mixture was rolled like dough, and the pildoras were shaped, the size of a fingertip, then put in the refrigerator to harden. Although this was not Loca's idea of a fun pastime (but the bedridden do suffer from constipation), she did on one or two occasions succumb to having the pildora applied with the aid of Vaselina and as doña Severa promised, was greatly relieved for it.

"I understand," Dr. Tolentino told doña Felicia as a way of showing his professional approval one day when they crossed paths in Sofia's house, one coming in to give Loca her own brand of healing and the other leaving after giving his and both maintaining the practice of praying before they did anything. So it may be said in the end that they did have much in common. There were "doctores invisibles," as they were called, in doña Felicia's homeland too, and she never found nothing disturbing about his practice. Likewise, on the islands from which he originated, he had heard of many of doña Felicia's treatments, although usually with a different variety of local herbs.

Sofia offered the doctor and doña Felicia un café and the two professionals sat down for a bit outside beneath the portal.

"In the Spanish flu epidemic of 1918," Doctor Tolentino said, thinking how pleasant it was to take a rest, which he rarely did, "as you might remember, doña Felicia, mucha gente died. At least one member in every family. More than half the people of Belen fell from it. Church bells tolled for a new death every hour in Socorro; the carpenters could hardly keep up with the demand for coffins . . ."

"No, I don't remember, Doctor," doña Felicia said, but despite his sad recollection, she was enjoying a good feeling too, sitting on Sofi's porch, watching a roadrunner make its way down to the acequia, and thinking how long it had been since she herself had taken a load off her feet.

"¡A poco!" the doctor teased her. For surely, if he remembered, she too, most certainly must recall . . .

"I didn't live here back then. I'm not a native either, like you, remember, mon ami?" doña Felicia reminded him.

"Ah, yes, forgive me," he said, smiling and sipping Sofi's café. "Many people died then, también, as I was saying. I was the only doctor around at the time and I couldn't keep up with los enfermos. Then, of course, I also didn't have enough vaccines to go around for everybody."

Sofi came out to the patio and sat to listen.

"What people came up with then was the 'cania de perro' cure," he continued.

"I know that one!" doña Felicia interrupted, "You mix a little water and peloncillo with the cania de perro . . ."

"Right!" he said with a smile, as if he had just given an exam to an intern.

Sofi stood up to go back into the house. "Well, we are not giving my 'jita spoonfuls of dog droppings! Kerosene is one thing . . . but caca de perro, never!"

She let the screen door slam and Doctor Tolentino, who shrugged his shoulders only, said to doña Felicia quietly, "Well, it saved a lot of people who would have died otherwise back then," and despite his cough, lit up his cigar. "And then we used barro with water for tuberculosis with good results, too . . ."

"Yes, I know," doña Felicia said. "And by the way, doctor, have you tried inhaling cachanilla fumes for that cough?"

"Yes, as a matter of fact, I have," Doctor Tolentino admitted. "Doña Jovita insisted on it when I went there to cure her little grandson of a chronic ear infection."

Doña Felicia made a face that went unnoticed, feeling slighted for some reason that she had not been able to recommend the remedio to Doctor Tolentino first. She studied him for a moment and then said, "You know, doctor, there's a way you could cure your baldness, I mean if you wanted to. Maybe you've gotten used to the draft on your head, but asufre would bring your hair back. And from what I remember, you had quite a nice mata once . . ."

"¿Asufre?" Dr. Tolentino asked.

"Yes, everybody knows asufre will prevent baldness *and* will bring back your hair if it has already fallen out!" Doña Felicia got a little animated by el Tolentino's attention. "You mix it with '*Aceite Mejicano*' and you leave it on for a week . . ." Noticing the doctor's skeptical look, she added, "Well, you probably will have to live in the woods until your hair grows because I'm sure not even la buena Mrs. Doctor would put up with the smell!"

They both laughed at the thought of Doctor Tolentino with a head full of sulfur spending his nights and days in the woods like a lone coyote for the sake of hair growth.

Perhaps la doña Jovita had beat her to it, after all, doña Felicia thought regretfully—lighting up the cigar Dr. Tolentino had just offered her—in giving el Doctor Tolentino a bit of special Rio Abajo medicine that he just couldn't have gotten nowhere else.

15

La Loca Santa Returns to the World via Albuquerque Before Her Transcendental Departure; and a Few Random Political Remarks from the Highly Opinionated Narrator

That year, Holy Friday was unlike all others for both La Loca and her mom for it was the only occasion in Loca's life—except at the age of three when she was taken to a hospital in Albuquerque and her death diagnosis was reevaluated as epilepsy—that Loca went out into the world.

For her debut, Loca wore the boycott jeans (upon Sofi's insistence, washed) that were now being held up by a pair of her father's suspenders left behind on a hanger in his ropero. Loca always rode barefoot with her soles thicker than moccasins and she had never owned a pair of boots, but for the occasion (and so that she wouldn't look like a motherless lamb, un penco, her mom called her), Sofi insisted that she put on a pair of her own Ropers.

That same day, Rubén, Esperanza's ex,

perhaps not too discreetly but well intentioned, brought over a chenille blue bathrobe that Esperanza had left at his place back during their sweat lodge days, and Loca immediately made that item her own and put it on, too.

Rubén, like others who had been close to Esperanza in life, had been having the sometimes unsettling feeling of being even closer to her after her passing. For his own part, it would not have occurred to him on his own to look behind the door in his bedroom where, on the hook beneath two flannel shirts, a pair of dirty jeans, some "lady's" nightgown (which had not belonged to Esperanza, by the way), and a pair of boxer shorts, was the chenille bathrobe.

He woke up that morning just before dawn and did that not really knowing why. When he found the blue bathrobe, he took it with him to the kitchen and laid it on a chair while he put some wood inside the wood-burning stove and got the coffee on. Then, just like that guy in that song by Rubén Blades (one of *our* Rubén's pop culture heroes), he had the unfortunate experience of stepping barefoot in dog pee on the way to the bathroom.

Rubén returned to the kitchen, picked up the chenille blue bathrobe and took it back to bed with him. He got under the covers and, wrapping the bathrobe up in a ball like a pillow, brought it up to his face. ¡Chingao, hombre! It still smelled of la Esperanza, not like any kind of perfume or nothing, but a feisty smell. EEE! Just like her! What a know-it-all she was, too! And how that woman loved to fight!

But for some people, fighting was good and led to good things. Back in college, if it wasn't for la Esperanza who led the protest, they never would have had one Chicano Studies class offered on the curriculum. If it wasn't for la Esperanza, who would have known about the struggle of the United Farm Workers on campus? Who would have ever told *him* about anything at all? How would he have known about

Salvador Allende of Chile removed by a military coup, or heard Victor Jara, the protest singer, or been told about his beautiful guitar-playing hands being smashed by soldiers' rifle butts?

Then he met this white *chick*, just before they finished college. She drove a new little sports car and the worst trauma of her life had been living with braces through high school. Her folks thought Rubén was such an "admirable young man," putting himself through college on grants and by working, and still being able to help out his own family up in Los Alamos. His father had died when he was twelve and he, as the second oldest of eight, had been helping his mom and familia get by ever since.

Her father offered Rubén a job with his business after college, and la Donna was pretty and loyal and most of all, really wanted him. She thought Rubén was just . . . everything.

Rubén really didn't know nothing about what love was, he had said to himself at the time, kind of as an excuse for dumping la Esperanza just like that. He didn't know nothing about soulmates or kindred spirits, except to say that he never forgot Esperanza, ever, even during his marriage. And here he still was, smelling up her bathrobe, rubbing his nubby morning face into it, the coffee boiling over on the stove and his tears flowing like they had never even flowed when his father died in the tractor accident and Rubén speaking softly to the robe, saying, "Oh baby, why did you have to go . . . ?" And nobody answering him but a single crow outside, calling for him to get up and start the day.

Instead of a jacket for that brisk Viernes Santo, Loca insisted on wearing the robe over her red plaid Pendleton shirt.

"Loca, please!" Sofi shook her head at Loca's "look," but no slave of fashion herself, she didn't say nothing else. After all, she was so glad that Loca was joining her that day that she didn't dare discourage her with a weak argument on personal style.

"What's wrong?" Loca said, looking down at her eclectic outfit and then, referring only to the chenille bathrobe, said, "It's blue. Blue is good." And this was no naive remark coming from a young woman who knew, among other things she was never given credit for knowing, that in her land, blue was a sacred color and, therefore, very appropriate for the occasion.

So it was that Loca, bareback on Gato Negro (Sofi fretted over Loca bringing the horse along but doña Felicia, who came with them, calmed her. "Leave her be! Anyway, there must surely be animals in heaven, too! Remember that dogs licked the wounds of San Lazaro!"), and her mother on foot joined their vecinos and members of various cooperative efforts in the Way of the Cross Procession through the main streets of the villages and then on to the city.

This Procession—which grew as it went along, comprising ultimately as many as two hundred people—did not flagellate itself with horsehair whips. There were no pitos blown nor alabadas sung, neither. As a kind of main feature, however, a supposedly famous woman singer named Pastora Somebody or Other did join the procession with her guitar and sang some of her own songs; and though they were not in the least religious in nature but about workers and women strikers and things like that, the way she sang them made some people sigh and some even sob and still others sang along with their eyes to the sky.

No brother was elected to carry a life-size cross on his naked back. There was no "Mary" to meet her son. Instead, some, like Sofi, who held a picture of la Fe as a bride, carried photographs of their loved ones who died due to toxic exposure hung around the necks like scapulars; and at each station along their route, the crowd stopped and prayed and people spoke on the so many things that were killing their land and turning the people of those lands into an endangered species.

No, there had never been no procession like that one before.

When Jesus was condemned to death, the spokesperson for the committee working to protest dumping radioactive waste in the sewer addressed the crowd.

Jesus bore His cross and a man declared that most of the Native and hispano families throughout the land were living below poverty level, one out of six families collected food stamps. Worst of all, there was an ever-growing number of familias who couldn't even get no food stamps 'cause they had no address and were barely staying alive with their children on the streets.

Jesus fell,

and people all over the land were dying from toxic exposure in factories.

Jesus met his mother, and three Navajo women talked about uranium contamination on the reservation, and the babies they gave birth to with brain damage and cancer. One of the women with such a baby in her arms told the crowd this: "We hear about what environmentalists care about out there. We live on dry land but we care about saving the whales and the rain forests, too. Of course we do. Our people have always known about the interconnectedness of things; and the responsibility we have to 'Our Mother,' and to seven generations after our own. But we, as a people, are being eliminated from the ecosystem, too . . . like the dolphins, like the eagle; and we are trying very hard now to save ourselves before it's too late. Don't anybody care about that?"

Jesus was helped by Simon and the number of those without jobs increased each day.

Veronica wiped the blood and sweat from Jesus' face. Livestock drank and swam in contaminated canals.

Jesus fell for the second time.

The women of Jerusalem consoled Jesus. Children also played in those open disease-ridden canals where the livestock swam and drank and died from it.

Jesus fell a third time. The air was contaminated by the pollutants coming from the factories.

AIDS was a merciless plague indeed, the crowd was told by a dark, somber man with sunglasses and an Eastern accent. It started in Africa, he said, among poor, black people, and continued sweeping across continents, taking anyone in its path. It was the Murder of the Innocents all over again, he said, and again, there was lamentation, and weeping and great mourning, not just in Rama as in the Gospels, but this time all over the world. Jesus was stripped of his garments.

Nuclear power plants sat like gargantuan landmines among the people, near their ranchos and ancestral homes. Jesus was nailed to the cross.

Deadly pesticides were sprayed directly and from helicopters above on the vegetables and fruits and on the people who picked them for large ranchers at subsistence wages and their babies died in their bellies from the poisoning.

¡Ayyy! Jesus died on the cross.

No one had understood the meaning of the brief war in the Middle East, and Sofi went up to the portable podium, a bit reluctantly at first, to talk about her eldest daughter who never returned, although she had gone not to fight but as a civilian, a news reporter, as part of her job, that's all. It was true that la Esperanza had always been outspoken, una mitotera. Everyone knew that. And now the Army said that although they knew she was dead they never produced a body for her to bury.

Christ was taken down from the cross.

At the hour that Jesus was laid in His tomb the sun set and

the temperature dropped immediately as it does in the desert. The crowd began to disperse, slowly and quietly. Sofi and doña Felicia led Loca—who only weighed eighty-five pounds by then and was very, very tired (although it had been one of her stronger days)—on Gato Negro back home.

No, no one had never seen a procession like that one before.

It was nearly six months later, and things went on pretty much business as usual around Tome, except that in Sofi's home they were quiet as they had never been before. The animals did not wander much inside no more. Loca was too weak to go out and tend to them.

And even though she didn't, she wasn't too lonely for the royal bird, or the dogs or Gato Negro, since, just around the Equinox, the Lady in Blue started coming to visit her, walked right into Loca's little room when no one was around one day and stood next to her bed on the same spot where el Doctor Tolentino used to stand and take out small bloody masses from Loca's body until she asked him not to no more.

This was not the woman Loca had known down by the acequia, by the way. This lady looked like a nun. In fact, she was a nun. But she didn't smell like nothing so Loca was not sure if she was a present nun or a past nun or maybe hasta una future subjunctive nun. Loca tried to find out by asking trick questions about la Esperanza, who also visited her occasionally, and questions about la Caridad and la Fe, who never did, but the Lady in Blue did not seem interested in talking about nobody besides La Loca and just making her feel better when she couldn't get out of bed no more.

Even if it was during the day when she came by, the nun carried a lantern; and on one afternoon, she pushed aside her manta, and opened up her habit to show La Loca the horsehair vest beneath that cut into her delicate white body, and that's when Loca decided that alive or not, the Lady in

Blue must be related to Francisco el Penitente. But when she asked the nun if she knew el Francisco, the nun confused her more by saying only that yes, she had known a few.

On another visit they played the game of "la Loteria," a kind of Mexican bingo that doña Felicia brought with her one day, making Loca laugh with all the little Spanish limericks that went along with calling out each card, like for El Gallo, for instance, the caller would say "¡Como el que le canto a San Pedro!", and things like that. Each played with three cards to better her odds and Loca beat the nun two out of three.

One early evening, just as the sky blazed orange, then red, then became purple like fire, the nun sang very softly for La Loca and put her to sleep. Although Loca liked the song, which was about a woman who had been left by her French soldier lover, she had never heard a *fado* before. The nun said that kind of song came from a faraway land called Portugal.

Loca went to sleep in the Lady's arms thinking that for a person who had lived her whole life within a mile radius of her home and had only traveled as far as Albuquerque twice, she certainly knew quite a bit about this world, not to mention beyond, too, and that made her smile as she closed her eyes.

16

Sofia Founds and Becomes la First Presidenta of the Later-to-Become World-Renowned Organization M.O.M.A.S.; and a Rumor Regarding the Inevitability of Double Standards Is (We Hope) Dispensed With

Sofi buried La Loca, or what was left of the body (it would be no exaggeration to say in this case the "remains"), in the camposanto of the Church of Our Lady of Guadalupe where her parents, grandparents, great-grandparents, great-great-grandparents, great-great-great-grandparents, great-great-great-great-grandparents, and their children, or at least, most of them, all lay to rest. Fe's urn was there and Esperanza and Caridad were there too, although in spirit and without headstones.

In the years to come, la pobre Sofia—encouraged not only by vecinos and comadres, but by the hundreds of petitions she received in the mail everyday, asking for prayers from the mother of the little crazy saint who died twice and her similarly ethereal sisters—became the founder and la first presidenta of what would later be known worldwide as the very prestigious (if not a little elitist) organization M.O.M.A.S., Mothers of Martyrs and Saints.

Furthermore, by then, it would be pretty evident that contrary to what people said during Sofi's thifty-eight-year presidency (appointments, like to the board of M.O.M.A.S., were for life, like judges), that you had to be the mother of a *daughter* to even be considered, it would eventually be about fifty–fifty. That is, there was an equal portion of male and female santos and martires represented by las M.O.M.A.S.; and by the middle of the new century, quite a few mothers of men were getting in with ease.

All that bad talk regarding M.O.M.A.S.'s discriminating against men, or rather the mothers of men, probably got its start back in Belen with la Mrs. Torres, the mother of Fe's one-time fiancé, Tom, who, on no fewer than twelve occasions over a period of twenty-five years—until her death, in fact—kept applying for nomination.

The thing was, of course, that the first and obvious reason why she was never eligible was simply because of the unfortunate but crucial criteria that the martyr or saint up for consideration would have to have transcended this life already, the form of "death" itself sometimes being the all-telling proof of qualification.

Everyone knew that.

Tom Torres, meanwhile, lived well beyond the national average for anybody and kept Mrs. Torres company as her dutiful son until his mother's passing. "What does she have to complain about?" Sofia would ask the committee every time it got a new application from Mrs. Torres. "I think it just kills her that her 'jito never 'mounted to nothing more than the manager of a gas station!" And of course, she was right.

The decision as to whether a " 'jito" of a M.O.M.A.S. member would be designated as a saint or a martyr was also very touchy for a lot of people. To be a martyr, of course, was a lot easier than to be considered a santo by anybody's standards. Saints had the unquestionable potential of performing miracles while martyrs were simply revered and considered emissaries to the santos. In many cases, this was nearly an impossible decision to make, except in the one of the original founding president's; there was never no question at all about that: Sofia had truly been the mother of a saint.

La Loca did not have to appear with the stigmata or thorn marks on her forehead before her final death to prove her sainthood to no one. And, remaining as ornery after she "transcended" as in her incarnated days, she made very occasional ectoplasmic appearances at the national and international conventions—although locally, back in Tome, for a long time people *claimed* to catch sight of her by her favorite acequia where a shrine in her honor had been built by don Domingo ("Father of the Saint"), shortly after her burial.

She was not particularly noted for answering the pleas of the desperate and the hopeless, neither, like el Saint Jude, for example, who is the patron saint of los desesperados.

In other words, people never really could figure out who La Loca protected and oversaw as a rule, or what she was good to pray to about. In general, though, it was considered a good idea to have a little statue of La Loca in your kitchen and to give one as a good luck gift to new brides and progressive grooms.

The truth of it was that she was just truly a santita from ever since her fatal experience at the age of three and she didn't have to prove nothing to no one. She didn't bother to do it when she was more or less among the living and people figured out eventually that she was not going to try to prove nothing afterward, neither.

Rather than all those gratuitous titles of La Patroncita de Todas las Pobres Criaturas or Patrona de la Cocina y la Comida (or, more formally, as she was referred to during Mass: Patrona de los Hambrientes, Patrona de las Enfermedades Misteriosas, and so on), if you ask me, nothing suited her better than La Loca Santa, which was her first and original title.

The annual conference of M.O.M.A.S. eventually became, as anyone could easily imagine, a world event each year, taking the cake over the World Series and even the Olympics, when they were held, winter and summer. Not only were Las Blessed Mothers present but droves of spectators attended with high hopes and often heavy hearts to catch a glimpse of their favorite martyrs and saints. In addition to the fact that few ever went away disappointed (since there was always a certain number among the faithful reported by the press to have been physically cured, spiritually redeemed, or otherwise saved from some human failing), you would, unfortunately, also get your share of charlatans.

Every year the number of vendors of basically more useless products and souvenirs than what a tourist could find on a given day at Disney World grew. For example, there were your T-shirts with such predictable stenciled phrases as "The Twenty Third Annual Convention of M.O.M.A.S., Flushing, NY," or "Perros Bravos, Nuevo Leon," or "Las Islas Canarias," or "My Mother Is a Member of Mothers of Martyrs and Saints—Genuflect, Please!", the usual posters, stationery, forever-burning votive candles with your favorite saint's or martyr's picture stuck on (or an instant photo of your own kid, if you preferred), "automatic writing" pens, and then, of course, the all-time favorite—La Loca Santa and her Sisters Tarot Deck drawn by a lovely and talented artist in Sardinia, Italy.

In this version, Sofia as a mother was simultaneously represented by the Empress card and by the Queen of Swords, a quick-witted, dance-loving strong woman who was nevertheless powerless to the sorrow she suffered. Esperanza also appeared as a court card in the suit of swords as the knight—for she had been driven by her yang as much as her yin for the sake of what she believed.

Caridad was simultaneously High Priestess and the Page of Wands for she had been guided by her spirituality. Fe had aspired to be Queen of Wands, tending to her home and garden and seeing herself as güera. And La Loca was represented by the key 0 of the Major Arcana, the Fool. The Fool card represented one who walked without fear, aware of the choices she made in the journey of life, life itself being defined as a state of courage and wisdom and not an uncontrollable participation in society, as many people experienced their lives.

This was more or less of a "circus" than mitoteros always went back home reporting, because as I said, the conference of M.O.M.A.S. was very serious business, hombre! It started out serious back in the days of La Sofia and stayed serious. After all, there was a lot of important information exchanged during these meetings when Las Mothers took time out from their city jobs, their ranchos, their all-too-mortal remaining children, lovers, and so on to travel regardless of whatever expense it ran them to meet with each other! Not to mention that, yes indeed, closed attendance was of utmost importance because the santitos did, in fact, make their sometimes shy appearances at these conventions.

It's not like Las Mothers had to hold séances or nothing like that. Usually after the First Mass, because a Mass always kicked off the convention, (eventually, Masses were held by women clergy, not just men, including some who were married), all the M.O.M.A.S. members went to have pan dulce y biscochitos with cafe in the main ballroom or church hall, meadow, or by the beach—that is, wherever they could all be together at one time where they had chosen to convene that year. And wandering among them, as fresh as a field of marigolds, would be their all-too-glorious (if hard to pin down) santito and martyred 'jitos.

They came to converse with their moms, as well as with each other. They brought all kinds of news and advice that was, as part of the bylaws, generously passed on to relatives, friends, the petitioning faithful, and community agencies, as well as to relevant local or federal governments. In the case of the very last mentioned, however, although accepted graciously, it was never done without some obvious skepticism on the part of officials, which, I guess, is the nature of politics.

But what a beautiful sight it all became at those reunions: 'jitos from all over the world, some transparent, some looking incarnated but you knew they weren't if you tested them in some way, like getting them to take a bite out of a taquito or something when, of course, after going through all the motions like he was eating it, the taco would still be there. Although, it really wasn't such a respectable thing to do to test a santo, even if he had once been your own chiple child! There were some who appeared just as they were in life when they were well and others as morbidly as they looked at the time of their death, or as the M.O.M.A.S. put it, transcendence, that is, all maimed and bloody or deteriorated, if that is how they met their end. But all seemed pretty happy to be there with everybody, no matter what their story in this life had been.

Y one final rumor I would like to dispense with once and for all that followed Las Mothers for a long time, but which I know for a fact was never true. To be a member of M.O.M.A.S. of course you had to have issued the *declared* santo or martyr from your own womb, coming out of that very place that some malcriado, like Saint Augustine, had so disgracefully referred to back in the fourth century as "being between feces and urine"!

If you applied as a mother and were accepted, your word of having given birth was honored. You were La Blessed Mom, la mother of the new santita or martyr, and as long as you could pay your own way, you got to attend the regional and international conventions y ya.

But for a long time, a rumor followed las M.O.M.A.S. that the appointed board member Mothers were made to sit on chairs much like the ones that popes back in the beginning of their days were made to sit on after a woman who passed herself off as a man had been elected pope. In other words, a chair that was structured to *prove* that you were in fact a "mom" or, at least, could have been. What happened to that woman pope way back when, by the way, was that she was not only thrown off the throne for not being a man, but dragged through the streets and stoned to death. Nothing like that never happened among the M.O.M.A.S.! ¡Hijo! Imagine las M.O.M.A.S. taking things that far to make sure that they all had wombs!

After all, just because there had been a time way back when, when some fregados all full of themselves went out of their way to prove that none among them had the potential of being a mother, did it mean that there *had* to come a time when someone would be made to *prove* that she did?